Thea felt her p

Somewhat above a
figure was distingui
shoulders, but it wa
that captured attention. A noble brow and arrow-straight nose were complemented by a firm chin and well-cut mouth. In addition to these glories he possessed the darkest, most long-lashed eyes Thea had ever seen. In fact, he was much too handsome for any girl's peace of mind!

Firmly curbing her wayward thoughts, Thea shook her head. 'I have no desire to know your name, sir,' she told him mendaciously.

Gail Mallin has a passion for travel. She studied at the University of Wales, where she gained an Honours degree and met her husband, then an officer in the Merchant Navy. They spent the next three years sailing the world before settling in Cheshire. Writing soon became another means of exploring, opening up new worlds. A career move took Gail and her husband south, and they now live with their young family in St Albans.

Recent titles by the same author:

CONQUEROR'S LADY
DEBT OF HONOUR
THE DEVIL'S BARGAIN
A MOST UNSUITABLE DUCHESS

MARRY IN HASTE

Gail Mallin

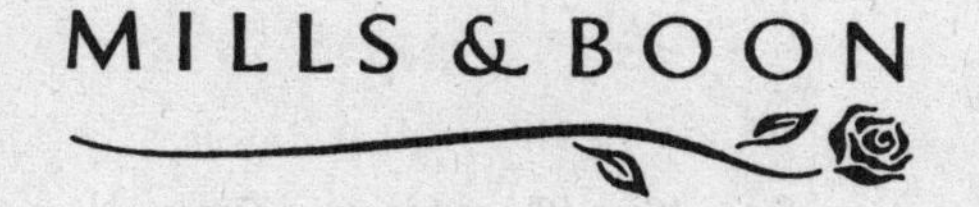

All the characters in this book have no existence outside the imagination of the author, and have no relation whatsoever to anyone bearing the same name or names. They are not even distantly inspired by any individual known or unknown to the author, and all the incidents are pure invention.

Harlequin Mills & Boon Limited,
Eton House, 18–24 Paradise Road, Richmond, Surrey TW9 1SR

ISBN 0 263 79462 8

Set in 10 on 10½ pt Linotron Times
04-9601-90211

Typeset in Great Britain by CentraCet, Cambridge
Printed in Great Britain by
BPC Paperbacks Ltd

CHAPTER ONE

'COME along do, you wretched animal! Grandmama will never forgive me if I am late.'

Mrs Howard's ancient pug favoured Thea with a baleful glare and promptly sank to the flagway. In despair she gave a sharp tug on his leash, but Nelson merely lowered his head to rest upon his front paws and closed his rheumy eyes.

Curbing an unladylike impulse to curse, Miss Howard attempted bribery. 'Good dog. You shall have a ham bone directly, if only you will get up and walk.'

This inducement, uttered through gritted teeth, caused Nelson to open one eye, and hope fluttered in Thea's merino-clad breast. If she hurried she might still have time to dress her hair in that new style she had seen in the *Ladies' Magazine*. . .

The sound of Nelson's snoring dashed this bud of optimism.

'Abominable brute! How am I to get you home?'

One rapid glance about her showed Miss Howard that no sedan-chair was to be had. The cloudy March afternoon was already well advanced, and the open space of the Orange Grove appeared deserted.

'I suppose I shall have to carry you all the way back to Beaufort Square,' she said bitterly. From unwelcome experience she knew that the pug was heavy, and the streets of Bath were steep.

With a faint sigh of resignation, she bent to pick up the old dog, a task made more awkward by Nelson awakening and resisting her attempts to hoist his considerable girth into her arms.

A half-smothered chuckle brought her efforts to a speedy close and, releasing Nelson, she whirled to find herself being surveyed by a well-dressed young man.

Flushing to the roots of her honey-brown hair, Thea said stiffly, 'I see no cause for amusement, sir.'

'I beg your pardon.' The laughter died out of his sun-bronzed face. 'I meant no offence.'

There was a note of contrition in his voice that instantly softened Thea's resentment. It was a very pleasing voice, she decided, becoming aware of the faint sing-song accent which marked his deep tones as he continued.

'My levity was misplaced. Do say you will forgive me, ma'am. I should hate to be at daggers drawn with anyone on my very first day in Bath.'

A civil bow accompanied this apology.

Thea acknowledged it with a little inclination of her head. Perhaps she had been too hasty, and had allowed Nelson's perversity to banish her sense of humour?

'You don't wish to forgive me? I assure you I am quite respectable,' the stranger added helpfully as she still hesitated for an answer.

'My sentiments are not at issue.' Thea lifted her eyebrows at him in a creditable imitation of one of her grandmother's snubbing frowns. 'Your garb proclaims you a gentleman, sir, so you must know that we ought not to be conversing in this manner,' she continued severely. 'We have not been introduced.'

'Oh, that's easily remedied.' He flashed a sudden smile at her. 'We need but exchange names and the deed is done.'

It was a very charming smile.

Thea felt her pulse quicken.

Somewhat above average height, his lean figure was distinguished by a pair of broad shoulders, but it was his finely-featured face that captured attention. A noble brow and arrow-straight nose were complemented by a firm chin and well-cut mouth. In addition to these glories he possessed the darkest, most long-lashed eyes Thea had ever seen. In fact, he was much too handsome for any girl's peace of mind!

Firmly curbing her wayward thoughts, Thea shook

her head. 'I have no desire to know your name, sir,' she told him mendaciously.

'But you will accept an apology for my rag-manners?' he persisted.

The sound of church bells, ringing out from the nearby abbey, startled Thea, reminding her that the hour was growing late.

'Oh, very well, but now you must excuse me, sir. I am in a great hurry.'

With a curt nod of farewell she turned away, intending to pick up Nelson once more.

'Pray, let me assist you.'

The dark-haired stranger had not accepted his dismissal.

'I do not require your help——' Thea began hotly, only to be interrupted by loud snoring.

'Incorrigible animal! I swear you put me to blush!' Unable to prevent it, a chuckle escaped Thea's lips. Of all the ridiculous starts!

'I think some form of transport is in order. May I procure a chair for you, ma'am?'

Recovering her composure, Thea nodded gravely, trying to ignore the twinkle in those black eyes.

A single wave of his well-kept hand brought the urchin who had been loitering by the obelisk in the centre of the grove—which had been erected in honour of the Prince of Orange—running towards them. An instant later, satisfied by the coin clutched in his grimy fist, he was dispatched to fetch the nearest chairman.

'Thank you,' Thea murmured. She opened her reticule and began to fish inside it. 'Please let me reimburse you.'

'Good God, it was the merest trifle! You can't imagine I would take your money? Or do I look such a nip-cheese?' he demanded, so indignantly that Thea hastily shook her head.

'No, of course not, but I do not care to be beholden to strangers,' she pointed out with a tart astringency.

'But I have already suggested the remedy for that,' he replied, with an engaging innocence.

Thea wanted to laugh, but instead she frowned at him, and said with all the severity she could muster, 'Do not try to cut a wheedle with me, sir! No doubt you think me brass-faced because I am out without a maid in attendance but——'

'No such thing, I swear, ma'am. Indeed, how could I make such a vile assumption when you are so closely chaperoned?'

Thea blinked.

A vivid grin split his gipsy-dark face, revealing excellent white teeth, as he pointed to the snoring pug. 'It would take a braver man than I to make up to a lady with such an encumbrance.'

'I see your point!' Thea was betrayed into a whoop of mirth. 'Nelson, at last you have earned my gratitude!'

She bent to bestow a swift pat of approbation upon the sleeping dog, but straightened quickly when her companion exclaimed, '*What* did you call him?'

The dimple at the left-hand corner of Thea's mouth quivered. 'I know—a ridiculous name for a pug, especially one such as this! In general I like dogs, but he is so lazy and spoilt! However, my grandmama was an ardent admirer of the late Admiral, and nothing else would satisfy her than to bestow his name upon her darling.'

He raised his thick black brows. 'I must take leave to doubt his lordship would have thanked her,' he murmured.

The fortunate arrival of the sedan-chair saved Thea from having to think of a reply to this wickedly accurate observation.

Stifling her amusement, she made him a neat curtsy.

'Thank you for your assistance, sir,' she said, but as she turned to pick up Nelson he stopped her with a crisp order.

'Get into the chair. I shall hand him in to you.'

Thea hesitated, uncomfortably aware that the manoeuvre must be fraught with difficulties if she refused his aid but resenting his easy air of command.

'You will get hairs on your coat,' she pointed out, adding virtuously, 'And he smells, sir.'

'So I had observed.'

Thea abandoned her objections and, after giving quiet directions to the chairmen, got into the conveyance.

'Here you are.'

So deftly had he scooped Nelson up, the pug was still snoring. Thea settled the dog comfortably on her lap and then held out her hand to the stranger who had so unexpectedly come to her aid.

'Goodbye, and thank you once again,' she said, a shy smile lighting up her grey eyes.

'My pleasure, ma'am.' He shook her hand with great politeness, but as he released it he added softly, 'But I hope this is merely *au revoir*.'

A tinge of pink stole into Thea's cheeks, but she answered him with composure. 'Why, as to that, sir, only the Fates can tell.'

'Then I must pray that they will be kind.'

Thea's colour deepened. He was flirting with her!

To her infinite relief she felt the chairmen swing her aloft, and the stranger stepped back.

Such impertinence... And yet it took considerable effort to resist the temptation to look back to catch one final glimpse of the most interesting man she'd ever met.

Gareth Rhayadar watched the sedan until it was out of sight, the smile lingering on his handsome face.

Something about that little filly certainly caught the attention! It wasn't her looks—she was no more than passably attractive—and her clothes were dowdy. He'd met dozens of prettier girls... But none with such laughing eyes. For a few moments she had managed to make him forget the depressing reasons which had brought him to Bath.

How he wished he might forget them completely! He longed to be back aboard the *Valiant*, with a brisk sea-wind to blow this fit of the blue devils away, but he had resigned his commission, and with his mother's pleas still ringing in his ears he knew he'd had no other choice.

'Damn Catari!' he muttered beneath his breath. How in Hades was he to persuade her to leave Castell Mynach, always provided he managed to find some seminary foolish enough to accept his wilful little sister?

Shaking off this uncomfortable reflection, he began to walk rapidly back towards Laura Place. It would not do to offend Simon's mother. She had plainly viewed his desire to take a stroll so late in the day as eccentric, but he had insisted on stretching his legs.

'I won't be long, ma'am. Just down to the abbey, perhaps,' he had murmured with steely politeness.

After being cooped up for endless hours in that damned mail-coach he had longed for some fresh air!

A faint smile touched his well-cut mouth. Mrs Murray had tried in vain to hide her surprise that he had not travelled post.

'But surely you keep teams of your own horses at the best posting-inns, my lord?' she had exclaimed, presiding over the teacups in her elegant drawing-room. 'I remember your father always did so.'

A warning cough from Simon had reminded her that Gareth and the late Viscount had frequently been at odds, and her inquisition had shrivelled into an embarrassed enquiry as to whether he would care for another of Cook's excellent macaroons.

Accepting it, Gareth had smoothed over the awkward moment by hinting that it was merely a fancy to broaden his experience which had led him to travel on the public mail-coach.

Such oddity would merely confirm Mrs Murray's

opinion that he had become an eccentric while in the Navy, but that was preferable to admitting that his pockets were sadly to let!

'Don't breathe a word to my mother of how badly your affairs stand,' Simon had advised, the moment Gareth had stepped over the threshold of the handsome town house in Laura Place and they had exchanged greetings.

Gareth had thrown him a quizzical look and Simon had ducked his blond head, his lanky body squirming with embarrassment.

'You are one of my oldest friends, Gareth, so I don't scruple to admit it; my mother is an excellent woman in many respects but she is a dreadful gossip! Mention one word of what a tangle your father left behind him and it'll be all over Bath in a trice!'

'Don't worry. I'll take care what I say.' Gareth reached out and gripped Simon's shoulder for an instant, touched by his concern.

'Good.' Simon nodded awkwardly, relieved to have got over such heavy ground so lightly. His constraint vanishing, he grinned. 'Come on, let's have a decent drink before Mama comes down and starts to rot your innards with her everlasting tea! I've got a very tolerable Madeira—or should I offer you Jamaica rum? That's what you naval fellows all drink, isn't it?'

'Madeira, if you please.'

Gareth wanted no reminders of the career he had been forced to relinquish, but he was happy to recall earlier days when Simon began to reminisce about the larks they'd got up at Harrow, and later at Jesus College, Oxford.

'I'm glad you accepted my invitation to come and spend Easter with us, Gareth. Letters are all very well, but it's been too long since we've talked like this!'

'Three years.' Gareth nodded. 'In London. Just before I joined the *Britannia* as a newly commissioned lieutenant.'

'Aye, you were bound for the West Indies and the

convey you were guarding was attacked by Spanish privateers.' Simon laughed a little enviously. 'Your letter made it sound dashed exciting.'

'It was lively, certainly,' Gareth agreed with dry irony.

Simon smiled. Trust Gareth to play down his adventures! 'Sometimes you make me feel a dull homebody!'

Gareth grinned back at him. 'Liar,' he retorted amiably. 'You were never one for travel. You got homesick at Oxford.'

'I must admit I've little taste for adventure.' Simon nodded, accepting this imputation with equanimity. 'If I had, I suppose I would have joined the Navy as you did, or purchased a pair of colours and gone gallivanting all over the Peninsular like my brother Andrew. But I like living here in Bath. It is no longer as fashionable as it once was but there's plenty to do, and one meets a great many new people, which I find entertaining.'

He paused and got up to refill their glasses. Glancing back over his shoulder, he continued casually, 'As a matter of fact, my mother has got it into her head you'd enjoy a bout of socialising. She's wangled several invitations on your behalf already, and she plans to give a dinner in your honour. I hope you don't mind?'

Gareth restrained a sigh. 'Of course not.'

The slightly strained note left Simon's tone. 'Well, that's all right, then!' he exclaimed. 'I did warn her that you might not like it. After all, you wrote to tell me that you were coming here on business, but I don't think she was listening.' He shrugged apologetically.

'I appreciate her kind concern.' Gareth injected conviction into his voice. Then, sensing Simon's unspoken curiosity, decided to explain further. 'I need to find a seminary willing to groom my sister. My mother wants to bring her out next year.'

'What? Little Catari?'

'She will be seventeen next February.'

'Aye, of course. She's a year younger than the twins.'

Simon shook his head. 'Who'd have thought time would fly so fast, eh? Is she still as much of a tomboy?'

'Unfortunately.' Gareth's clear features twisted into a grimace. 'She's been left too much to her own devices—especially since my mother became ill. She has no sense at all.'

'Even the best of females don't seem to have much,' Simon pronounced, with all the authority of a man saddled with no less than five younger sisters. 'Liza, Mary and Sally are all wed now, of course, and off my hands, but I sometimes doubt if even a matchmaker like Mama will ever find husbands for the twins. They'd drive any normal fellow mad with their chatter. All they ever talk about is new hairstyles or what gowns they are going to wear to the next party!'

'I wish Catari would discover an interest in such innocent preoccupations. At least they are acceptably feminine,' Gareth muttered. 'She'd rather practise fencing or ride her pony barebacked along the beach than sew a seam!'

He gave an impatient shrug of his broad shoulders. 'To be frank with you, Simon, I don't know what to do about her. She's too old to beat and, in spite of what my mother seems to think, she don't pay much notice to what I say.'

Simon watched his friend's hands clench upon the arms of his chair. Gareth would never criticise his mother, but he'd already guessed that Lady Rhayadar had applied pressure to force Gareth to leave the Navy. Not that one could altogether blame her for wanting her only son home. It was eighteen months since the fourth Viscount had died—a long time for a woman in frail health to hold together a large estate.

'I dare say a few months in a strict seminary will teach Cati to mind you better,' he declared, with deliberately cheerful optimism. 'Tell you what, why don't I ask Mama if she knows of a suitable place? Even if she doesn't, one of her acquaintance is bound to.'

Since this thought had already occurred to Gareth, he was happy to agree to this sensible suggestion.

'I just hope they are accomplished at miracles,' he concluded grimly. 'You see, my mother is determined on a London Season. Nothing less than a grand match will do! God alone knows, I've tried to convince her such a scheme won't wash—but you know my mother!'

Several school holidays spent at Gareth's ancestral home on the coast of South Wales enabled Simon to understand exactly what his friend meant. Lady Rhayadar's pride was a legend throughout the Gower Peninsular!

'Just be grateful she ain't interesting herself in *your* nuptials,' he retorted, with a wealth of meaning in his tone.

Gareth guessed from this dark remark that Mrs Murray was plaguing her elder son to embark upon the married state.

'Marriage is an encumbrance a man of sense can do without.' He proffered the advice with a wry smile. 'Stay single, *bach*. I mean to. Life holds enough vexations as it is.'

Simon's crack of laughter had been cut short by the arrival of Mrs Murray, and perforce the conversation had reverted to more decorous lines.

The classical façade of the Murray dwelling hove once more into view, but Gareth remained wrapped in his thoughts.

He had meant every word.

'You must find yourself a rich heiress, Gareth,' his mother had urged, the moment she'd laid eyes on him on his return from the Navy. 'Or do you wish to see the castle fall down around our ears?'

'I can afford neither the time nor the energy to look for a bride, Mother. As you so rightly point out, there is much for me to do here to restore the estate.'

His unyielding retort had prompted a frown.

'Are you sure it isn't because you are still pining for Nerys Parry?'

'No!' Gareth strove to control his temper.

Warned by the flash of fury in his dark eyes, the Dowager had prudently abandoned the topic, but the next day she had begun again.

Gareth was heartily sick of the subject. He had no desire to settle down—least of all to some worthy heiress who would bore him to distraction.

Women were a luxury. He had learnt to do without their charms during the last nine years. An officer in His Majesty's Navy had more important things to think of, and, while he was no longer in command of a frigate, he did have other, equally weighty responsibilities.

So why couldn't he stop thinking about a pair of laughing grey eyes?

'And what, pray, took you so long, miss?'

The sharp voice arrested Thea's swift progress towards the stairs.

Her grandmother was standing in the doorway of the small salon, an impatient expression pulling her heavy features into a scowl.

'Come in here. I want to speak to you.' Without waiting to see if her order would be obeyed, Mrs Howard sailed back inside her domain.

Smoothing her face into submissiveness, Thea unwillingly followed.

I detest this room, she thought to herself as she watched Mrs Howard carefully lower her bulk on to one of the pink satin-covered sofas that littered the thick, richly patterned Aubusson carpet. Vivid shades of rose and gold assaulted the eye at every turn while numerous knick-knacks competed for attention with the intricate furniture.

It was like being inside the heart of some overblown rose!

Strange that her grandmother, whose personal taste in dress ran to severe blacks and greys, should have chosen to decorate their new home in such a florid manner. The whole house had been refurbished to the latest kick of fashion since their removal to Bath two months ago. Thea didn't understand it. They had lived in a much more simple style in Bristol, but since Papa's death Grandmama had seemed determined on change.

One thing, however, remained constant. The salon was stiflingly hot. Unlike many overweight people, Mrs Howard felt the cold, and took care that her favourite retreat was heated to the kind of high temperature she preferred. In spite of the mildness of the spring evening, an immense fire of sea-coals burned in the vast white marble fireplace, and the thick pink velvet curtains which draped the long windows had been tightly closed to exclude any possibility of stray draughts.

'Where is Nelson?' Mrs Howard did not invite Thea to sit down.

'I took him to the kitchen, Grandmama. He appeared to be hungry.'

'Humph! And no wonder, miss, keeping the poor animal out until this hour! You were told to take him for some exercise, not to go jaunting halfway to Bristol and back. I only hope you did not walk the legs off him.'

'No, Grandmama.' Thea carefully kept the irony from her tone. She had learnt long ago the utter folly of trying to explain anything to her grandmother.

Mrs Howard eyed her with disfavour. 'Oh, very well!' She waved a dismissive hand. 'You had best go and change. But hurry, mind! I'll not have you creating a bad impression by being late.' Her dry, rasping voice shook with sudden anxiety. 'Everything must go off well tonight!'

Thea's expressive face betrayed her surprise. Of course she knew that this soirée was important. It was the first formal entertainment they had offered in their new home, and all the leading citizens of the town had been invited. Every aspect had been endlessly discussed and planned down to the tiniest detail. Georgy had been in a dither for weeks, but Thea hadn't expected her self-confident grandmother to be so on edge.

'Don't be dense, girl!' Mrs Howard's patience snapped. 'This is Georgy's big chance. The Murrays are bringing their guest with them. He is a nobleman—a viscount.' Her pale eyes held a greedy gleam. 'I intend Georgy to marry him.'

'But we don't know anything about the man. We haven't even met him.' The objection sprang impetuously to Thea's lips.

'Nonsense!' Mrs Howard glared at her. 'According to Sarah Murray he owns half of Wales.'

'Mrs Murray could be mistaken, and even if she isn't, surely wealth isn't everything?'

Thea tried to keep her tone calm, but she could feel her anger rising. In the past her grandmother had beaten Thea with a leather strap, or locked her overnight in the cellars, and out of necessity she had learnt to control her tongue.

But now Georgy's future was at stake.

'My sister is barely eighteen.' Bravely she met Mrs Howard's angry eyes. 'I see no hurry for her to marry yet, but when she does it ought to be to someone who will treat her with care and consideration. We don't know what this man is like. He might be old or cruel. . . or anything!'

'You talk like a fool!' Mrs Howard's hard mouth twisted in a look of scorn. 'I'll grant you Georgy's young for her years, but she's plenty old enough to be wed. As for Viscount Rhayadar, he ain't yet reached thirty—and if the Murrays vouch for him he's hardly likely to be a rogue.'

She nodded her elaborately dressed grey head, causing her many chins to wobble. 'He sounds an ideal match, but I won't force her if she takes him in dislike.'

Thea released a sigh of relief. 'I am thankful to hear it, Grandmama.'

Mrs Howard shrugged, dismissing her remark with indifference. 'If Rhayadar don't come up to the mark,

I'll find someone else.' She jabbed one fat beringed forefinger in Thea's direction and wagged it to emphasise her meaning.

'I want a man of wealth and title for Georgina. Why else do you think I uprooted us from Bristol to come and live here, eh? It weren't from any sentimental attachment to my birthplace, if that's what you've been thinking. No, I said my goodbyes to Bath when I left it as a bride. I never expected to come back, but Georgy stands a better chance of catching a fine husband here.'

Hidden by the folds of her dull gown, Thea's slim fingers twisted angrily together. She might have known!

'What a face! Disapprove, do you?' Mrs Howard snorted.

'I'm only surprised you didn't decide on a London season, Grandmama.'

'None of your sauce, miss!' Mrs Howard's big square face flushed. There was a tiny silence and then, her eyes narrowing, she gave Thea a considering look.

'Maybe it's time you knew the truth. Sit down.'

She pointed to a spindly-legged little chair opposite her sofa, and when Thea had obeyed she continued in the same grim tone.

'As you know, your grandpa made his fortune by building up the family trade of ships' chandlery. But he didn't reckon on dying before he'd trained your father to take over from him. It grieves me to have to say so of my only child, but Richard was a fool. He had little interest in the business and no talent for it.'

She paused.

Thea wondered how to reply. In truth, she had hardly known her father. Throughout her childhood he had been a remote figure, seen only in brief glimpses. Even when she had been old enough to leave the schoolroom he had rarely exchanged more than a dozen words with her. Nor had Georgy fared any better.

'I think Papa preferred his painting to anything else,' she remarked at last.

'Art!' Mrs Howard sniffed deprecatingly. 'What good did that ever do? If it had been left to him, we all would have ended up in the poorhouse!'

Thea goggled at her in surprise.

'You may well stare, miss. Five years—that's all it took your father to bring us to the brink of ruin. I did my utmost to check his folly, but if he hadn't fallen that day I dare say there would have been nothing left.'

Denied the opportunity to travel to Italy by war, Richard Howard had gone on a sketching holiday to the English Lakes some fourteen months ago. Ignoring the advice of his guide, he had attempted to climb a steep cliff and had slipped to his death.

'But all this!' Thea indicated their lavish surroundings with a bewildered wave of her hand. 'If there was no money——'

'This house is mine,' Mrs Howard interrupted. 'I paid for it out of my own pocket. Your grandpa left me well provided for. He knew what Richard was like!' She shook her head. 'He destroyed your inheritance. All I managed to salvage was a few thousand pounds, which must be shared between the pair of you.'

Struggling to absorb this shocking information, Thea had to force herself to concentrate on what her grandmother was saying.

'I decided we'd do best to sell up and make a fresh start away from Bristol once our mourning was over. Bath seemed the obvious choice.' She smoothed her dark satin skirts in a small, satisfied gesture. 'Although we've no close relatives left here, I am still acquainted with plenty of folk who count. Now we are ready to start entertaining, I intend to ensure that everyone will be glad to accept my hospitality.'

Thea gave a reluctant nod. She might not like this house but it was impressive. 'You have spent a lot of money, Grandmama.'

'It'll be worth it.' She fixed Thea with a gimlet stare. 'However, I won't waste my blunt. There's no need for a fancy London season. Plenty of rich visitors still come to Bath, and Georgy's pretty enough to attract any man.'

'Does Georgy know of your plans for her?' Thea asked stiffly.

'Aye, why not? She's a sensible girl. She knows it's just as easy to learn to love a rich man as a poor one.' Mrs Howard gave a short bark of laughter. 'She ain't like you. Her head's not stuffed full of romantic nonsense.'

Thea coloured. Her grandmother frequently made fun of her liking for novels.

'Be that as it may, Grandmama, *I* have no intention of selling myself to highest bidder,' she declared hotly.

'Hoity-toity, miss! You'll take the first respectable offer that comes your way or I'll wash my hands of you.'

'I'd as lief earn my own living.'

Mrs Howard laughed. 'Don't be a fool. You've been reared a lady.'

Thea bit her lower lip. Papa had insisted that both she and Gregory attend a select school as day-pupils. In addition to their academic studies they had been taught etiquette, deportment, music and dancing.

Georgy had disliked the school—she had found studying tedious and had wanted to leave. Grandmama had supported her, but for once Papa had exerted his authority and left them in no doubt of his views.

'Your mother was cousin to Sir George Ashby. You will learn to become ladies and honour her memory,' he had shouted at his startled daughters, his vehemence all the more frightening for being incomprehensible.

'Marriage is the only realistic option open to you.' Her grandmother's harsh voice wrenched Thea back to the present. 'Unless you want to turn all that book-learning to account. Well, have you a fancy to becoming a governess?'

'No, I do not, Grandmama.' Thea answered bluntly, knowing that most governesses were badly treated. 'If Papa left some money——'

'Not enough to last you the rest of your life.'

'I could learn to economise,' Thea replied spiritedly.

'Talk sense! You've not been bred to live hand to mouth in some hovel!'

Thea's hands clenched on her skirts.

'You need a husband, my girl. And may I remind you that you're in no position to be choosy?' Mrs Howard's pendulous jowls shook with malicious amusement. 'You're already two and twenty, with no looks to speak of and no fortune either. So you'd best pray some man does ask for you, and soon—for you needn't imagine I mean to go on supporting you once Georgy is wed.'

Thea sucked in her breath in suprise.

Mrs Howard gave a cold smile.

'Oh, don't worry——I'll do my duty by you. You'll leave this house with a respectable dowry. *If* I approve the man you choose.' Her voice was mocking. 'But understand this. Georgy shall inherit my fortune. I'm not leaving you a penny of it.'

'You have never liked me,' Thea declared angrily.

'No.' Mrs Howard admitted it with bald indifference.

'May I ask why?'

'Another time.' Mrs Howard flapped her hands in irritable dismissal.

Thea rose stiffly to her feet. She had always known that Georgy was her grandmother's favourite, but she had never dreamt that her aversion went so deep! And for the life of her she couldn't understand why!

Mrs Howard fixed Thea with her pale gaze. 'Just remember what I've said, Dorothea. I've no mind to be saddled with you for life, so you'll do as I say and take this chance to find yourself a respectable *parti*, or be damned to you!'

'Thank you for making your feelings so plain, Grandmama,' Thea replied, with all the dignity she could muster. 'Believe me, I shall do my best to relieve you of my unwelcome presence as soon as possible.'

Dropping a swift curtsy, she hastened to the door, but the hateful laughter followed her from the room.

'Thea! What an age you've been. I've been ready for hours!'

Her sister's impatient sigh greeted Thea as she entered the small back bedroom which was her personal domain.

'Do hurry, or Grandmama will be cross with you again.'

'She already is,' Thea retorted, but then relented when Georgy's exquisite face creased with anxiety.

Taking a deep breath, she subdued her quivering nerves and banished the memory of her grandmother's gloating smile.

'Don't worry—it's all right. I've already apologised for keeping Nelson out so late.'

She began to strip off her drab clothes. The water in the ewer on her wash-stand would be cold but it would have to do. There was no time to ring for more.

'Thank goodness for that!' Georgy exclaimed with artless satisfaction. 'I should hate any unpleasantness to spoil tonight.' She beamed at Thea. 'Oh, Thea! Aren't you excited? Just imagine, my first grown-up party!' She gave a little giggle. 'I never thought the day would come. We seem to have been in mourning forever!'

'Do you miss Papa, Georgy?' Laving water over her bare arms, Thea glanced her sister curiously.

Georgy shrugged, and flung out her hands in a careless gesture. 'Why should I? He never cared a straw for me. In fact, I think he used to regard us as a nuisance! I'm sorry he's dead, but I can't pretend it makes much difference to me.'

She watched Thea towel herself dry for a moment and then added, 'It's probably very wicked of me to say so but it seemed typical of him to choose to die just at that moment, when I was getting ready to make my come-out!'

'I dare say he didn't mean to be selfish,' Thea murmured, suppressing a pang of unseemly amusement.

A regretful expression appeared in Georgy's big blue eyes. 'No,' she agreed, 'but if we hadn't gone into mourning I would mostly likely have been betrothed by now.'

Thea blinked. 'Do you *want* to be married so young?'

'What nonsensical questions you do ask, Thea!' Georgy's silvery laughter rippled throughout the room. 'Of course I do! The sooner the better! And tonight is going to be the start of it all!'

She bounded up from the window-seat where she had been sitting and began to twirl around the room, her lovely face alight with anticipation. Pirouetting to a halt in front of the long cheval glass, she peered at her reflection with sudden anxiety.

'Do you think this white sarcenet suits me? Perhaps the blue silk would have been better.'

'It's perfect,' Thea replied, hastily donning fresh underclothes and trying to reconcile herself to the idea that her little sister was all grown up.

'I asked Alice to press your pink lustring for you.' Restlessly Georgy swung round from the mirror and indicated the gown laid out in readiness on the bed. 'But I do wish you had let Grandmama buy you a new evening gown. You won't do yourself justice in that old thing!'

She surveyed her sister with a critical eye.

'You are too thin, but your complexion is good. You

could look quite pretty, you know, if only you would try!'

It was on the tip of Thea's tongue to retort that a new gown had not been been offered to *her*, but instead she forced a smile.

'You know I'm not interested in fashion,' she lied smoothly.

Sometimes she almost believed this pretence herself. Not for the world would she have admitted how hurt she had been when she'd first realised that Georgy's dress allowance was more than three times her own—to say nothing of the expensive presents Grandmama was always buying her.

'At least let Alice arrange your hair. I'm not at all clever at playing the pianoforte or painting in water-colours the way you are, but I know the importance of dressing one's hair nicely,' Georgy said, giving her own immaculate silver-gilt curls a satisfied pat.

'There isn't time,' Thea answered, concentrating on fastening her pink silk sandals. One of the ties was loose. She must sew it before she wore them next.

'You shouldn't have taken Nelson out,' Georgy remarked carelessly, turning back to examine her reflection once more.

'It was Grandmama's wish, not mine,' Thea replied impatiently.

She decided that it was futile to point out that Georgy never offered to exercise the pug. Georgy would only deny it and start crying—and besides, it never did any good to argue with her sister!

'Did Grandmama tell you that the Murrays are going to bring a real viscount with them?' Georgy demanded eagerly as Thea began to brush the tangles out of her thick honey-coloured hair.

'She did mention it,' Thea answered drily before changing the subject.

Her sister was equally happy to discuss the numerous floral tributes that had been delivered to the house. Although this would be her first evening party, Georgy had already caused a stir at Sunday services at the abbey and in the Pump Room, and several enterprising young gentlemen had dragged their mamas and sisters along to pay a morning call in Beaufort Square.

By the time this topic was exhausted, Thea had arranged her hair in a plain neat coil at the nape of her neck and begun hunting round for the fan which matched her dress.

'Oh, don't you remember?' Georgy exclaimed. 'I borrowed it last week. I'll get it from my rooms and meet you at the top of the stairs. But do hurry, Thea, or Grandmama will scold us both!'

Taking her silence for consent, Georgy disappeared in a whirl of silken skirts.

Thea picked up the simple sheath of pink lustring from the bed and slipped it on. It had pretty, short puffed sleeves and a flattering neckline but, as Georgy had so tactlessly pointed out, it was no longer in its first flush.

Still, the colour is becoming, Thea told herself firmly.

A quiver of excitment shot through her. In spite of everything, she was starting to look forward to this evening after all.

During the five years she had been out Thea had rarely attended parties. In Bristol their circle of acquaintance had been composed mostly of older people. Sedate evenings of whist or music had been considered adequate entertainment by her grandmama. Even before strict mourning had put an end to all thought of such frivolity, Mrs Howard had point-blank refused to countenance any of the assemblies that Thea had longed to attend.

Why, oh, why, did her grandmother dislike her so much? Surely it couldn't be just because she wasn't as pretty as Georgy?

Thea's slender frame stiffened as she remembered the ultimatum Mrs Howard had flung at her head not an hour earlier.

In a strange kind of a way it was almost a relief to

know where she stood. Whatever its cause, her grandmama's animosity was genuine, and not a figment of her imagination!

Her grandmother desired to be rid of her. Very well. She would start making her own plans. Whatever happened, she was not going to allow herself to be bullied into some loveless marriage just to suit her grandmother's convenience!

CHAPTER TWO

'DOROTHEA, are you deaf, girl? Go and fetch me another glass of water at once!'

'Yes, Grandmama.'

Thea hadn't heard Mrs Howard above the noise of the crowd that thronged the Pump Room. Although it was still very early in the season, this was one of the most fashionable meeting-places in Bath, and it was full of people seemingly intent on drowning out the tune being played by the group of musicians in the gallery.

Mrs Howard had procured a chair for herself in a good position near the doors, from where she might observe everyone entering. Several people had already come flocking up to them, congratulating her on last night's soirée, and although she smiled and answered them gracefully Thea wasn't fooled. Grandmama was furious because Viscount Rhayadar had cried off!

Making her way through the throng to the pump, Thea silently cursed the Viscount. Even Georgy was in a somewhat dejected mood this morning, in spite of her undoubted triumph.

Thea had also experienced the dizzying thrill of success. No less than three gentlemen had paid her compliments, and she was much too content to care whether or not a haughty aristocrat had thought them beneath his touch! Mrs Murray, of course, had pretended that her guest was fatigued after his long journey, but very few people had actually believed her.

On her return from the pump, a glass of the lukewarm, rather flat-tasting mineral water in her hand, Thea's progress was blocked by a gentleman standing with his back turned towards her.

Thea checked, her pulse suddenly unquiet. Surely

there was something familiar about that pair of broad shoulders?

'Excuse me, sir.'

He swung round. It *was* her impudent stranger!

'So we meet again, my fair unknown.'

Today, dressed in a smart coat of blue superfine worn with a yellow waistcoat and pale cream pantaloons, he looked even more handsome than she remembered.

Thea's chin tilted, and, ignoring the treacherous stab of pleasure that fluttered along her veins, she said severely, 'Pray let me pass, sir.'

'What? Without a word of cheer to brighten up my day?'

Gareth smiled at her, his spirits rising. Suddenly this tedious gathering had taken on a new aspect.

His dark gaze raked up her and down. What was it that he found so attractive about her? Of medium height, her figure was neat, but she lacked the ripe curves he preferred. Her hair was thick and shiny, but not a particularly striking colour. Except for that small dimple by her mouth, her features were similarly unremarkable.

Only her eyes were out of the ordinary. A clear, luminious grey, they had the ability to reflect her mood. When she smiled their sweetness transformed her small face, lending her a rare charm.

A charm he found quite irresistible!

'I see you left your charge at home today,' he observed, with an innocence at variance with the glint of amusement in his expression. 'Did you give him the ham bone you promised him?'

Thea found it impossible not to return his smile. How could she go on pretending to be missish when they shared the same sense of humour? 'He ate every scrap of it.'

'I hope he was grateful.' The deep voice hesitated. '*I* should be very grateful if you would favour me with a few moments' conversation.' He indicated a pair of empty chairs over by the big windows.

Looking up into his midnight eyes, Thea realised that he wanted to get to know her better.

'I promise I will be on my best behaviour,' he added lightly.

'I'm sorry,' Thea murmured with great reluctance. 'But I'm afraid I must refuse, sir.'

For a moment she thought he was going to press her to change her mind, but then he bowed polite acquiescence. 'Of course.'

'I'm here with my family, you understand,' Thea added quickly, experiencing a sudden longing to see his smile again. 'My grandmother is waiting for me. I have to take this water back to her.'

'Thank God.' His engaging grin returned. 'For one horrible moment I thought you might be intending to drink the disgusting stuff yourself.'

Thea gave a little choke of suppressed mirth. 'No, indeed! I tried it once and that was enough.'

He laughed out loud at this, and several heads turned in their direction.

'I must go,' Thea said hurriedly, becoming aware of her indiscretion.

'Wait. Won't you at least tell me your name?'

There was a note of urgency in his deep, musical voice that almost persuaded her, but with a quick shake of her head Thea brushed past him.

The cluster around her grandmother had thinned.

'About time too, miss, you know it should be drunk hot,' Mrs Howard said grumpily as she took the glass from Thea's unsteady hand. 'Heavens, you clumsy girl! You have spilt it—it's half-empty!'

'I'm sorry.' Thea apologised automatically, her thoughts elsewhere.

The instant her grandmother's attention was diverted, her gaze scanned the room.

He was gone! She hadn't dared risk a glance in his

direction with her grandmother's reproving eye on her, but now he had disappeared and she didn't know where.

A crushing sense of disappointment swept over her. If he had been interested in her, why hadn't he found some means of obtaining an introduction?

'Don't look so distressed. I don't think anyone else overheard Grandmama scolding you,' Georgy whispered.

Thea put on a bright smile. 'I'm all right,' she answered.

It's your own fault if you are feeling miserable, she told herself sternly. You've let last night's success go to your head. He was just amusing himself. Ten to one, you'll never see him again!

The thought should have been consoling—so why did she feel so unutterably depressed?

Gareth surveyed the results of his valet's handiwork in his bedroom mirror. The plain dark evening coat sat across his broad shoulders without a crease, its elegant severity a tribute to his tailor, and a ruby pin gleamed amid the snowy folds of his necktie. Satisfied, Gareth nodded dismissal to the man.

He rose to his feet, curbing a sense of reluctance.

Damn this party anyway. Simon's mother seemed incapable of understanding that he did not wish to become involved in the social round. He had refused most of her invitations these last two weeks but, conscious of his obligations, he could not avoid tonight's affair.

Mrs Murray had invited fifteen of her closest friends to join them for dinner, which was to be followed by cards and dancing for sixty more.

'You need not fear it will be stuffily formal, my lord,' she had told him a few days ago, with a coy smile more suited to a new débutante than a widow in her fifties. 'Just a few young people enjoying themselves, you know.'

Simon had hooted with laughter when Gareth had reported this conversation to him later that same day.

'Don't you believe it,' he had warned. 'Mama will seize this chance to impress everyone. I dare say we will have as many as thirty dishes and an Italian band!' His wide grin faded. 'What's worse, I expect she will invite the Howards.' Gareth directed a look of enquiry at him and Simon shrugged.

'Set of mushrooms,' he announced succinctly. 'Mama wanted to drag you to the old lady's soirée the night you arrived, but I put my foot down and told her not to bother you.'

'Then I owe you my thanks,' Gareth commented drily.

'Indeed you do! She is just the kind of toad-eater you despise,' Simon laughed.

Gareth raised his brows.

'Mama met them while out paying a call,' Simon elaborated obligingly. 'Old Mrs Howard claimed acquaintance with m'father. Said she knew him in his salad days when she lived here in Bath!' He chuckled. 'I'm not sure if Mama cared for such revelations, but before she knew how to prevent it she found herself invited to take tea in Beaufort Square.'

'Isn't that where all the rich cits live?' Gareth enquired.

'Aye. I've told Mama she ought to give her the go-by, but she says she likes the girls.'

'Girls? Good God, are there more of them?'

'Two granddaughters. Orphans. Their father—the old lady's heir—died about a year ago, I think.' Simon shrugged. 'Trade, of course, but pretty enough manners—and the younger one is a real beauty too.'

'Do I detect an ulterior motive behind your consideration for my ancient bones?'

Simon chuckled. 'Nay, you know I'm not much in the petticoat line. Not that little Miss Georgina couldn't tempt me, mind,' he added reflectively.

'Rumour has it that they are as wealthy as Croesus, but the old lady is a regular horror!'

'Then why does your mother continue to favour the acquaintance?' Gareth asked with lazy amusement.

'Beats me,' Simon replied with a cheerful grimace. 'Unless, of course, it is to humour the twins. They are inclined to cling together, which Mama dislikes, but they have taken a shine to Georgina Howard. They all giggle together for hours.'

Another answer to this riddle had occurred to Gareth, but he kept a still tongue, not wishing to disturb his friend's harmony.

Now, as he descended to the drawing-room, he wondered if his suspicion was correct. Could Mrs Murray have settled on this Miss Georgina Howard as a prospective daughter-in-law? It would be interesting to see what this heiress was like.

God knew, the rest of the evening promised to be exceptionally tedious. He disliked formal affairs, but even more he hated to be made a fuss of merely on account of his rank. Only good manners had prevented him from seeking some excuse to escape.

Dinner proved as lavish as Simon had predicted. The first course offered a choice of three soups, a rack of lamb roasted with apricots, a fricassee of chicken, pork escalopes with sauce *à l'indienne* and a sauté of veal, all accompanied by several side-dishes. These were followed by timbale of macaroni in the Neapolitan style, a seafood gratin, various omelettes, cheese dishes, and assorted vegetables done in different ways.

'You are not eating, my lord. May I tempt you to try some of this praline gateau?' Mrs Murray trilled.

Gareth declined. 'I fear my appetite has become dulled after life in the Navy, ma'am,' he added politely, softening his refusal.

This unwary remark unleashed a flood of questions from the middle-aged lady seated on his left, and by the time he had satisfied her curiosity concerning his former career Gareth was glad that the meal was over.

'Come, ladies, let us leave the gentlemen to their port for a few moments.'

Encouraged by this parting shot from their hostess, the gentlemen did not linger, and Gareth soon found himself heading for the pale blue drawing-room to rejoin the ladies.

'Ready for the fray, my lord Viscount?' Simon whispered.

'Sapskull!'

The new influx of guests began to arrive. Exchanging polite inanities with an elderly couple who claimed acquaintance with one of his aunts, Gareth suddenly stiffened.

Excusing himself at the first opportunity, he sought out his host.

'I want an introduction,' he announced baldly.

Simon's gaze followed the jerk of Gareth's dark head, and he let out a tiny chuckle.

'So you've fallen victim to our beauty's charms already. And I thought you preferred brunettes.'

Gareth's brow creased for a second and then cleared.

'No, not that one,' he said impatiently. 'I want you to introduce me to the girl standing next to her. The one in pink.'

'You mean you prefer Miss Howard to her sister?' Surprise coloured Simon's ejaculation, but he had the sense to keep his voice down.

Gareth nodded vehemently. The little blonde was indeed the stunner Simon had claimed, but his mild curiosity had died an abrupt death. He had found his grey-eyed charmer again, and this time he was determined not to let her escape.

'Very well.' Simon began to thread his way towards the little group near the fireplace. 'But don't say I didn't warn you. She's a regular dragon!'

Correctly interpreting this remark, Gareth allowed his glance to rest upon the old lady guarding the two girls.

She was a remarkable figure. Almost as broad as she was tall, her fashionably cut gown of dark grey silk strained to contain a vast expanse of flesh. A lavishly beplumed turban and a dazzling assortment of jewels thickly scattered about her person added to the impression of wealth run tastelessly riot, reminding Gareth of nothing so much as a decorated elephant he'd seen once while in India.

'Still game, Saint George?' Simon teased.

Gareth raised his brows. 'Saint David, if you please,' he retorted with a mocking grin. 'We Welshmen know all about taming dragons!'

'May I present our guest, Viscount Rhayadar, to you, ma'am?'

Looking up, Thea saw the man standing at Mr Murray's side and almost let out an involuntary squeak of surprise.

In a daze she watched him bow over her grandmother's veined hand with elegant grace.

'I was desolate to have missed your soirée the other night, ma'am,' he was saying in that lovely deep voice of his. 'I hear it was a great success.'

Thea could have kicked herself. Oh, why hadn't she realised earlier that his distinctive intonation was Welsh!

There could be no mistake. Her impudent stranger was the eligible *parti* her grandmother schemed to capture!

'Charmed to meet you, I'm sure, my lord.' There was a girlish breathlessness in Mrs Howard's normally harsh voice, and she fluttered her fan at him in delight. Compliments from a viscount! And him such a handsome young man! Wait until her cronies heard about this!

She turned to introduce her granddaughters and her beaming smile faded. What on earth was the matter with that idiotic girl now? How dared she frown at a moment like this?

'Dorothea, make your curtsy to his lordship this

instant,' she ordered sharply, and Thea reluctantly obeyed.

'Delighted to make your acquaintance, Miss Howard.'

Aware of his dark eyes upon her, Thea struggled for composure. 'I trust you are enjoying your stay in Bath, my lord?' she said in her primmest tone.

'Indeed. One may see such unusual sights here,' Gareth replied, with such perfect innocence that Thea guessed his meaning at once.

He was teasing her! Oh, how dared he?

Gareth enjoyed the sudden flush of colour that enlivened her clear complexion, but his attention was demanded by Mrs Howard, who was introducing her younger grandchild.

'Miss Georgina.' Gareth bowed politely.

She was certainly a beautiful little creature, with those enormous blue eyes and that silver-gilt hair. Her figure was good too, with a full bosom enticingly displayed in a surprisingly low-cut gown of ivory spider gauze.

'Do you like parties, Lord Rhayadar?' Georgy asked, fluttering her eyelashes at him.

'It depends on the company, ma'am.'

Georgy giggled, taking his factual reply for a compliment, and, thinking she had made a conquest, began to prattle in her usual artless fashion.

After a few moments Gareth decided that she was empty-headed, and impatiently began to wonder how he could detach her sister.

At length, catching Simon's eye, he smoothly handed the conversation over to his friend and turned back to Mrs Howard.

'I wonder if Miss Howard would favour me with the next dance? I believe they are about to form sets for a cotillion in the yellow salon.'

Watching the disappointment flicker over her grandmother's broad face, Thea thought that she would refuse permission.

Her relief was short-lived.

'Of course. You must dance with the *elder* first—must you not, my lord?' Mrs Howard's arch smile remained firmly in place as she turned to Thea. 'Well, go along, Dorothea,' she said, trying to disguise her annoyance. 'Do not keep his lordship waiting.'

Much as she would have liked to disobey, Thea had no desire to cause a scene, so she took the arm held out to her and allowed Gareth to whisk her away.

'You are very silent, Miss Howard.'

All Gareth could see was the top of her downcast head. She had refused to meet his gaze since he had led her away from the drawing-room. Throughout the cotillion, a dance which she had performed with a skilful grace that had enchanted him, she had remained silent. Now it was over, and in a moment it would be too late for private conversation.

'I have no desire for your conversation, sir.' Thea glanced up, her eyes flashing.

'Have I offended you?' Surprise coloured Gareth's question. 'What did I do to——?'

'I do not wish to discuss it. Please return me to my grandmother,' Thea replied, striving to maintain her appearance of calm. It was becoming more difficult by the minute to control herself. If she didn't get away from him soon she would explode!

Gareth's thick black brows drew together, but he nodded and held out his arm to her.

Gingerly Thea laid her hand on his sleeve. Beneath the smooth fabric she could feel the hard muscles in his arm. Her fingers began to tingle and she swallowed nervously.

They left the yellow salon and began to make their way back to the drawing-room.

'Must you walk so fast?' Thea found it difficult to keep up with his long legs.

'I thought you wanted to be rid of me.'

This brutally honest answer robbed Thea of the power of speech.

Oh, how had things got into such a horrid muddle? For two long weeks she had looked everywhere in the hope of seeing him again, but the shock of discovering that he was none other than the wealthy aristocrat her grandmother desired for Georgy's husband had destroyed all her pleasure in finding him.

She felt such a fool!

In spite of his failure to follow up their conversation at the Pump Room, Thea had cherished the memory of his warm smile. Not being vain, it was hard for her to accept that his interest might be sincere, but she had allowed herself to dream. The realisation that he was a peer of the realm had instantly put paid to her tentative hopes.

Not only was he a very attractive man, but he was also rich and titled. Such a paragon could never want to have any dealings with an ordinary mortal like Thea Howard. It was highly unlikely that even her beautiful sister would tempt him!

'This way.' They turned into the long corridor which led past the library and Thea let out a little cry of vexation.

'Oh, no! It's snapped.' She halted, raising the hem of her gown a discreet inch. The strap on her left sandal dangled uselessly. 'I knew it was loose. I should have remembered to sew it,' she groaned.

'Take it off and I'll try and fashion a temporary knot to hold it together.'

'I will do no such thing.' Thea stared at him indignantly. 'Would you have me make a public spectacle of myself, sir? Why, anyone could come along!'

'It will only take me a moment.' Gareth made a slight movement towards her, and Thea hastily drew back.

'No! I will not stand here on one leg like a. . .a stork!' she protested.

'Then we'd best remove ourselves from sight while

we effect repairs, ma'am.' He grinned at her mischievously. 'And since you cannot easily walk——'

Before she could guess his intention, he swept her up into his arms and carried her into the deserted library.

'Put me down!'

'In a moment.'

Thea was trembling, but she didn't know whether it was his outrageous behaviour or his nearness which affected her more.

She could feel his heart beating against her own as he kicked the door shut and carried her over to one of the leather-upholstered sofas near the fire. His arms were gentle but she could feel the strength in them.

They were so close that she could see the network of fine lines that traced his eyes.

Perhaps they are the result of too much staring into the sun; his skin is very bronzed... Thea's thoughts drifted dreamily as she inhaled the scent of the light cologne he used. It was mixed with the clean, fresh smell of his healthy male body, and she was beginning to feel deliciously intoxicated.

Just as the longing to slip her arms around his neck became unbearable, he set her down on the sofa and stood back.

'You are very high-handed, sir.' Thea forced herself to reprimand him.

'So I've been told.' He grinned at her unrepentantly.

By all that was holy, she had felt adorably fragile in his arms!

Thea frowned at his flippancy.

'Forgive me. Shall I fetch Mrs Murray or one of her daughters to act as chaperon?' He paused, and his tone became serious. 'Or will you trust me?'

Thea nodded, suddenly breathless.

He was smiling at her with that special warmth again, just as he had done that day in the Pump Room, and her tension dissolved. She was a fool to let anger get the better of her common sense. It wasn't his fault he was a viscount!

'Then hand me your shoe, please.'

Thea removed her sandal and gave it to him with a shy smile.

Gareth sat down next to her and stared with assumed concentration at the broken tie.

She was so close that he could feel the warmth emanating from her slender body, and smell the delicate perfume she wore. . .

'Is it hopeless, sir?'

'Not at all.' Gareth gathered his wits. 'I can rig a knot to last you the rest of this evening, but you'll have to put it back on first.'

Reaching out to take back the sandal, Thea hesitated, and then blurted in a sudden rush, 'Please forgive my bad temper.'

'Only if you will tell me what I did to displease you tonight,' was his swift answer. 'You looked at me as if I had crawled out of the worst ship's bilges!'

Thea hung her glossy head. 'I know. It was abominably rude of me.' Taking a deep breath, she raised her gaze to his. 'You see, when we met earlier I didn't know that you were a viscount.'

'It makes that much difference?'

'You know it does!' Thea abandoned caution and spoke with her usual honesty. 'You ought not to have started up a flirtation with me, sir. The daughter of a tradesman and a peer of the realm can have nothing in common!'

'I will not insult you by pretending there is no truth in what you say, but you exaggerate the case, Miss Howard.' Gareth met her troubled gaze with a level look. 'You may be of merchant stock but you are undoubtedly a lady. Rank need not concern us.'

'It is easy for you to say so, my lord,' Thea flashed back at him. 'I have to be more practical. After all, it is my reputation that will suffer from the gossips if. . .if. . .'

'If I pursue you,' he finished for her.

Thea nodded stiffly.

He was silent, and she watched him, wondering if she had gone too far. Was he offended? Or was he turning over what she had said in his mind?

A tinge of colour crept into her pale cheeks. She could hardly believe she had taxed him outright with being a flirt! He might easily claim that it was all in her imagination!

'Please forgive my lack of forethought, Miss Howard. I should have considered tongues might wag.'

A surge of relief dissolved the tight knot of apprehension in Thea's chest. 'Bath is a very small place,' she murmured.

'And the gossips very active!' he agreed, accepting her olive-branch. 'It is a handsome town but I should find it hard to live here.'

'I must admit I prefer Bristol, which is where we lived until very recently,' Thea confided. 'I liked being near the sea.'

'My home, Castell Mynach, is on the coast. It lies on a headland overlooking a small bay, which is excellent for sailing.' He laughed, a shade ruefully. 'Perhaps it inspired my choice of career.'

'My grandmother told me that you served in His Majesty's Navy. But she thought that you had recently resigned your commission.'

The pair of interested grey eyes raised to his somehow robbed this question of its sting.

'Two months ago.' He supplied the answer with a faint shrug. 'For family reasons.'

'But you still miss your ship.' Thea spoke her thought aloud and then blushed. 'Oh, I'm sorry. I didn't mean to pry.'

'You are quite correct, Miss Howard. I *do* miss the *Valiant*.' Gareth acknowledged her apology with a stiff inclination of his raven head.

'It seems very natural to me that you should do so,' Thea said bluntly, sympathy for his sacrifice prompting her to speak her mind. 'If you hadn't been whole-hearted in devoting yourself to your career you wouldn't have been successful.'

'You think I was a success, Miss Howard?' Gareth enquired lightly, hiding his surprise at her directness behind a show of amusement. 'I was a mere captain, you know, not an admiral!'

Thea ignored his teasing tone. 'To have reached that rank so young proves my point, sir,' she said firmly. 'Of course you must miss the Navy. How could you not?'

Gareth hadn't considered the matter in this light before. He had seen his restless dissatisfaction as weakness. 'Perhaps you are right.'

It was odd how she seemed to understand his innermost feelings. 'However, I dare say I shall get over it in time, and settle down to the life of a country gentleman again.'

'Then you do not intend to live in Bath?' Amazed at her own daring, Thea quickly sought for a less emotional topic. 'Only, there are rumours circulating that you mean to buy a house in the Royal Crescent.'

'*Annwyl Crist*!' Gareth exclaimed, and then hastily apologised so she knew it must have been an oath.

'Towns make me feel confined, Miss Howard,' he explained. 'I like space to breathe. Buying a house here would not suit me at all.'

Thea knew it was foolish to feel disappointed at his answer but her spirits sank still further when he added, 'In fact, I mean to leave Bath quite soon. I am needed at home.'

Thea nodded, and then quickly pretended to admire one of the handsome mahogany bookcases that lined the room. 'Mr Murray possesses an excellent library,' she murmured inconsequentially.

Gareth stared intently at her neat profile. What an odd girl she was! Full of contradictions. One minute surprisingly bold, the next as shy as a harvest mouse!

Beneath her reserve he sensed a warm heart and a

penetrating intelligence. For some reason she preferred to hide these admirable traits. But why? Was the shyness she had displayed earlier in the drawing-room genuine or just a mask? He didn't know.

Admit it, Rhayadar, she intrigues you. She seems so cool, but there is passion there behind those stiff company manners!

'Would it bother you very greatly if our names were linked by the scandalmongers?' he asked, with sudden gruff abruptness.

Startled, Thea answered with devastating honesty. 'That, sir, would depend on your intentions!'

'Of course.' Gareth's dark eyes twinkled. 'But there is no law that says we cannot not be friends, is there?'

Thea found herself shaking her head.

'Then I may call upon you tomorrow?'

'It might not be to my grandmother's liking.' Thea felt it was only fair to confess this fact.

Her grandmother would probably think that she was trying to steal him away from Georgy, but he'd shown no sign of wanting Georgy's company!

Her cool answer rang an alarm in Gareth's head. He would have laid odds that the old dragon would have welcomed the acquaintance!

'May I ask you a question?' Thea said hastily, in the hope of diverting his puzzled frown.

'Whatever you wish,' he replied simply.

Thea coloured shyly. When he smiled at her like that it was all holiday with her!

'Why did you not seek an introduction when we met that day in the Pump Room?'

'I thought you might wonder at my dilatoriness!' He gave a rueful shake of his dark head. 'To be perfectly honest with you, Miss Howard, I had gone there to meet an acquaintance of Mrs Murray's, and he came up to me just after we had finished speaking. He is related to a lady reputed to run the foremost seminary in Bath, and when he immediately offered to escort me to Queen Square to view these premises I accepted.

You see, I am here to find a place for my sister at a good school.'

'Thank you for telling me, sir. I. . . I did wonder.'

'I have looked for you everywhere since then,' Gareth added softly.

Unable to prevent it, Thea beamed at him, delighted by this unexpected admission.

How pretty she looked with that shine of happiness lighting up her fine grey eyes. Her other features were quite ordinary, but you didn't notice it when she smiled.

'May I have my shoe now, sir?' His intent gaze had set her heart thumping, and, thrown into confusion by the violence of her feelings, Thea blurted the first thing that came into her head.

'Of course.' Of their own volition, Gareth's long brown fingers closed over hers as their hands met.

The silken slipper fell unheeded into Thea's lap and she caught her breath.

His hand felt so warm, so vital! It was as if his light touch had set the blood in her veins on fire. . .!

The clatter of running footsteps and a loud, high-pitched giggling out in the corridor penetrated into the library and shattered the sudden taut silence.

'It sounds as if someone has been imbibing too freely of Simon's excellent champagne,' Gareth said lightly.

Thea nodded and bent to slip on her sandal, glad to turn away in case her inner turmoil might be showing on her face. 'It must be getting late.'

'Aye. We ought to get you back to your grandmother before she starts worrying what has happened to you.'

Gareth indicated her sandal. 'If I may.' He took her hesitantly extended foot on to his lap and bent forward, dipping his raven head a little to see better. 'This won't take a moment, Miss Howard. Please keep still.'

Desperately aware of his nearness, Thea strove to obey. An insane longing to stretch out her hand and stroke his thick black hair tormented her.

Gareth could feel the tremors that shook her slim,

silk-stockinged leg as he began to fashion a stout knot to hold the sandal in place, and it instantly cured him of the impulse to praise her neatly turned ankle.

Beneath the façade of her quick tongue, she was unexpectedly vulnerable. This discovery aroused an urge in him to protect her, although with a touch of ruefulness he realised that it was his own instincts that might be the source of danger.

Duw, but he wanted to kiss her! But his promise prevented him from attempting to find out if she would welcome his embrace.

Face it, man, you're sailing in uncharted waters! You don't know the first thing about handling innocent maidens. Expensive barques of frailty or dashing widows are more in your line!

'There. It's done.' Concealing his reluctance to let her go, he released her. 'It should hold, provided you don't dance too much.'

'Thank you.' To her annoyance, Thea's voice emerged as a squeaky whisper. For a moment she'd been sure he was going to kiss her!

'Come, let me escort you back to your family.'

Gareth rose to his feet and Thea copied him, her thoughts in a whirl.

I suppose I ought to be glad his touch was coolly impersonal, she told herself as they left the room.

But her absurd disappointment that he had behaved like a perfect gentleman stayed with her for the rest of the evening.

Faithful to his promise, Lord Rhayadar arrived in Beaufort Square the next morning.

'The mistress is out, sir,' he was told by Dutton, the high-nosed butler hired to give tone to the establishment.

Gareth experienced a disturbing stab of annoyance. But perhaps. . .

'Are the young ladies at home?'

'Miss Georgina accompanied Mrs Howard, but I believe Miss Howard is in.'

'Ask her if she will receive me.' Gareth's spirits rose.

This request set the butler frowning.

'At once, if you please.' Gareth smiled politely but his tone was crisp, and, recognising authority, Dutton obeyed.

He returned a moment later. 'This way, my lord,' he announced disapprovingly.

Gareth doffed his high-crowned hat and stripped off his York tan gloves and tossed them casually on to the hall table. 'Thank you.'

Dutton sniffed.

The morning-room into which he was shown was a large apartment, hung in expensive green and white striped wallpaper and furnished with a great quantity of gilded furniture.

His grey-eyed girl was seated in the centre of all this splendour on an uncomfortable-looking green satin sofa with gold clawed legs. The workbox at her elbow and the piece of sewing in her lap told of her occupation, but as he advanced across the thick Turkish carpet she cast her sewing aside and stood up to greet him.

'Lord Rhayadar. How kind of you to call.' Thea spoke the conventional words demurely but her smile was warm.

Gareth gazed in fascination at her dimple.

A cough from the butler recalled him to his senses.

'Miss Howard.' He bowed politely over her hand.

Thank goodness she had taken the precaution of wearing her best morning gown! The lilac-sprigged muslin had been made last year, when they were in half-mourning, but the fabric was pretty and Thea knew that its simple lines suited her. She had taken extra care with her hair too, spending far longer than usual before her looking-glass although she had warned herself that she was being foolish.

'My grandmother will be sorry to have missed you, but I hope you will stay for a few moments?'

For once she had been quite happy to be left behind while Mrs Howard took Georgy to buy the new hat she'd admired in a milliners in Milsom Street!

'I should be delighted, Miss Howard.'

'Then pray be seated, sir.' Thea indicated one of the least spindly-looking chairs, and resumed her own seat before addressing the butler who still hovered in the doorway.

'That will be all, thank you, Dutton.'

The butler nodded reluctantly. 'Yes, miss.'

When he had gone Thea said, 'I am glad you came.'

'So am I.' Gareth grinned at her. 'Though I suspect your butler disapproves. Look, he has carefully left the door ajar.'

There was a tiny silence.

'Should *you* prefer me to come back later?' Gareth asked carefully.

Thea shook her head. Taking a deep breath, she met his eyes. 'I'm no longer a green young miss in need of constant chaperonage,' she said firmly. 'I shall be twenty-three come September—quite old enough to choose my own friends.'

Gareth found her frankness delightful. 'In that case, Miss Howard, may I hope to persuade you to take a stroll with me? I'm told that the Sydney Gardens are of interest.'

'Indeed. They are delightful.'

'Then you'll come? We could even attempt the labyrinth if you wish.'

The thought of being alone with him in such privacy was tempting, but Thea paused. She was willing to risk her grandmother's wrath—she had already been scolded for monopolising his company—but would he think her fast if she accepted?

'I'm not sure I should, sir. It might give you the wrong idea of my character.'

Gareth was taken aback by her directness. She had

the disconcerting habit of saying exactly what she thought in that quiet, cool voice of hers.

'I know I have little experience of the world,' Thea continued, with an earnestness he thought enchanting, 'and I don't want you to mistake my ignorance. I am not a flirt, whatever you might think to the contrary.'

Gareth's eyes twinkled. 'You are too fond of honest speaking to make a successful flirt, Miss Howard.'

She laughed, as he had intended, but then her expression sobered. 'Last night you offered me your friendship. I should like to accept, but I must make my position plain.'

She met his interested gaze with a level look.

'I have no wish to insult you, sir, but we both know that gentlemen of your station do not usually offer friendship to daughters of tradesmen without ulterior motive.'

He grinned at her. 'I cannot promise not to flirt with you occasionally, but you have my word I won't try to make you my mistress.' He stretched out a hand in laughing appeal. 'Does that reassure you?'

Thea smiled, but before she could frame a reply the door was flung wide and Mrs Howard swept into the room, Georgy at her heels.

'My lord! Fancy us being out when you arrived! I wouldn't have had it happen for all the world.' She gave him an arch smile. 'Do say as you'll forgive us.'

Gareth had risen to his feet at her abrupt entrance and now he bowed politely, concealing his irritation. 'There is nothing to forgive, Mrs Howard.'

'I hope you've made his lordship welcome, Dorothea.' Mrs Howard turned to her elder granddaughter. Her glance became severe. 'Did you offer him refreshment?'

'Not yet, Grandmama.'

Mrs Howard frowned at her. 'Then pull the bell at once and summon Dutton, you stupid girl!' she snapped.

'Please do not trouble on my account, ma'am,'

Gareth intervened swiftly, startled by her harshness. No wonder those lovely grey eyes had lost their sparkle! Was the old dragon usually so hard on her?

After some fussing, Mrs Howard accepted his reassurances that he required neither food nor drink and came and settled herself in the chair next to his. The younger girl, whose name he could barely remember, went to join her sister on the sofa.

'Did you enjoy the party last night, my lord?' she asked immediately, fluttering her eyelashes at him.

Gareth nodded, wondering whether she ever stopped to think before she opened that pretty rosebud mouth. What did she expect him to say? The party had been hosted in his honour!

'And you, Miss Georgina?' he responded politely, knowing that she expected it.

The floodgates opened. Georgy began to chatter, monopolising the conversation with a flow of girlish inanities, while her grandmother looked fondly on.

The Murrays' party exhausted, the talk turned to their shopping expedition.

'And do you know, my lord, after we had finished at the milliners we had to try no less than three drapers to match some ribbon for my new dress.' Georgy rattled to a breathless halt at last. 'I declare I am quite exhausted!'

'Perhaps you ought to go upstairs and rest for a while?' Thea intervened, seeing that his lordship's eyes were beginning to glaze over with boredom.

'No one asked you for your opinion, miss!' Mrs Howard stirred in her chair and glared at Thea.

Inwardly seething, Thea fell silent, knowing that there was no point in arguing if her grandmother was going to condone Georgy's hoydenish behaviour!

Gareth was aware of gathering anger. There had been no call for the old woman to speak so severely!

'I'm not *that* tired, Thea!' Georgy broke the tension with one of her little giggles. She reached out to pat her sister's arm in a pretty little gesture of forgiveness.

'Oh, by the way, you remember Mr Harley, don't you? We met him just now, coming out of the last shop, and he was obliging enough to carry my parcel for me. Not that it was very heavy. It only contained an ell of satin ribbon. But he said that he longed to serve me.' She turned to their visitor. 'Only fancy, my lord! Don't you think it romantic of him!' she exclaimed with a giggle.

Gareth smiled obligingly, but he wasn't listening. His attention had been caught by the use of her sister's nickname

Thea. It was very pretty. And a touch unusual. It suited her.

Poor girl. She was horribly embarrassed by her relatives' antics!

In his years at sea Lord Rhayadar had consorted with people from all walks of life. His judgement of character had been honed by necessity, and he'd already taken their measure.

The old woman was frankly vulgar. He suspected that she possessed a shrewd business brain but her manners were ill-bred and grasping. Under certain circumstances, he'd wager that she could turn into a regular harpy!

As for Miss Georgina, her behaviour revealed that she'd been thoroughly spoilt and overindulged. God help Simon if his mother did persuade him into offering for her—she'd bore him to tears within a week!

'We were thinking of attending a performance at the theatre the day after tomorrow, my lord. Would you do us the honour of accepting a seat in our box?' Mrs Howard proffered the invitation with one of her arch smiles.

'Thank you, ma'am. I should be delighted.'

Gareth noted the triumphant look she threw at her younger granddaughter. Good God, so that was the way the wind veered!

He glanced quickly at Thea. A slight tinge of colour stained the skin over her cheekbones. So, she knew that this assiduous cultivation of his rank went beyond mere social ambition.

But two could play at that game!

'In return, ma'am, since it is such a fine day, may I beg the favour of escorting your granddaughters on a walk to the Sydney Gardens?'

'What? Both of 'em?'

'But of course, ma'am.' Gareth gazed at her serenely, hiding his grim amusement. 'The young ladies may chaperon each other.'

'Oh, aye. I see.' Mrs Howard nodded, and, shifting her bulk in her chair, flapped her hands energetically towards the sofa. 'Go along, girls. Put on your bonnets and don't dally about it. His lordship don't want to hang around all day.'

Georgy bounced to her feet with alacrity, and Gareth moved to open the door for her. Thea followed more slowly, delight at the thought of enjoying his company for a little longer warring with disturbing uncertainty.

Had he guessed Grandmama's scheme or not?

'Miss Howard.' Gareth willed her to look up at him as he held the door for her to pass into the hallway.

And when she did, he winked.

CHAPTER THREE

THE visit to the Theatre Royal was an undoubted success. The Viscount pronounced himself delighted with the performance, and Mrs Howard revelled in his courteous attentions. Georgy, a fairytale vision in blue-spangled silk, took the other chair next to his and chattered whenever there was a pause on stage, happily aware that their box was attracting envious looks from most of the females in the audience.

Although more decorous, Thea's pleasure in the evening was equally intense. Thanks to her grandmother's restrictive presence she was unable to exchange more than a few conventional remarks with his lordship, but she was able to sit back and enjoy the play with the additional treat of feasting her eyes upon his elegantly turned out figure.

'Take care that you don't go pushing yourself forward tonight, miss!' her grandmother had warned Thea before they had set out.

In view of the tirade which had blasted her ears after the Murrays' party, Thea had thought it prudent to obey. However, listening to Georgy's squeals of delight during the interval over the wine and cakes that his lordship had thoughtfully provided, she decided that short of setting her hair on fire it would be impossible to outdo her sister.

To put it bluntly, Georgy's behaviour was abominable. She was acting like a coquette! She had flirted shamelessly with the Viscount for the entire duration of their walk in the Sydney Gardens, in spite of his lack of encouragement.

She is determined to enslave him if she can, Thea concluded, and, remembering his conspiratorial wink, was moved to drop a word of caution into her sister's ear when they made their way upstairs to bed later that evening.

'Oh, pooh! What nonsense you do talk, Thea!' Georgy gave a yawn. 'Didn't you think those crab patties were wonderful? The Christopher is such a superior hotel. I am glad his lordship thought of taking us there.'

'It was very polite of him to invite us to supper,' Thea agreed impatiently. 'But you mustn't mistake his good manners for anything warmer, Georgy.'

Her sister emitted a little trill of laughter. '*You* are the one who is mistaken.'

They mounted the last stair and Georgy trailed her small white hand along the top of the polished oak banister for an instant in silence, before lifting her golden head to give Thea a look of satisfaction. 'I shall make an excellent viscountess.'

Momentarily robbed of speech by this overweening self-delusion, Thea watched her sister drift daintily towards her bedroom.

In the act of reaching for the doorknob, Georgy paused and glanced back over her shoulder. 'Don't fuss, Thea. I know what I'm doing. I have always wanted to marry a titled gentleman, and Rhayadar will do as well as any other.'

Thea followed her into a large front bedroom, which had been lavishly decorated and furnished to Georgy's own expensive tastes.

'Georgy, what do you mean?' she demanded.

Her sister merely tugged the bell to summon Alice, the maid they shared. 'I'm tired,' she said pettishly. 'Can't this wait until morning?'

'Do you find him attractive?' Thea persisted.

'He is handsome, I suppose.' Georgy stripped off a gold bracelet and tossed it casually on to her dressing-table. 'But I wish his manner was less formal. He is so reserved it is often hard to tell what he is thinking.'

Thea blinked. Reserve had not marked the Viscount's dealings with her! By nature he was easy-going rather than top-lofty. It was only Georgy's vanity that kept her from seeing the truth: Lord Rhayadar was keeping her predatory advances at bay with a shield of formality.

Georgy lifted a hand to the glittering fillet that confined her curls and pulled it free. Then, becoming aware of her sister's disapproval, she shrugged petulantly. 'If you must know, I find him overbearing. Mr Harley is much more amusing, and he dresses better too.'

They had first met Anthony Harley, the son of a local Somerset baronet, in the Pump Room a month ago. He had paid half a dozen calls in Beaufort Square since then, and had been invited to Georgy's début party. Thea thought him pleasant enough. About her own age, he was slightly formed, with delicate features and an inclination to dandyism.

Thea strove to recall anything striking about this young man. But her mind's eye could only envisage a black-browed face with eyes as dark as jet.

Could Georgy *really* prefer Anthony Harley?

Giving herself a mental shake, Thea rapidly reviewed the situation. It was obvious that Georgy was attracted only to Lord Rhayadar's rank. His air of command and potent aura of virility, which hung around him like an invisible cloak and which Thea found so disturbing, clearly frightened her.

'Mr Harley is gentry, and rumour has it that his family is well-to-do,' she murmured. 'Perhaps we can persuade Grandmama——'

A loud outburst of giggles interrupted her.

'I don't mean to *marry* Anthony! I like him much better than Rhayadar, but he isn't a viscount.'

Thea stared at her in disgust. 'Georgy!'

Georgy began to fiddle nervously with her sapphire earrings. 'Oh, Thea, don't be so. . .so romantic! It isn't necessary to be in love with one's husband!'

The discarded earrings followed her bracelet on to

the dressing-table. One caught the edge and fell to the floor, but Georgy carelessly ignored it.

'After all, I can always take a lover once I have presented him with an heir.'

Thea didn't know whether to laugh or to cry. 'Georgy, you can't mean any of this!'

'Why not, pray?' The china-blue eyes hardened. 'I may not have your learning, but I don't want for sense.'

Thea swallowed hard. Subconsciously she had always known that her sister was shallow, but she had never dreamt that she could be so selfishly self-centred.

'My advice to you is to give up this mercenary plan before you get hurt,' she said slowly. 'Marry some nice boy like Anthony Harley.' She paused significantly. 'If you can find one who will have you after the way you've been behaving.'

Georgy's lovely face twisted into an expression of petulant affront.

'You have no right to criticise my behaviour! Grandmama said you were jealous. You only want to spoil things for me.'

'That isn't true.' Thea denied this charge with more calmness than she felt. 'I simply want to stop this folly. Lord Rhayadar isn't interested in marrying you, believe me.'

Georgy tossed her head. 'What do you know anyway!' she demanded angrily. 'No suitor has ever offered for *you*! I don't need your advice. I shall be the Viscountess Rhayadar before the summer is out—just you wait and see!'

'If you choose to deceive yourself, then all I can do is warn you to be careful.' Thea forced down her own anger. 'It might be dangerous to tease him too far.'

A look of doubt flashed across the exquisite oval face, but then it vanished. 'I'm not worried. I know how to hang on to my virtue,' she retorted.

'You misunderstand me. It is his temper you should fear. They say the Welsh are a fiery race, and I think it true of Lord Rhayadar.'

'What, that polite icicle?' Georgy mocked.

'I believe him to be a man of deep passions.' Thea's instincts told her that it was true. Beneath his veneer of easy-going charm, Gareth Rhayadar was a full-blooded passionate Celt!

'Oh, fiddle-de-dee! I know how to handle him.' Georgy threw up one prettily rounded arm in an airy gesture. 'Besides, I have Grandmama to help me. She has plenty of ideas on how to bring him up to scratch.'

Thea grimaced at this confident assertion. 'I don't doubt it,' she murmured. 'But I shall keep my fingers crossed that you won't regret throwing yourself at his head.'

'At least I'm honest about what I want.' Georgy flung herself sulkily into the armchair by the bed and surveyed her sister through narrowed eyes. 'What about you? You are practically an old maid! Don't you want to find a husband?'

Thea lost patience.

'Of course I would like to marry and have a home of my own,' she snapped. 'But not at such a cost to my self-respect! How can you be so mercenary, Georgy? You don't appear to have the slightest affection for Lord Rhayadar.'

'I know better than to expect love to go hand in hand with the bargain. That's a fairy-tale for fools!' Georgy answered with a sneer, but she failed to meet her sister's level gaze.

'Oh, go away, Thea, do! I am sick of your mealy-mouthed preaching,' she burst out with shrill petulance. 'I *won't* waste myself on a nobody! I want the best out of life, and I won't let you or anyone else stand in my way!'

Thea swallowed hard.

'Do you know, Georgy?' she said at last. 'People have always remarked upon the resemblance between you and Papa, and now I can see it too.'

'What. . .what do you mean?'

A knock at the door heralding the arrival of Alice

saved Thea from the trouble of replying, but as she turned to leave she knew from the guilty look in her sister's limpid eyes that Georgy understood her meaning only too well.

During the next few days Thea frequently regretted that she had let her temper run away with her. Far from helping her sister to see sense, she had only made the situation worse!

Observing the look of strain in those lovely grey eyes, Gareth guessed that she had quarrelled with her family—a suspicion strengthened by the fact that whenever he called in Beaufort Square only his polite intervention prevented the old dragon from dismissing her from the room.

'Is there anything I can do?' he asked without preamble one evening, when he had at last managed to snatch a moment alone with her during the interval of a concert of music held in the Octagon Hall at the Upper Assembly Rooms.

Thea did not pretend to misunderstand him. 'Thank you for asking but I must sort matters out myself,' she replied with a faint smile.

He nodded slowly, impressed by her quiet determination.

'In any event, I dare say I shall be forgiven in the end,' Thea added lightly. 'Grandmama needs me to exercise Nelson. He prefers me to the servants, you know.'

Her attempt at levity didn't fool his lordship.

'It is damnable of them to treat you in this manner. They act as if you *were* a servant. I should like to keelhaul the pair of them,' he declared violently, a sudden flash of intense anger surprising him.

'Please!' Thea clung to her composure. 'I know you mean well, sir, but you must not say such things. If the worst comes to the worst, I shall leave Beaufort Square and earn my own living.'

Gareth stared at her in astonishment.

'Good God, you cannot be serious!'

His exclamation caused heads to turn in their direction, and Thea hastily implored him to lower his voice.

'I beg your pardon.' Gareth shrugged impatiently. 'But I don't understand. Young ladies do not go out into the world on their own. It is unheard of.'

'Unless they undertake a post as a governess,' she reminded him. 'I mean to find a suitable employer as soon as I can.'

Gareth raised his dark brows. 'You would hate it,' he replied succinctly.

'Perhaps.' Thea acknowledged his remark with a wry smile. 'But I should be independent, sir, and no longer at the beck and call of my grandmama.'

A little sigh escaped her.

'It is doubtless very wrong of me, but I cannot go on living in her house. Our ideas are too different! I know there are difficulties involved in the path I have chosen, but at least I may find some peace of mind.'

He frowned. Everyone knew the indignities and hazards governesses were subjected to. Catari had run through dozens of the poor creatures! Aye, and driven them half-mad!

'You do realise you would be neither part of the family nor one of the servants?' he said abruptly. 'Your daily life subject to the whim of your employer and the good nature of your charges? You could be turned off without notice and lose both your home and your livelihood in an instant.'

'You think me foolish.' Despondency swept over Thea.

Her plan to leave Bath was already under way. She had written in response to an advertisement she had seen in the *Morning Post*, and was awaiting a reply.

'Perhaps you are right,' she sighed. Then, her tone hardening, she added, 'However, I am determined to leave Bath.'

Gareth came to a rapid decision to keep his doubts

to himself. He admired her courage in facing the future so fearlessly, and he did not wish to add to her worries.

Instead he said mildly, 'This storm will blow over. Don't cut yourself adrift too soon, my dear Miss Howard.'

'I promise you I won't do anything hasty.'

'Good. But let me know if there is anything I can do to help.' Her gallant fortitude deserved his support. *Duw*, she hadn't complained once!

'Thank you.' Thea smiled at him, her heart warmed by his concern.

He didn't know, of course, how intolerable life had become in that overheated, luxurious house in Beaufort Square. The buffer of Georgy's support had been withdrawn, and her grandmother's snide comments made it painfully clear that she was no longer welcome to join their pursuit of pleasure unless she was required to act as chaperon for her sister when Mrs Howard was tired.

Taking their cue from their employer, even the servants had begun to treat her orders with disdain. When she had protested, Mrs Howard had laughed in her face.

It was better to strike out and win her freedom now, before her spirit was broken by such Turkish treatment!

'The concert is about to resume. Here comes your grandmother, with Mrs Murray and the others.'

Gareth's quiet warning wrenched Thea from her unhappy reflections.

'May we speak of this matter another time? Tomorrow, perhaps? I promised your sister that I would give her my escort to take an airing up on the Heights if the day is fine. Your grandmother said that she did not wish to make the climb, so you will be required to accompany us.'

He smiled at her with a touch of wicked amusement. Mrs Howard was so fat that she disliked trying to squeeze herself into a sedan-chair—the normal mode of transport in hilly Bath—and declined to go anywhere that entailed more than a short walk.

'In the meantime, I shall cudgel my brains to think of some distraction which will give us a chance to talk in private.'

'As you wish, sir,' Thea replied mechanically, her fingers clenching upon her programme as her grandmother came towards them, wearing a frown.

She thinks I am putting myself forward again, and trying to outshine Georgy!

There would be another angry scene the minute they got home!

This realisation brought a bitter taste of resentment into her mouth and strengthened her determination.

I will get away from here! I must! And soon!

The sound of angry raised voices greeted Lord Rhayadar's arrival at the Howard residence the next morning.

'What the devil is going on, Dutton?'

The butler's haughty countenance flushed at this abrupt demand, and his manner was unusually flustered as he tried to persuade his lordship to wait in the marble hallway while he ascertained if Mrs Howard was receiving.

'Don't fuss, man.' Gareth sensed trouble, and he had no patience with polite prevarication. 'The ladies are expecting me. I will announce myself.'

Accepting the inevitable, Dutton stepped aside, and Gareth walked into the morning-room.

The dramatic tableau that met his gaze would have astonished him if he had not already guessed that a fierce dispute was taking place.

Mrs Howard, flanked by her younger grandchild, stood on one side of the vast fireplace, where a fire burned even on this bright April morning. Her arm was outflung in an accusing gesture, and the vein at her temple throbbed alarmingly.

Facing them, Thea reminded Gareth of a hind at

bay, but her chin was defiantly raised and her voice was firm as she declared, 'I am no thief, ma'am, and well you know it. This is just another excuse to humiliate me.'

She would have said more, but she suddenly realised that they were no longer alone and, her cheeks burning, fell silent.

Mrs Howard, who was so incensed that she had not noticed his lordship's quiet entrance, let out a scream that would have done credit to a banshee.

'Excuse? Let me tell you, miss, this is my house, and I need no excuse to say what I think. You are nothing but a troublemaker.'

'Grandmama, please don't——'

'Nay, Georgy, I have been patient for far too long.' Mrs Howard ignored this urgent attempt to interrupt her tirade. 'The pearl necklace I gave you is missing. It is my belief she took it out of spite.'

She glared at Thea.

'Miss Hoity-Toity! You've always thought yourself above the rest of us, haven't you? So full of book-learning and fancy notions, but when it comes down to it you are just jealous of your sister.'

'You have no right to accuse me in this manner.' Thea was agonisingly aware of his dark eyes on her. Now he would know the full extent of her humiliation, and she could hardly bear it!

'Perhaps I did mislay my necklace, after all, Grandmama,' Georgy fluttered, flicking a nervous glance in the Viscount's direction. 'It could have fallen down behind my dressing-table.'

In her heart Mrs Howard knew that this was the most likely explanation, but she had worked herself up into a rage and she was unwilling to abandon her satisfying hysterics.

When she finally halted, in response to Georgy's persistent tugging at her puce satin sleeve, her pale eyes bulged with dismay. 'Your lordship! Pray. . .pray come in and be seated.'

Thea watched him advance into the room. His expression was thunderous.

'What is the meaning of this, ma'am?' he demanded, with a coldness Thea had never heard in his attractive voice before. 'Are you accusing Miss Howard of theft?'

'It has all been a misunderstanding.' Georgy flashed her brightest smile at him.

'Aye, just a lttle family dispute—but it's over now. There's no need for you to concern yourself, my lord.' Mrs Howard spoke up quickly. 'Georgy shall be ready to accompany you in a trice—won't you, love?'

Georgy fluttered assent, and ran out of the room to fetch her hat.

'Tell you what, my lord, why don't the pair of you enjoy the sunshine on your own?' Mrs Howard held out the lure with an ingratiating smile. 'I reckon I can trust you by now to behave without the need of a chaperon.' She threw a darkling look at her elder grandchild. 'Dorothea can bide at home. There's plenty for her to do here.'

Thea held her breath. Would he accept? The thought made her feel suddenly giddy, as if his leaving her behind would deprive her of her only friend. I am being absurd, she told herself. But her pulse was racing so fast that she felt sick. . .

'I think not, ma'am. I find I have no taste for Miss Georgina's company, either alone or accompanied. Her behaviour is disgraceful.' Gareth's tone was cool, but Thea had never heard him sound so angry or so distinctively Welsh.

Mrs Howard goggled at him. 'My. . .my lord?'

'Come, ma'am. You know exactly what I mean.' Gareth was blunt. 'It is my belief that you have been encouraging the child to flaunt herself like a piece of Haymarket ware. Well, I'm no greenhorn, to be taken in by a pretty face and cheap tricks.'

He fixed her with a stern look.

'Give me leave to inform you, ma'am, that no man wants to take a flighty little baggage to wife. If you wish to marry her off to a gentleman of rank—as you have made painfully clear—you'd do better to teach her a little decorum than to drop heavy hints concerning the fortune you mean to leave her in your will.'

Mrs Howard's broad face took on a flush that gave it a resemblance to a boiled ham.

'Here's plain speaking indeed!' she gasped, looking so disconcerted that in spite of everything Thea couldn't help feeling a flicker of sympathy for her.

'Furthermore, on the subject of proper behaviour, I think she owes her sister an apology,' Gareth continued remorselessly. 'It was patently absurd of her to accuse Miss Howard of theft. You must know it!'

He eyed her with contempt.

'When considered in the light of previous unfair treatment I have seen handed out to Miss Howard, I can only conclude that the motive of both yourself and Miss Georgina in this matter was sheer spite.'

A tiny gasp escaped Thea.

I don't think anyone has ever dared speak to her in such a way before! Heavens, she will go off in an apoplexy, Thea thought, watching her grandmother's cheeks swell purple, but a strange elation mingled with her astonishment.

'Now, see here, young man, you might be a viscount but you've no call to speak to me so sharp.' Mrs Howard rallied. Her cherished plan had gone awry, but she was determined to find out why he had changed his mind. 'Not after all the hospitality you've received in this house!'

'Believe me, ma'am, I regret the necessity.' Gareth gave her a cool look.

He flicked off an imaginary speck of dust from his immaculate blue sleeve and then raised his dark eyes to her flustered face.

'However, the needs of justice must be rated higher than propriety, don't you agree?'

Discomposed by his manner, which was suddenly as

haughty as his rank, she began to stammer assent before her natural pugnaciousness reasserted itself.

'Well, sir, I'll go to the devil if I know what to make of you,' she snapped, planting her balled fists upon her wide hips. 'A fine thing, to insult me in my own morning-room! If you think so little of us, then why have you been coming round here, eh? You made it pretty plain just now that you've no fancy to either Georgy's face or the fortune she'll inherit. So what is the attraction? Tell me that!'

'Gladly, ma'am.' Gareth executed an exquisitely graceful bow in her direction.

He straightened and, turning to Thea, smiled at her.

'My purpose in coming here was to become better acquainted with your *elder* granddaughter.'

Thea's heart began to slam against her ribs. His honesty was commendable, but liable to cause nothing but trouble!

'My lord, please. . .' She attempted to intervene, but couldn't force another word from her dry throat.

'*Dorothea?* What do you want with her?'

Ignoring Mrs Howard's snort of amazement, Lord Rhayadar answered calmly, 'I would like to marry her.'

Mrs Howard was the first to break the resounding silence.

'Well, I'll not deny this is a surprise, my lord,' she gasped, collapsing heavily into her favourite chair. 'Still, I'm not one to cut off my nose to spite my face, so I won't withhold my consent,' she continued more briskly, regaining her usual florid colour. 'Now, when did you want the wedding to take place?'

'As soon as possible, ma'am.'

Not by so much as a flicker did his lordship's expression betray his inner perturbation.

What the devil had possessed him?

'Excellent! I'll have my lawyer draw up the settlements right away.'

The avaricious gleam in her grandmother's eyes jolted Thea out of her stupor.

'No!'

Two pairs of startled eyes swung round to fix on her.

Thea took a step forward and dropped a neat curtsy to the Viscount.

'Thank you for your kind offer, sir, but we both know that I cannot possibly accept.'

'Have you run mad, girl?' Mrs Howard let out another banshee wail.

Thea shook her glossy head. 'I will not enter into such an unsuitable union, Grandmama,' she said firmly.

He didn't really wish to marry her. He had only made the offer to annoy her grandmother.

It was a shock to realise just how much she wanted it to be genuine!

'Of course you will marry him!' Mrs Howard's pale eyes bulged.

Again Thea shook her head. 'No, ma'am,' she said softly. She flashed Gareth an apologetic look before turning back to face her grandmother. 'I am going to be a governess.'

'What, turn down the chance to be a viscountess just so you can teach a parcel of brats? I've never heard such nonsense! You'll do as you are bid, miss!'

'Thea——' Ignoring Mrs Howard's angry outburst, Gareth took a swift stride towards Thea and held out his hand to her.

A small part of her brain registered that he had used her Christian name, but her spurt of pleasure died instantly.

'I'm sorry, it. . .it is impossible!' she muttered incoherently, backing away from him.

'Wait!'

With a final shake of her head, Thea whirled and fled from the room.

Later that afternoon Thea emerged from the house. She wore a sober walking-gown of grey jaconet and had Nelson on his leash. Her manner appeared brisk as she urged the little dog along, but an acute observer might have noticed that her eyelids were reddened.

She had barely reached the end of the road before she was brought to a sudden halt by the sound of his familiar voice.

'Miss Howard. May I walk with you for a while?'

Thea read determination in his tanned face, and instead of uttering a refusal gave a small nod of acceptance.

They walked in silence for few yards and then Gareth said carefully, 'As you may have guessed, I was waiting to catch a moment alone with you.'

A wry smile twisted his features for a brief instant.

'I hoped you would take Nelson for his usual walk. I didn't think you would wish me to call at the house.'

Thea stared fixedly at a point between Nelson's ears.

'No,' she replied with blunt honesty.

'Was it very bad?'

The sympathy in his voice prevented her from snapping back at him, and she contented herself instead with a heartfelt nod.

Her grandmother had raved, calling her an ungrateful imbecile, but even that had been preferable to Georgy's hysterics!

'I'm sorry. The last thing I wanted was for you to be made unhappy,' Gareth said, and found that he meant it.

'You need not worry, sir,' Thea replied in a low voice, avoiding his gaze. 'I will not let my grandmother take advantage of your impetuous offer. Somehow I shall find the means to persuade her to silence.'

'I don't intend to withdraw my offer.'

Thea felt as if a giant fist had squeezed all the air out of her lungs, leaving her breathless and shaking.

The look of shocked disbelief on her face prompted Gareth to continue gruffly, 'I esteem you greatly, and I should count myself a fortunate man if you will accept my suit.'

Thea gave a little choke of laughter that bordered on hysteria. 'Oh, sir, I appreciate your chivalry, but the whole idea is absurd!'

A dull flush coloured Lord Rhayadar's lean cheeks.

'I admit I spoke in haste this morning, but the damage has been done,' he said stiffly. 'Your grandmother will not let the matter drop even if you release me.'

Summoning all her reserves of self-control, Thea managed to school her expression, but his choice of words had made her wince inwardly.

'She will have to, sir. Marriage between us is out of the question. My birth cannot compare with yours, and I lack the fortune that might make me acceptable to your family.'

Thea hoped her cool voice did not betray the tumult of confused feelings that rioted within her breast.

'I shall always treasure your kindness, but I hope I am not fool enough to think you spoke from any real wish of the heart.'

His proposal had been prompted by nothing more than impetuous generosity, but how she wished she might accept!

But it was impossible!

Gareth's mouth set into a grim line.

'Pray, let me be the judge of your suitability, Miss Howard. You may have no fancy to take me, but if I choose to make you my viscountess then you can be sure I will not permit anyone to say a word against you.'

'Your family may accede to your wishes, but you cannot stop other people's tongues! And I have no desire to be thought an adventuress,' she declared with a flash of spirit.

'I understand how you feel, but you must see that my honour is involved,' Gareth answered impatiently.

Duw, he had imagined that she would be pleased!

'I'm sorry if I have offended you, my lord, but I have other plans to safeguard my future.'

Lord Rhayadar raised his brows, his expression cynical.

'A letter was delivered soon after your departure this morning.' Thea decided to explain. 'A family in Norfolk I applied to wish me to take up a position as their governess as soon as possible. So you see, there is no need for you to be concerned.'

'And I suppose you prefer to be a governess rather than become a lady of title?' Gareth asked bitingly.

Thea struggled to think of a reply and failed.

They were now approaching the abbey, and the flagway was soon too crowded to allow privacy.

'We cannot talk here.' Gareth bit off an exclamation of impatient annoyance. Glancing along the street, the sign-board of an inn caught his eye. 'We could try there.'

She followed his gaze. 'Are you suggesting a private parlour, sir?' she gasped.

'Don't you trust me, Miss Howard?'

'Well, yes, but—' She began a flustered reply and then saw the faint smile in his dark eyes.

He was teasing her!

Glad that he was no longer angry with her, Thea grinned back at him, a spark of warmth igniting in the pit of her stomach. After all his kindness, the last thing she wanted was to quarrel with him.

'I think my reputation is safe with you, sir,' she said demurely.

'I'm glad to hear it,' Gareth replied with a dry irony. 'Believe me, I have no desire to risk your good name.'

'Then you had the coffee-room in mind?'

Gareth nodded, adding persuasively, 'It looks a respectable place.'

'I wonder if the landlord would think the same of us!'

A muscle twitched at the corner of his well-cut mouth. 'Shall I flaunt my title?'

Thea laughed, but shook her head.

'We still have much to discuss,' he reminded her.

'Perhaps you could call on me tomorrow?' Thea hedged.

'I should prefer to settle matters today,' he replied with inexorable politeness, and held out his arm to her.

With a little sigh of resignation, she placed her fingers upon the smooth broadcloth and allowed him to steer her into the inn.

Within a very few moments they were installed in the most comfortable corner of the modest coffee-room, which was fortunately deserted.

'Be so good as to leave the door open a trifle, if you please, ma'am.'

'Of course, sir.' The landlady, who could recognise the Quality, bobbed a deferential curtsy. 'But I shall see to it that you are not disturbed.'

She bustled off, shouting for the waiter to hurry up with the gentleman's coffee, leaving Thea to hide her awe at his lordship's deft handling of the lower orders.

'This is a snug little berth.' Gareth came to join her on the polished oak bench. 'I think we shall be comfortable here.'

A fire was burning in the hearth, and the late afternoon sunshine lanced into the room through the narrow windows.

'Indeed, sir. Even our chaperon approves.'

As if to echo her words, Nelson concluded his tour of exploration and sank down before the hearth where, adopting his favourite pose, he promptly fell asleep.

It was no use wishing that she could just sit here and enjoy his company. 'What was it that you wished to say to me, my lord?' she asked, taking the bull by the horns.

'You remember that I told you I was looking for a suitable school for my sister?'

Thea nodded, surprised.

'Unfortunately there is no place available in the seminary I have chosen.'

'I am surprised they did not make an exception for someone of your rank,' Thea murmured. 'Surely it would be to their advantage to number a viscount's sister among their pupils?'

Gareth coughed. Her perceptive comment was too near the mark!

'They might have done so if I had not been fool enough to confess that my sister is a handful,' he continued hastily. 'Instead they suggested I try hiring someone to teach her the rudiments before I sent her to them to apply the final polish.'

'That sounds sensible, sir. But what has this to do with me?' Thea asked in a puzzled tone.

Gareth ran a finger around his neckcloth. The Mathematical he had tied earlier suddenly felt much too tight.

'It is quite simple,' he answered, taking the plunge. 'You informed me just now that you are willing to take up that post in Norfolk. Won't you come to Wales instead, and teach Catari how to be a lady?'

Thea blinked at him. 'You are offering me a position as a *governess*?' she enquired faintly.

Gareth took a deep breath and tried again. 'What I am offering you, Miss Thea Howard, is a marriage of convenience.'

'What. . .what did you say, sir?'

Thea stared at him, her eyes wide.

Gareth shrugged, pretending nonchalance. 'I need help with Catari. You need to get away from Bath. If you agree to marry me both problems will be solved.'

Thea swallowed hard and found her voice. 'I should be happy to teach your sister, sir, but surely there is no need for talk of marriage?'

'No one would believe I had hired you as a governess.'

Thea bit her lip.

'You are too young and pretty.' Gareth saw that she understood his meaning. 'The gossip would make things intolerable for you—particularly as it would be bound to come out that we had spent these last few weeks enjoying the social round in each other's company.'

'People would think the worst.' Thea nodded reluctant agreement. It was hardly *comme il faut* to discuss such matters, but his neighbours might imagine she was some lightskirt that he was brass-faced enough to entertain beneath his own roof.

He laughed, albeit a trifle harshly. 'They would say I am following in my father's footsteps.'

An unaccustomed tinge of colour warmed his olive skin.

'My parents did not have a happy marriage. My father spent much of his time in London. When he did return he made no secret of his infidelity.'

A welcome knock at the coffee-room door, heralding the arrival of their coffee, gave Thea time to collect herself. Her head was spinning!

Once the waiter had departed she broke the silence.

'Thank you for being so frank, sir, but do you not think you should give more thought to the business of choosing a bride? Surely a marriage of convenience must be repugnant to you?'

'On the contrary. My parents' example encourages me to think it an excellent idea. You see, theirs was a love-match, but they had nothing in common and it turned sour before the first year was out.'

Her pretty mouth formed a circle of astonishment, and Gareth was sorely tempted to seize her in his arms and kiss her objections into oblivion. But she would never trust him again if he betrayed her confidence in such a flagrant manner.

He rose to his feet and began to pace the floor, his hands firmly clasped behind his back, just as he had used to do on his own quarterdeck whenever he had a problem.

'Won't you have some coffee?' Thea wished he would sit down. His restless pacing made it even harder to concentrate. He reminded her of nothing so much as some great caged beast!

Gareth shook his head.

Thea left the coffee-pot untouched.

'Sir, I am honoured that you have confided in me. I wish I could help you, but I still fail to see why you need to go to such lengths. You can easily hire someone else to teach your sister.'

'Catari has had dozens of governesses. None lasted longer than a few months.' Gareth fixed his dark eyes on her face. 'My wife would possess a greater authority. She would assume the role my mother is now too frail to undertake. Catari would have to pay heed.'

Thea acknowledged the force of his argument. 'No doubt you are right, sir, but I am not the bride you need. The idea is absurd.'

'Why? You were prepared to sentence yourself to a life at the beck and call of strangers,' Gareth answered. 'Think me a coxcomb if you wish, but surely marriage to me would be better than such a fate?'

Thea's fingers curled tightly into her palms. How could she deny it?

Gareth came back to the bench and sat down.

'I can offer you a home and the comfort of security, Thea.'

Thea was disturbingly aware of his nearness, but she ploughed on with conscientious determination. 'Your family may not share your view that rank is unimportant.'

'Members of the peerage have married into trade before.' Gareth laid his hand gently over hers. 'Besides, your mother was of good birth.'

'But I'm no rich heiress,' Thea muttered.

Her hand was tingling, as if he had ignited a fire in her veins. What would it be like to feel his mouth against her own?

'Thanks to my father's extravagance, we are more equal than you suppose.'

Giddy with the strange longing that had overtaken her, it took Thea a moment to realise that he was explaining he was not as wealthy as the Bath gossips had painted him.

'My inheritance was much reduced by his gambling. There were many debts, and Castell Mynach is in sad need of repair.' He gave her a crooked smile. 'I hope to come about in time, but I cannot promise you luxury.'

Slowly, so as not to alarm her, he lifted her hand to his lips and kissed it.

'I need a wife, Thea,' he murmured softly. 'My mother has been urging me to marry and she's right. It's high time I settled down.'

A strange recklessness began to fill Thea. Listening to the deep, persuasive music of his voice, she was sorely tempted to agree to his crazy scheme.

It took considerable effort to go on putting the sensible objections she knew she ought to make!

'There must be several other ladies who would suit you better, my lord.'

'But none whose company I enjoy as much.'

Thea dropped her eyes in confusion, but not before he had seen the sparkle of delight his compliment had aroused.

Heartened by this sign, Gareth slid his arm around her waist. 'Say you agree, *cariad*. You'll not regret it, I swear.'

'I don't even speak Welsh,' she murmured desperately, wondering what the strange word he'd used meant. It sounded like an endearment!

'Very few of the gentry do. In any case, English is widely spoken in the Gower, so you needn't fear you won't be able to communicate.'

Thea shook her head wildly. 'You will need an heir one day, my lord. Have you thought of that?'

'You are right to think I should like children of my own,' he admitted. 'However, I have a cousin who could carry on the family name if need be.' He smiled at her with all the charm at his disposal. 'The choice would be yours.'

She stared up at him in wary silence.

'Do you really imagine I would coerce you into my bed?' Gareth let a hint of amusement fringe his tone. 'I hope you don't think me such a brute.'

He shrugged lightly.

'If you doubt my capacity for self-control, pray consider that for the last nine years I have managed to do without a woman for many months at a time.'

Dropping his bantering manner, he gazed deep into her eyes. 'I won't break my word, Thea. I won't demand anything you are not ready to give.'

Thea blushed, but innate honesty forced her to murmur unsteadily, 'You must know I am not indifferent to you, my lord.'

Gareth felt a flicker of triumph.

His proposal had been a quixotic impulse born out of a strange desire to protect her from that old harridan. The words had been out of his mouth before he'd had time to stop and think. Naturally once the offer had been made there was no way he could honourably withdraw it.

His immediate reaction had been to damn himself for a fool, although he had too much pride to show it. Thea's refusal had startled him, and he had left Beaufort Square with very mixed feelings.

Realising that nothing could be decided until they had spoken in private, he had returned to wait for her. And now, perversely, the more she objected, the more he wanted to convince her!

'It pleases me to hear you say so,' he told her now. 'For I have enjoyed your company from the first moment we met.'

His smile was warm, and Thea's heart turned a somersault. She was having great difficulty in thinking straight! His nearness was affecting her in a way she had never imagined possible!

'You are too kind, sir.' Thea spoke the conventional words in a breathless whisper. 'But. . .but. . . I feel such a marriage would be taking advantage of your good nature!'

'Thea, listen to me.' His dark eyes burned into hers. 'If I didn't think we had an excellent chance of building a successful life together I would never have put this proposal to you. I *want* you to come to Wales with me.'

Thea shivered at the intensity in his tone but she remained silent.

'You need more time to consider?'

A slight frown passed over Gareth's face as she nodded.

'Unfortunately this trip was meant to be a short one. My return home is already overdue.'

Thea smoothed her skirts with a nervous gesture. Of course. After his long absence he was needed at home. He couldn't just drop everything to stay here and pay court to her, and it was a long journey between Bath and Wales.

'I fear we are at an impasse, my lord.'

'Then let me propose a solution,' he said swiftly. 'Come with me, and in six months' time, if you agree that our platonic marriage is a success, I shall ask you to become my true wife. However, if you think we have failed to find happiness together, I give you my word of honour that we will seek an annulment on the grounds of non-consummation.'

She took a deep breath and considered his suggestion.

'This arrangement would be a private one between us?

'Of course. We would simply appear an ordinary married couple. Not even our families need know. Unless you wish it?'

Thea hastily shook her head.

'Very well. But, naturally, in the event that we decide to part, I should make full provision—both financial and practical—for your future.'

Thea's heart was pounding so fiercely that she

thought he must hear it. It was an enormous risk...
and yet...

'Well, *cariad*?' Gareth hoped he sounded calm. He hadn't dreamt that her answer would matter so much.

'I agree, my lord,' she said, throwing sanity to the winds. 'I will marry you as soon as it can be arranged.'

CHAPTER FOUR

IT WAS dark when the *Gwendolyn* put into Swansea's calm harbour. All Thea could see was a huddled mass of houses, dotted here and there with lights that appeared to twinkle as the merchantman bobbed gently up and down in the water.

'Welcome to Wales, *cariad*.'

Thea turned to smile at her husband of a few hours. 'Thank you.'

'We will be ready to disembark shortly.' Gareth, who had been talking to the Captain, came to join her at the ship's rail. 'It's a pity we didn't arrive in daylight so you would have got a better first look at your new home.'

'I can hardly believe I am here at all,' Thea murmured.

It was only yesterday that Gareth had obtained a special licence, and they had been married early this morning in Bath's fashionable Octagon chapel, where the Howards rented an expensive pew.

Simon Murray had acted as Gareth's best man, but in view of the haste with which the wedding had been arranged few guests other than the Murrays had been able to attend. Mrs Howard had been disappointed, but Thea hadn't minded. She had no taste for fashionable fuss.

In any event, there had been little opportunity to linger over the wedding breakfast.

'I'm afraid it is time for us to leave,' Gareth had announced, consulting his gold-cased verge watch once the final toast had been drunk. 'Or we risk missing the tide.'

'Take care to put on your new velvet pelisse, my

dear.' Mrs Howard had given Thea an affable smile. 'It won't do to catch a chill today of all days!'

Thea had hurried off to change into her travelling costume, reflecting with wry amusement that her standing with Grandmama had risen enormously in the last three days!

She had even insisted on organising a lavish feast and paying for Thea's wedding clothes.

'It's bad enough wanting to hold the ceremony at such short notice. I'll arrange a proper wedding breakfast here,' she had informed Thea. 'I don't want people hinting there is anything havey-cavey going on.'

Her stern expression had softened. 'You've done well, girl. Far better than I ever dreamt you would.'

'I thought you would be displeased because of Georgy,' Thea had murmured, struggling to come to terms with this *volte face*.

'Where is the sense in letting such a prize slip our grasp, eh?' Mrs Howard had shrugged with worldly-wise resignation. 'Oh, I won't deny I wanted Georgy to have him, but she'll never go short of an eligible suitor.'

She had given Thea a considering look.

'God knows what that young man sees in you, but I won't waste this chance.' A smile of triumph had spread over her broad face. 'We are about to form an alliance with a noble family. If Georgy don't like it, then she must hide her feelings!'

Thea had restrained a sigh. She might have known that it was only ambitious vanity that had inspired this change of heart. Her grandmother still didn't care a rap for her.

Nonetheless, she had quickly discovered that it was pleasant to be on the receiving end of her grandmother's favour. After so many years of having to choose clothes within the framework of a meagre allowance, she had revelled in the freedom to purchase whatever she liked.

Sadly, there had been no time for a dressmaker to

create a trousseau for her. She had had to buy clothes already made up, but by a stroke of good luck she had found a particularly pretty white muslin sprigged with tiny pink roses to wear for the wedding.

It had been painstakingly sewn for another client by one of the town's leading modistes, who had been furious when that lady—a visitor taking the waters—had abruptly decided to return home and cancelled her order. After one or two slight alterations this dress had fitted Thea as if it had been made for her.

Thea thought that she had never worn anything that suited her better. Heel-less slippers in white kid, a pink silk hat and an elegant parasol striped in both colours completed her ensemble, and Gareth had given her a slightly surprised but wholly appreciative smile as she had joined him at the altar.

He was smiling at her now, as he began to point out landmarks that might interest her.

'You'll find Swansea quite civilised,' he reassured her. 'There is a theatre and assembly rooms as well as a subscription library and some elegant shops.'

Thea regarded the twinkling lights with fresh appreciation. 'It sounds as if I won't lack for amusement,' she replied without thinking.

'I hope not.' Gareth's tone was dry.

Wishing she had kept her mouth shut, Thea quickly embarked on a slightly breathless tale of how she had heard that the war had brought many visitors flocking to Wales, for, in spite of Lord Wellington's recent victories in the Peninsular, Boney's stranglehold on Europe still prevented people travelling to the Continent for their pleasure.

'Those with antiquarian interests find Wales particularly interesting, I hear,' she concluded. 'There are many stone circles and other ancient remains, are there not?'

Gareth nodded. 'We have a ring of standing stones near Llanrhayadar—' he began, but halted as one of the sailors came up to them.

'Beg pardon, sir,' the man said, doffing his woollen cap. 'Captain said to tell you that the gangway is down and your bags are on their way to the Golden Harp, like you ordered.'

Gareth thanked him, slipping him a coin that brought an appreciative grin to the sailor's face as he hurried off.

'I should think you will be glad to get on to dry land,' Gareth said, escorting her towards the gangway.

The sea had turned rough as the merchantman had left the Bristol Channel, and Thea had turned quite pale, although she had staunchly refused to go and lie down!

Thea chuckled. 'I did feel queasy, but actually I have enjoyed this voyage. It is a much nicer way to travel than by coach.'

They had joined the *Gwendolyn* at Avonmouth, and once Thea had found her sea-legs she had savoured the new sights and sounds all around her—particularly the novelty of dining in the Captain's cabin.

'I shall make a sailor of you yet.' Gareth grinned at her, pleasantly surprised by her reply.

He had thought she would be bored, and had anticipated a string of complaints, but she had endured the long journey with a cheerfulness that had impressed him.

The Captain was waiting at the head of the gangway to say farewell to them. Watching him exchange polite pleasantries with Thea, Gareth noted the appreciative gleam in the older man's eyes.

Turning to gaze at his new bride, Gareth decided that he could hardly blame the fellow! She looked decidedly fetching in that jade velvet pelisse and matching bonnet with its fashionable high poke.

It was surprising what a difference proper dressing and an expertly cut and curled hairstyle could make!

'Do we travel on to the castle tonight?' Thea asked, once they had reached the quay.

'I had intended to do so. Unless you have some objection?'

Thea instantly shook her head, but Gareth suddenly realised that she was nervous.

'If you wish we could put up at the Harp until the morning. I'm sure my family won't mind.'

Thea refused, quashing the temptation to seize the opportunity to delay meeting her new in-laws.

There had been no time for his family to make the journey to attend the wedding, but Gareth had airily assured her that his mother would understand their need for haste.

Thea wasn't convinced.

Thank goodness Gareth had sent news of their marriage on ahead. With any luck they would have had time to get over their surprise by now.

Guessing what was going through her mind, Gareth said firmly, 'You mustn't worry, Thea. They will soon learn to like you.'

'I hope so,' Thea answered, with a plucky grin that Gareth found strangely touching.

He cast a weather eye over the clear sky as they made the short walk to the Golden Harp—the hostelry Lord Rhayadar favoured with his custom whenever he was in Swansea.

'We'll be home in little more than an hour,' he promised.

The landlord of the Harp was delighted to see them, but expressed surprise when Gareth asked if his carriage was ready.

'I'm sorry, my lord. I had no message to say you was coming,' he apologised. 'But you are welcome to borrow my gig.'

Gareth frowned and then accepted this offer.

'Come, we'll take a glass of wine to hearten us while they put the horses to,' he said to Thea.

The private parlour into which they were shown was warm and snug. Thea sat down by the fire. It still felt a little odd being alone with him like this. It made her think of the day Gareth had proposed in that little inn in Bath.

She glanced across to where he was pouring out two glasses of wine.

How handsome he looked in the dark blue coat and cream pantaloons he had worn for their wedding. A rush of pride had overwhelmed her when he had slipped the heavy gold band on to her finger. For an instant she had felt like a real bride. . .

She suppressed a sigh. She was being foolish beyond permission!

Gareth handed her a glass of Madeira. 'It is unfortunate that my mother didn't send someone to meet us, but there's no need to worry about your reputation. I told Roberts we were wed.'

So he was remembering the past too! A little shiver ran up Thea's spine. It was uncanny how often their thoughts seemed to mesh!

Gareth remained standing as he sipped his wine.

'Are you sure you are not tired?' he enquired, resting his foot negligently on the fender. 'If you wish to rest, I dare say we would be comfortable enough here for the night, although I think we would have to share a room. Roberts said they were busy and it might seem odd if we kicked up a fuss about separate rooms.'

His casual words conjured up a picture of such intimacy that Thea could feel a sudden heat spreading all over her body.

'I would prefer to go on. You must be longing to get home,' she said quickly.

Aghast at her wanton thoughts, she scarcely listened to his reply.

For heaven's sake, stop behaving like some silly schoolgirl! You have no business wondering how it would feel to be kissed by him!

Thea knew that infatuation made the pulse race. For one entire school term she had imagined herself in love with the young man who taught Italian. But infatuation had a nasty habit of fading into oblivion when confronted with reality.

You have six whole months to get to know him, she scolded herself. Wait! Don't let your heart rule your head or you might regret it.

It was good advice. But how did she deal with this slow, insidious longing for his touch that filled her whenever he came close?

Gareth observed her sudden blush and wondered at it.

How pretty she looked with that rosy colour in her cheeks. A temptation to draw her into his embrace assailed him. She had felt so deliciously fragile in his arms the night of the Murrays' party!

He took a step towards her, and then remembered he had given her his word of honour.

A flash of wry humour shot through him. You will not kiss her, *bach*, unless she gives you some sign of encouragement!

'Have you finished? Good. Then we had best be on our way, or everyone will be abed before we arrive,' he said lightly, setting down his wine glass.

The gig was waiting for them.

'I'll send someone for the rest of our luggage tomorrow,' Gareth informed the landlord.

Thea had never had the opportunity to watch him handling the reins before, and she was surprised at the speed with which he drove. The narrow twisty road seemed to fly past.

'I know this road very well,' Gareth assured her.

'You drive with considerable skill, sir.' Thea resisted the impulse to cling on to the side of the vehicle.

'For a sailor,' Gareth corrected, wry amusement in his deep tone.

Thea said hastily, 'I meant no offence.'

'They probably wouldn't have me in the Four-Horse Club,' he admitted cheerfully. 'But you need have no fear you'll end in a ditch.'

Thea relaxed. His confidence was infectious!

'Are you warm enough?' he asked a few moments later. 'Would you like another rug?'

Thea reassured him of her comfort.

The bright moonlight cast a silver glow over the landscape and she could smell the fresh green scent of growing things. In the stillness she could hear an owl hooting.

'So this is your Wales,' she whispered, overcome by an inexplicable wave of happiness.

It was so peaceful and quiet. They could have been alone at the dawn of creation. Like Adam and Eve in the Garden of Eden, Thea thought dreamily, her eyelids beginning to droop. . .

'Thea. Thea, wake up. We've arrived, *cariad*.'

Thea's eyes snapped open. In bewilderment she saw that they had halted in a cobbled courtyard. The dark shape of a house loomed before them, but she was too sleepily confused to try and take in any details.

'I'm sorry.' Hastily she straightened up. 'You must have a cramp in your shoulder. You should have woken me.'

He denied it with a laugh, reluctant to admit even to himself how much he had enjoyed the feel of her slight body resting against his shoulder.

'Let me help you down,' he said, springing to the ground with a lithe ease that Thea envied. She felt stiff and sadly dishevelled, her elegant outfit crumpled after their fourteen-hour journey.

She had barely alighted when a servant came running, roused from his slumbers by the sound of their arrival to judge by his tousled hair and untucked shirt.

'My lord!' He held up the lantern he carried. 'We were not expecting you.'

Gareth's brows drew together but he said calmly, 'See to the gig, will you, Owen? You can take it back to the Golden Harp in the morning. Dai can go with you.'

The man, who was middle-aged and bow-legged,

nodded his grey-flecked dark head, but his gaze flicked curiously to Thea.

'This is my wife. Thea, meet Owen Richards, our head groom.'

'My lady.' He looked stunned, but managed a rough and ready bow.

Thea acknowledged his clumsy salute with a friendly smile.

'Shall I fetch Mr Howell, sir?'

'No need. It is nearly midnight. I see no sense in rousing more of the household than necessary.'

Gareth waved aside Owen's offer of help and hefted the two bags they had brought with them from the carriage.

'Go back to bed when you've finished, Owen. Goodnight.'

He turned to Thea. 'We'll go through the kitchens. If I know Mrs Jones, nothing will be locked up yet.'

Thea blinked. After living with her grandmama's rigid notions, she found his casual informality disconcerting.

Glad of the moonlight which guided her steps, she followed him to an enormous oaken door. It swung open at his touch and he stood aside to allow her to precede him.

The kitchen was enormous, a great whitewashed barn of a place, dominated by an old-fashioned wide hearth cluttered with various blackened iron cooking implements.

A large scrubbed deal table occupied a central position on the stone-flagged floor. To one side of this, placed to catch the cosy glow from the banked down fire, was a rocking-chair in which sat the sole occupant of the room.

'*Duw*! Master Gareth, what a fright you gave me!'

The woman sprang up, dropping her knitting in her haste, and Thea saw that she was a round, plump body, with a head of abundant crow-black hair and smooth rosy cheeks that belied her forty odd years.

'Mrs Jones.' Gareth moved forward, and to Thea's surprise gave the cook a hug and kissed her soundly on both cheeks.

'You'll need a hot drink after your journey, sir.' Mrs Jones beamed fondly at him and bustled to the hearth, where she added more coal to the fire, blowing it into brighter flame with a pair of bellows before adjusting the chimney crane to swing a large kettle over the heat.

'Won't take a moment, now.' The cook began to load a tray with cups and saucers, but she kept glancing curiously at Thea.

'This is your new mistress, Mrs Jones.' Gareth decided to stop teasing her. 'We were married this morning.'

Astonishment widened the cook's brown eyes.

'Didn't my mother warn you?' Gareth's tone sharpened.

'Nay, Master Gareth, she never said a word.' The cook looked flustered. 'But your room is ready anyway. Shall I run a warming-pan through the sheets?'

'I don't think that will be necessary.' Gareth had a brief vision of the outcry there would be if he asked her to make up the spare bed in his dressing-room!

Mrs Jones turned to smile at Thea. 'Welcome to Castell Mynach, my lady. I hope you will be very happy here.'

Thea thanked her shyly.

'Can I get you anything to eat?'

'I am too tired to be hungry,' Thea admitted, with a simple honesty that won a smile from the cook.

Gareth surveyed her. In the dim light she looked ghostly pale, and he suspected that the strains of the day had caught up with her.

'Then we'll leave further introductions until the morning,' he said firmly.

Thea experienced a flicker of relief. It was important that she didn't make a poor first impression.

Mrs Jones began to measure out the expensive

leaves of Chinese tea. 'Actually, your mother went to bed early, sir. And so did Miss Cati.'

Gareth flashed Thea a rueful look. 'I'm sorry. This is a poor homecoming for you.'

Unexpectedly, he raised her hand to his lips and kissed it.

Thea felt a strange tingling burn her skin, and she was glad when the cook diverted Gareth's attention by saying, 'Shall I bring this tray up to the drawing-room, Master Gareth?'

'I'll take it. You get off to bed, Mrs Jones. And don't bother rousing Ifan. I'll fetch those bags myself later on.'

The cook nodded and, handing him the tray, hurried to hold the door out into the passageway open for them.

'Goodnight, sir. Goodnight, my lady. Sleep well.'

There was a hint of a giggle in her lilting voice and Thea could feel herself begin to blush.

By the time she had recovered her composure they had traversed a bewildering maze of corridors and flights of stairs leading up from the service area of the house to the family apartments. The shadowy darkness only added to her sense of confusion.

How on earth shall I ever find my way around this labyrinth? she thought, bumping her shin on a low chest placed against the wall. Gareth hardly seemed to need the aid of the branch of candles that she carried. He moved as surefooted as a cat, seemingly untroubled by the darkness.

'Here we are.' He kicked open a door and led the way into a large, high-ceilinged apartment.

The coals in the ornate iron firebasket were dead but the room was still warm, and Thea sank gratefully into an armchair.

Gareth placed the tea-tray on to a low mahogany side-table.

'Drink this,' he said, handing her a delicate porcelain cup and saucer. 'Then you must go straight to bed.'

Thea's eyes flew to his.

'I will sleep in my dressing-room. Don't worry, I shall occupy another set of rooms in future, but it will only occasion talk if we don't appear to be sharing the same bed for tonight at least.'

'Of course.' Thea forced the answer out from her tight throat.

They sipped their tea in silence for a few moments and then Gareth put his cup down.

'Thea, I know this is difficult for you,' he said softly. 'Believe me, it will get easier once you have met my family and settled in.'

She nodded. 'You may be sure I shall do my best not to let you down, sir.' A look of determination appeared on her weary face. 'I will do all in my power to teach your sister the things you wish.'

It wasn't quite what Gareth had meant.

Damn it, but he wanted her to be happy here!

Before he could begin to question why this mattered so much to him, the sound of a loud thump and a muffled curse broke in on them.

'What in Hades?' I strode to the door and flung it open.

Sprawled on the floor of the corridor, having obviously tripped over the portmanteaux which Mrs Jones had helpfully brought up, was a young girl, dressed in stout outdoor boots and a dark riding-habit.

'Catari! Where the devil have you been at this hour of the night?'

Catari Rhayadar scrambled up into a sitting position, a look of apprehension on her narrow face.

'I didn't know you were back.' She pushed back her windblown tangle of raven curls.

'Obviously,' he replied tightly. He shot out a hand and hauled her to her feet. 'Well, where have you been? And don't pretend you've just got out of bed—not in that rig!'

Catari didn't answer, but looked beyond him to where Thea stood framed in the open doorway.

'Who's your guest?'

The demand checked Gareth's rising tide of anger. 'Didn't Mother receive my letter?'

'We haven't heard from you since you wrote to tell us how you spent Easter.'

Thea watched her great dark eyes, so like her brother's, become sharp with suspicion.

'Well, who is she?'

Gareth enlightened her, and Thea thought she might faint at his feet.

'Your *wife*!' Shock had reduced Catari's voice to a whisper.

'I am very pleased to meet you, Catari. Gareth has spoken of you very often.'

She ignored Thea's outstretched hand.

'Why?' Her small thin body was as taut as a bow-string. 'Why did you have to marry? She isn't beautiful. Is she rich?'

'Catari, control yourself. You disgrace us both with such vulgarity.' Gareth crushed an impulse to comfort her.

'Why did you marry in such a hole-and-corner fashion?' White-faced, she ignored his reprimand. 'Mother will be furious!'

'I do not intend to discuss my reasons with you,' Gareth retorted. He took a deep breath. 'It is very late. I have been travelling all day and I'm in no mood for insolence. Please go to bed. We will discuss your escapade another time.'

'I will not go to bed.' She spat the words at him. 'You cannot order me around like a child.'

'Catari, I won't have one of your displays of temper,' Gareth warned. 'Say goodnight and leave us.'

She shuddered, and Thea saw how her sharp little teeth made an indentation in her lower lip as she struggled with herself.

It was a surprisingly sensuous mouth, red-lipped and generously curved, in an otherwise undeveloped young face. She might grow up to be a beauty, Thea thought, but just now she is all arms and legs and bubbling emotions she cannot control!

'Goodnight.' Catari jerked her head begrudgingly at Thea and, spinning on her heel, stalked away.

'What an unfortunate beginning.' Thea kept her tone light, but she felt shaken by the dislike in Cati's eyes.

Gareth returned her rueful look with a wry nod of agreement.

'Thank you for your forbearance, *cariad*. I'll see to it that she is more polite in future.'

'Be careful, Gareth.' Thea moved closer and laid her hand on his arm. 'If you are too hard on her she will resent it.'

'I know.' He covered her hand with his own and pressed it gently. 'What's worse, I suspect she will blame you. We used to be close and she may be jealous.'

The touch of his hand on hers drove Cati's rudeness from Thea's mind. The heat from his skin was igniting that strange tingling in her veins again. . .

With a sudden sense of shock she realised that she wanted to throw her arms around his neck and be held close against his broad chest.

Idiot! You are merely tired and in need of comforting reassurance, she told herself sternly.

But she knew that she was lying.

'Come, let me show you your bedchamber.' Gareth picked up the portmanteaux.

Thea followed him along another set of corridors which brought them to an odd sloping passageway riddled with fierce draughts.

'This is the bridge which leads to the tower, which is the oldest part of the castle,' Gareth explained. 'You see, Castell Mynach is really a castellated house.'

Thea nodded. She wasn't quite certain of the difference, but wisely decided to save her breath for the flight of ill-lit winding steps they were now facing.

'My room is at the top.' Gareth led the way up. 'Not very convenient but it is a tradition, I'm afraid.'

The stairs were so narrow and steep that Thea was glad she didn't suffer from a fear of heights. A fall would certainly have resulted in injury.

They twisted upwards in a dizzying spiral until they emerged on to a shallow landing permeated with more cold draughts.

'Here we are.' Gareth opened a heavy door and ushered her into a large room.

For a brief instant Thea was surprised by the fact that it was almost circular in shape. She ought to have expected that, of course, but the shabby furnishings were certainly strange.

An enormous four-poster bed occupied the centre of the room, its faded hangings visibly stirring in the draught that was whistling around her ankles. Several heavy wooden chairs, cushioned in the same crimson velvet, and a high-backed oak settle provided seating near the stone hearth.

'Shall I light the fire?'

She nodded gratefully, and he set to work while Thea continued to take stock of her surroundings.

That vast, lavishly carved chest ranged against the far wall also looked old—Tudor, perhaps—but the wash-stand near the bed was modern, with a basin and ewer of fine porcelain in a pretty blue and white design.

'It's local ware,' Gareth told her when she admired it. 'There's a pottery in Swansea which produces excellent quality goods.' He laughed. 'I have a share in it. One of our few good investments.'

The matching pair of tapestries adorning the stone walls were also of Welsh origin. Studying them, Thea realised that they depicted the story of King Arthur. They were in sad need of cleaning, but the workmanship was very fine.

The stark simplicity of the bare stonework was otherwise unrelieved, except for three narrow slit windows piercing the outer walls. Thea suspected that they would once have been covered by stretched membrane, but thankfully modern glass reduced the intensity of the draughts.

'I suppose the wind comes off the sea,' she murmured.

'The beach is almost directly below us. A path leads down to it from the gardens. I'll show you tomorrow.' Gareth stood up and dusted off his hands. 'Come and get warm, *cariad*.'

Thea moved towards the fire, which was beginning to put forth welcome heat.

'I feel chilled to the marrow,' she confessed, knowing that it was a combination of exhaustion and the depressing knowledge that Catari didn't want her here which was making her feel so drained.

'Perhaps a glass of brandy would help.' Gareth gestured to a tray laid out with a variety of bottles and glasses on a side-table.

'I am not in the habit of consuming spirits, sir,' Thea retorted, with more asperity than she had intended.

'It relieves my mind to hear it.' Gareth's eyes twinkled.

Thea blushed. 'Oh, dear, did I sound priggish? I didn't mean to, only Grandmama was forever warning us of the evils of strong drink.'

Gareth laughed. 'Thank God—I thought you'd decided I was a toper. Actually, I keep those bottles there to save myself or the servants a long walk.'

A smile curved her pretty mouth in response to his mild joke, and Gareth found himself staring in fascination at her little dimple.

Annwyl Crist! He hadn't dreamt he would feel like this! With every fibre of his being he longed to draw her into his arms. He wanted to unpin her hair and feel it slide like silk through his hands. He wanted to divest her of that crumpled dress and explore her slender body. Her skin was lovely, with a milky white sheen that made his fingers itch to stroke it. Her breasts would be tender and sweet and. . .

Gareth slammed the door firmly shut on his imagination.

'Is there anything I can get you before I say goodnight?' he enquired somewhat hoarsely.

'I don't think so. Your housekeeper seems to have thought of everything.'

'Then I shall leave you. If you need me, just pull that bell over there in the corner.' He pointed it out with one long forefinger. 'Another disadvantage of living in this tower is that my dressing-room is actually on the next level, but my grandfather had that bell installed to improve communications.'

'To save his voice, I assume?'

He grinned at her. 'Of course.'

He took a step closer and Thea's pulse began to hammer.

'Goodnight, my lady. Sweet dreams.'

He possessed himself of her hand and, raising it to his lips, pressed a kiss upon the soft skin of her inner wrist.

'Goodnight, sir.' Thea forced the words past the obstruction in her throat.

She watched him depart and then collapsed on to the wide bed in a boneless heap, every nerve in her body quivering.

For one crazy moment she had longed to beg him to stay!

'So it seems I must welcome you as my new daughter-in-law. . . *What* did you say her name was, Gareth?'

Stifling an urge to wring his mother's fragile neck, Lord Rhayadar supplied this information once more, his tone a warning growl.

The Dowager merely smiled.

'You must forgive me,' she murmured in her cultured accents. 'I am apt to be sleepy-headed in the morning—particularly before I have breakfasted.' She gave a delicate little laugh. 'However, I shall endeavour to make an effort. It isn't every day I receive such. . . such delightful news.'

'Would you prefer it if I came back later?' Thea asked in an equally polite voice.

Her mother-in-law shook her beautifully coiffured head. 'However, I am in the habit of rising late and breakfasting in my room. Normally you must not expect me to receive you before noon.'

Thea felt that Angharad Rhayadar wished to reduce her to the level of a scolded schoolgirl, and she was very glad that she had chosen to wear her new morning-gown for this interview. At least she would find nothing to cavil at in her appearance. Her cream-coloured Indian mull was both fashionable and becoming.

'Come, take this chair.'

Raising her chin in an unconscious gesture, Thea obeyed, and sat down near to her mother-in-law's *chaise-longue*.

Gareth came to stand behind her chair. He bent forward to whisper in her ear under the pretence of brushing an imaginary speck of dust from her gown. 'Courage, *cariad*.'

He left his hand resting against her shoulder and Thea was glad.

'Ring for a bottle of champagne, Gareth. We must drink a toast to your bride.'

'Thank you for the thought, Mother. However, the doctor says it is bad for you.'

'Nonsense. Pugh is an old woman.'

Gareth disputed it, and a spirited exchange followed.

Thea tried to concentrate, but she was very conscious of his touch burning her through the thin muslin. She could feel the already familiar dizzying rush of pleasure burning through her veins.

To distract herself from her improper imaginings, she focused on the wealth of Dresden ornaments and numerous fine watercolours that decorated the Dowager's sitting-room. The delicate rococo furniture, upholstered in pale blue to match the expensive silk wallpaper, and the elegant flower arrangements in their crystal vases proclaimed the Dowager's expensive tastes.

Gareth had spoken of economising—and from what she seen so far the rest of the castle was shabby—but his mother dwelt in luxury.

Thea eyed the older woman thoughtfully.

To be honest, the Dowager was a surprise. Thea had been expecting a middle-aged matriarch, but Angharad barely looked old enough to be Gareth's mother. She must be nearly fifty, but beneath that frivolous lace cap her black hair showed no trace of grey, and her olive skin was still smooth. Only the painful thinness of her elegantly clad body hinted at ill-health.

'Gareth tells me you did not bring your maid with you. We must find one for you.' The Dowager turned back to Thea 'We do not entertain as much as I should like these days, but as the new Viscountess Rhayadar you will, of course, be required to meet all the neighbouring families. You will want to look your best.'

Thea resisted an urge to raise a hand to check that her curls were still in place. 'Thank you, ma'am.'

The Dowager smiled graciously. 'Your appearance does you cridit, my dear. Are you interested in fashion?'

Thea nodded cautiously

'Excellent. It will be pleasant to have someone with whom I can discuss the latest styles. Catari has no taste whatsover.' An irritated sigh escaped her painted lips. 'She would wear the same gown week in, week out if I let her! Perhaps you will have a reforming influence.'

'Thea has already agreed to my request to help curb Carari's unladylike habits, Mother.'

Angharad raised her thin brows at her son.

'I won't deny I should be glad to see your sister brought to a better understanding of her position, Gareth, but do you think your wife is the right person to effect this miracle?'

She smoothed a fold in her striped gauze skirts and then glanced up at Thea. 'Pray do not take this amiss, but are you qualified to instruct my daughter?'

Thea did not pretend to misunderstand her.

'My mother was related to the Ashbys, a very good Wiltshire family, ma'am, and I was reared as a lady in spite of my connections with trade,' she said with assumed calm, but she was grateful for the increased pressure of Gareth's fingers against her shoulder.

'Does that satisfy you, Mother? Or would you care to inspect Thea's teeth while you are about the business?' he asked sweetly.

The Dowager glared at him. 'Do not be impertinent, Gareth. Surely I am entitled to ask a few simple questions?'

The arrival of a servant come to answer the bell provided a distraction.

'What an age you have been, girl!' The Dowager rounded on the unfortunate maid. 'Pray tell Howell to bring us up a bottle of the best champagne at once!'

'Yes, ma'am.' The maid bobbed a curtsy and fled.

'Useless! That girl is as useless as the rest of her family!'

'Megan does her best, Mother. There is too much work for her to manage.'

'Then hire more servants.' The Dowager gave him a sullen look. 'Do you realise we are reduced to a half-dozen women and only two footmen?'

'I realise a house of this size needs more staff,' Gareth replied drily. 'However, you know there is no money to pay for extra maids or a new housekeeper. You ought to be thankful that Mrs Jones is willing to take on both tasks.'

The Dowager swished her fan angrily at him, but refrained from answering his blunt statement.

Heavens, matters must be in more desperate case than I had realised, Thea thought to herself.

Hot water had been brought to her bedchamber earlier by the same dark-haired little maid, who was the cook-housekeeper's younger daughter. Another of Mrs Jones's progeny had carried into the breakfast-parlour their substantial meal of eggs, ham, oatcakes and strange little sausages, which had turned out to be filled with hard white cheese—a local delicacy, her husband had informed her.

It explained why most of the furniture could have done with a thorough polishing. Cobwebs flourished in the more remote corners and she'd seen dust rising from the rather threadbare carpet in the morning-room where she had waited for Gareth to inform his mother about their marriage.

'Speaking of Catari, have you seen your sister this morning?' the Dowager asked, abandoning Megan's inadequacies.

Thea's concentration sharpened.

'She did not appear for breakfast.' Gareth's expression was grim, but he had no intention of disclosing Catari's latest misdemeanour until he had heard the truth from her own lips.

The Dowager frowned, but her expression brightened when the elderly butler arrived, carrying an ancient silver tray on which resided a bottle of champagne and three glasses.

'Thank you, Howell. I'll open it,' said Gareth.

The butler thankfully handed him the folded linen cloth he carried over one arm and bowed himself out of the room.

'I don't know why you continue to employ that old fool,' the Dowager remarked pettishly.

'He served my grandfather, ma'am.' Gareth poured the wine and handed his mother a small glassful.

'Your sentiments do you credit, Gareth,' she retorted sarcastically. 'I just hope you can afford to keep them and a wife.'

Thea watched how his well-cut mouth tightened, and hastily stepped into the breach.

Her admiration of the Dowager's collection of

Dresden figurines restored the smile to her mother-in-law's face, and she even insisted on toasting the bride.

A little while was spent in amiable discussion of fine chinaware, and then the Dowager asked Thea if she liked dancing.

'Indeed I do, ma'am.'

'Good. We must arrange a party to welcome you to Castell Mynach.' The Dowager's dark eyes slid mockingly to her son. 'Oh, don't look so alarmed, Gareth. I'm not planning anything elaborate, but we must do *something* to celebrate your marriage!' Her tone was honey-sweet. 'Or do you want even more gossip than there is bound to be? If you marry a tradesman's daughter you must put a brave face on it, or they'll think you are ashamed of her.'

Thea winced. It was easy to see that her mother-in-law was fond of getting her own way—and none too scrupulous about her methods of achieving it!

'I hope you are not going to continue to refer to Thea in that manner,' Gareth said quietly, but a wealth of annoyance fringed his tone.

'Naturally I meant no criticism of Thea. I am sure I shall find her charming once I get to know her.' The Dowager smiled and reached to pat Thea's hand.

Detecting Angharad's insincerity, in spite of the sweetness of her voice, Thea had to resist the desire to snatch her hand away.

She hides it more skilfully but I don't think she likes me any better than Catari does, she thought, with a stab of dismay.

Gareth decided that it was time to bring the interview to an end. 'I've promised to show Thea the gardens, Mother.'

'Of course. They are somewhat neglected, I'm afraid, but I dare say that won't surprise Thea.' There was a wealth of bitterness in the Dowager's tone.

Deciding that it would be politic to remain silent, Thea rose and made a graceful curtsy.

'Thank you for receiving me, ma'am.'

'A moment, if you please.' The Dowager stopped them with an imperious gesture as they reached the door. 'There is one last question I would like to ask.'

She twirled her fan delicately.

'Forgive me if I offend, but there was no reason for you to marry my son with such indecent haste, was there?'

Colour flooded Thea's pale cheeks as her meaning sank in.

'*Annwyl Crist*! You go too far, Mother!'

Ignoring her son's angry imprecation, the Dowager continued to survey Thea closely.

'Only it would be most unfortunate if an heir arrived early. Think of the gossip! I really do think you must warn me if there is any prospect of such an event occurring.'

'There is no such possibility, ma'am.'

Thea met her dark gaze with a steady dignity, and knew that she had successfully survived the first test when Angharad nodded reluctant approval.

CHAPTER FIVE

A STIFF breeze was blowing when they began their tour of the grounds. Thea could taste the salt on her lips and smell the seaweed tang in the air.

'It must be difficult trying to get things to grow so close to the sea,' she said.

'So old Trebor—our head gardener—complains.'

They entered the flower garden and Thea looked about her with interest. There was a rustic bench placed in the centre. It would be pleasant to sit out here on a fine day, but the beds and paths were in sore need of tidying up and weeding.

'Do you think Trebor would object if I tried to restore some order here?'

'I should imagine he would be delighted.' Gareth cocked his head to one side in enquiry. 'Am I to take it that you like gardening?'

Thea laughed. 'I cannot claim much experience, but I enjoy pottering about in a garden.'

They turned back to the main path and Gareth said, 'My mother likes to amuse herself making floral arrangements and often demands exotic flowers, but Trebor tells her he has no time to cultivate them.' He shrugged. 'As with the house, more help is needed.'

'Until this morning I hadn't realised your finances were in such a parlous state,' Thea admitted carefully.

'Regretting your bargain, *cariad*?'

A spurt of annoyance shot through Thea. 'Not so far, my lord.'

'Forgive me. That was a crass thing to say.'

Thea was mollified by his apology. 'If you are wondering whether your mother upset me, the answer is no. I never believed she would welcome me with open arms.'

'Her bark is worse than her bite.'

Thea shrugged.

'Shall we venture along the clifftop?' Gareth changed the subject. 'The view over the bay is attractive, and you will be able to get a good impression of the castle as a whole.'

Thea had taken the precaution of wearing a cloak over her pelisse, and she hugged it to her as they left the shelter of the gardens and the wind came rushing at them.

'The fishing boats are out.' Gareth pointed seawards and, straining her eyes, Thea could just make out two dots on the horizon.

What good vision he had!

'They are from Llanrhayadar.'

Thea nodded. She had already discovered that the village lay about half a mile to the east below the castle. Gareth had promised to take her there soon.

'It is a lovely view,' she remarked, enjoying the way the sunshine made the waters of the bay sparkle.

There was a house on the opposite headland. A large, modern-looking brick mansion.

'That's the Cwrt—Parry Cwrt,' Gareth informed her when she asked, and Thea was surprised by his tone. He sounded almost angry!

Tactfully she turned her back on the sea, and looked inland.

Set high on its headland, Castell Mynach was an impressive sight. Built in the local sandstone, it shone fiercely red in the sunlight, and Thea could imagine no sharper contrast to the sedate house in Beaufort Square.

It stood four-square to the elements, its thick, battlemented walls declaring its purpose as a refuge and stronghold—a house that was as strong as a castle, with a defensive tower to prove it. Sixty feet high, the tower where she had slept last night was hexagonal in shape and joined to the main building by an arched bridge.

'The tower is the oldest part of the castle—the

original keep, in fact. It was built in the thirteenth century. Local legend has it that a hermit once lived on this spot—hence the name: monk's castle.' Gareth gave her a crooked grin. 'I don't know if it is true about the hermit, but my remote ancestor, Llwelyn the Strong, was no monk! My grandfather used to tell me that he built those walls thirty-two feet broad each side and ten feet thick to keep out the husbands he'd cuckolded!'

Beneath his amusement, Thea heard the pride in his voice. Notwithstanding all the worry and frustration of the debts that hung about his neck, Gareth loved his heritage.

'Shall we go down to the beach? The path is quite safe, although it can be slippery in wet weather.'

Thea was happy to agree. 'Are those caves in the cliffside?' she asked as they descended.

He nodded, but again she sensed a reticence in him and wondered at it.

'I feel quite guilty at depriving you of your own room.' She changed the subject, abandoning her curiosity.

'There's no need.'

'It is kind of you to reassure me, sir——' she dimpled at him '—but I think you are merely being polite.'

'Believe me, I've slept in far more uncomfortable places than my dressing-room,' he insisted, firmly ignoring the fact that he had spent a restless night.

Lying awake in the darkness, he had begun to realise what a trap he had dug for himself.

It had been a damnable way to spend a wedding night!

'And you? Did you sleep well?'

Thea nodded. In spite of her expectations to the contrary, her eyes had closed the instant her head had touched the pillow. It was only when she had awoken this morning that she had found herself fretting about the future.

Crushing this memory, she said with mock severity,

'I hope, sir, that you aren't going to warn me that the tower is haunted.'

His black eyes danced with merriment. 'Actually, they do say that Llwelyn's ghost walks on certain nights of the year. Mrs Jones claims to have seen him more than once.'

'Gareth, you just made that story up!' Thea's eyes widened. 'Didn't. . .didn't you?'

His laughter sparked her own, and, momentarily careless of her footing, she slipped as her heel caught in a tussock of coarse grass.

Her shriek of fright was as instinctive as Gareth's swift reaction.

'It's all right, *lili'r môr*,' he murmured, catching her in his arms. 'You are safe now.'

Gazing down into her upturned face, his eyes darkened.

'What. . .what did you call me?' Thea whispered, trying to recapture her own composure and failing dismally.

'It means lily of the sea,' he answered hoarsely, forgetting his good resolutions. 'You make me think of a cool sea-nymph, slender and delicate. Your eyes are clear like sparkling water, and your skin is white like the lily, soft and pure. . .'

His deep voice slowed to a halt and Thea's pulse began to hammer. Her heart was beating so wildly that she felt sure he must be able to hear it!

His arms tightened.

'Thea! *Annwyl Crist*, but you are driving me insane!'

Breathless, she could only stare at him, her eyes enormous in her pale face.

His dark head began to dip towards hers. . .

'I'm sorry. I have no right to say such things to you.' Gareth ground the words out jerkily between clenched teeth, and forced his arms to release her.

He stepped back.

'Perhaps it would be better if I returned to the

house. No doubt you will wish to enjoy the view alone. Shall I send a servant to escort you home?'

His breathing was still ragged, but she saw that he had regained control of himself.

'Thank you, I can find my own way.' She managed a polite smile, hiding her feeling of bitter disappointment.

Gareth bowed with precise formality. 'As you wish.' With a curt nod of farewell, he turned away.

The sound of his footsteps faded.

Thea stared blindly at the wind-ruffled sea. What was the matter with her? He was behaving in an exemplary fashion and she wanted to burst into tears!

You are a fool, my girl, she told herself sternly.

Infatuation or love, she didn't know. But in spite of all her fine resolutions she was already in too deep to draw back. Gareth Rhayadar had become a fever in her blood.

Her whole body ached for his touch! She couldn't stop thinking about him.

And yet she still knew so little about him. Oh, he desired her—she had seen the passion in his eyes just now, and it had taken every ounce of her will-power to resist the urge to wind her arms around his neck and press her lips to his—but if they became lovers, what then?

He had asked her to be his bride, but he had never spoken one word of love.

If she gave in to longing, would he tire of her once desire was satisfied?

Wishing she had the experience to answer her own question, Thea sighed.

One thing she *had* learnt this morning. Her virtue was safe.

Gareth meant to keep his promise. But she no longer wanted him to!

'What a pity to waste such a dashing creation on a quiet family dinner,' Gareth announced when he arrived to escort her downstairs that evening.

The gleam of appreciation in his eyes sent Thea's spirits soaring.

The fashionably cut eau-de-nil silk was her finest evening gown. Unfortunately her hope of impressing her mother-in-law was quickly crushed.

The Dowager was in a mood to be critical.

She pestered Gareth with trivial complaints throughout dinner and found fault with everything from the buttered crab which began the meal to the cheesecakes that ended it.

Catari did not help soothe her mother's ill-temper by arriving late. To make matters worse, she was clad in a gown that had seen better days.

'Why did you not change?' the Dowager demanded, glaring at the mud staining her daughter's skirts.

'It was too late.'

'You could at least have brushed your hair!'

Cati shrugged carelessly. 'I've been swimming.'

Her superb disregard for convention aroused a reluctant flicker of admiration in Thea.

'What's the matter? Why are you staring at me? Don't people swim in Bath? They certainly ought to!' Catari let out a shriek of laughter at her own wit.

'Don't be so childish, Cati.' Gareth frowned at her and she subsided sulkily.

'Mostly people just drink the waters in Bath,' Thea said in a conciliatory manner. 'Or sit in the hot baths for their ailments.'

'How boring.' Catari's sensual mouth curled with scorn.

Thea had the uncomfortable feeling that this remark was meant to apply to her as well.

'Try to behave, brat.' Gareth flashed Thea an exasperated look of apology. 'Or you go to bed hungry.'

Cati glowered at him.

'Pray ignore my daughter, Thea. She has no idea how to behave.' The Dowager's mouth compressed to a thin line of aggravation.

'Then I think it about time she learnt,' Thea retorted briskly.

Cati's mouth fell open in surprise.

'You are capable of understanding a few simple facts, are you not?' Thea continued, in the same pleasant but firm tone.

'Of course I am! Do you take me for a mooncalf?'

'To be honest, I wasn't sure. And unless you want other people to make that assumption you will have to amend your manners. Young ladies do not come to the table looking like scarecrows. They do not pull sulky faces when reprimanded. And they most certainly do not insult their elders.'

Thea held the rebellious gaze steadily.

'I didn't meant to be insulting. Sorry.' Catari muttered the words ungraciously.

Relief flooded over Thea. She had spoken on impulse but her instinct had been correct. Catari needed a firm hand. She would not respect weakness.

'If you have both finished arguing, it is time to leave Gareth to his port.' The Dowager snapped the order, her expression irritable.

Gareth rose politely to his feet as they left the table.

'Well done, *cariad*,' he murmured to Thea as she passed him. 'Stick to your guns.'

Encouraged, Thea took her seat in the drawing-room with every appearance of calm.

It was a pleasant room, which bore the marks of its many years of age with pride. The walls were half-pannelled in oak, with several landscape paintings and family portraits above. The furniture was equally old-fashioned, but Thea found it comfortable and more to her taste than the formal dining-room or the Dowager's lavish retreat.

She was not allowed to enjoy the peaceful atmosphere for long.

'In future, Thea, I should prefer it if you could curb your enthusiasm for taking Catari to task. Save your reprimands until we have left the table. I do not find it an aid to digestion.'

There was a waspish note in her mother-in-law's voice that set Thea's back up.

'I understood it was your ladyship's wish that Catari be sent away to school as soon as possible?' At the Dowager's nod of assent, Thea continued. 'Then I fail to see your objection, ma'am. Surely you want her to behave as a lady at mealtimes too?'

The Dowager flushed and seeemd to struggle in vain for an answer.

'I don't want to go to some seminary.' Catari waded into the fray. 'I want to stay here.'

'Be silent, miss! No one asked for your opinion.'

A flicker of sympathy for the younger girl shot through Thea. Unless she missed her guess, the Dowager regarded her daughter as a nuisance.

'Ring for Williams, Catari. I am tired. I will not stay for the teatray tonight.' The Dowager turned to Thea with a grim smile. 'Pray convey my compliments to my son, and tell him I wish to see him before he retires.'

When her mother had withdrawn, on the supporting arm of her personal maid, Catari let out a low whistle.

'She means to complain to Gareth, you know. She hates being bested in an argument or anything else.'

'No doubt you are right, but it isn't very polite of you to speak of your mother in that way,' Thea replied.

Cati tossed her untidy braids. 'Much I care.' She gave Thea a sharp look. 'What does it matter to you, anyway? You are not my keeper.'

'Actually, Cati, in a way I am. You see, Gareth wants me to help you. He feels you will be happier at school if you learn to fit in easily with your new companions.'

Cati stared at her indignantly. 'I am sixteen. I don't need another governess.'

'Your brother thinks you do.'

Cati bit down on her full lower lip. 'It is all Mother's

fault,' she muttered rebelliously. 'She wants to be rid of me. She has never liked me.'

Cati's bitter remark merely confirmed Thea's suspicion that the Dowager was not a loving parent. After all, she knew the signs only too well!

'I'm sure your mother wants the best for you,' she said firmly, crushing the desire to sympathise. It wouldn't help Cati to agree with her. She had been overindulged for long enough.

'All my mother wants is for me to make a grand marriage,' Cati retorted in an oddly flat tone.

Thea regarded the tips of her Denmark satin slippers. Really, this conversation was raising too many uncomfortable ghosts!

'It might help if you could view the seminary as an interesting opportunity rather than a banishment,' she said, after a moment's strained silence. 'There will be lots of new things for you to see and do.'

'I am quite happy making my own amusements, thank you.'

'You will be able to make new friends of your own age at school. From what Gareth has told me there aren't many young people for you to mix with here.'

Cati began to laugh in a strange, harsh way, but before Thea could ask her what was wrong, Blodwen arrived with the teatray.

The fresh-cheeked maid, who was the image of Mrs Jones, set the heavy tray down in front of Thea and bobbed a curtsy.

'Mam says to ask you if you want to have me until you can hire a proper lady's maid.' She gave Thea a hopeful grin. 'I know what to do, my lady. I've helped Miss Williams.'

'Thank you, Blodwen, I'm sure you will manage very well. You may tell your mother that I am happy to give you a trial.' Thea dismissed her with a smile.

'I don't want any tea.' Cati got to her feet.

'Won't you stay and keep me company?' Thea said in her friendliest fashion.

'Gareth will be here in a minute. You don't need me.' Cati snorted derisively. 'And I don't need you.'

Thea's heart ached at the loneliness she could hear behind the bravura defiance.

'Please don't regard me as an enemy, Cati. I am obliged to follow Gareth's instructions——'

'I don't believe you. You are a new bride.' Cati glared at her. 'If you wanted to, you could persuade him to change his mind and drop this stupid scheme to send me away.'

'It is not my place to interfere.' Thea objected mildly, but she was bitterly aware of the irony in Cati's mistaken assumption. 'Our lessons need not be formal. I shall do my best to make them entertaining for you.'

'Don't bother. I have no intention of wasting my time on such rigmarole.'

'Cati, please, you are not being fair.' Thea curbed a spurt of annoyance. 'At least give me a chance.'

'Why should I?'

'We could be friends.'

For a second indecision showed on the narrow young face, but then Cati shook her head. 'I don't trust you.'

Thea's spirits sank as she gazed at her sister-in-law's mulishly obstinate expression. It was going to be even harder than she'd thought to win Catari Rhayadar's friendship.

Thea was the solitary occupant of the breakfast-parlour the next morning. A tentative enquiry revealed that his lordship had breakfasted early.

'Miss Cati was down first thing too,' Megan added, setting a pot of coffee in front of Thea. 'I think she has gone out.'

Thea thanked her for the information and picked up her knife and fork.

She was just finishing her meal when Gareth strode in. He was wearing riding-dress and she thought he looked particularly handsome.

Refusing coffee, he said, 'Would you like to ride into the village with me?'

Thea hesitated, and Gareth experienced an unexpected stab of disappointment.

'I haven't ridden in years.' Thea was anxious that he should not misunderstand her reluctance. 'Not since I left school.'

'I'm sure we could find you a quiet mount.'

She shook her glossy head apologetically. 'I'm afraid I don't even possess a riding-habit.'

For an instant he thought of suggesting she borrow one from Cati, but she was taller than his sister.

'Then we must get one made for you.'

'I should like that.' Thea's face brightened.

'Are you brave enough to risk my curricle instead?'

'I'll go and change my dress,' Thea laughed.

Gareth grinned back, and admonished her not to take too long.

'It will take me longer climbing all those stairs up to my eyrie,' she riposted.

'I'll arrange for you to move out of the tower once the honeymoon is over.' Gareth's smile faded.

Unable to think of an appropriate answer, Thea quickly nodded and hurried off to change.

Entering her chamber, she became aware that she would regret giving it up. It might be shabby and old-fashioned, but she had grown to like it.

With Blodwen's help she donned her best carriage-dress. Made of almond-green French cambric, it was extremely elegant—an excellent choice to wear for her first trip to the village.

Tying the ribbons of her chip-straw hat into a saucy bow beneath her chin, she paused.

Did she relish this room because it was Gareth's?

Five minutes later she rejoined her husband, who was waiting for her outside the main front entrance. A thin young groom, whom Gareth introduced as Dai, was holding the heads of a pair of well-matched greys.

Thea imagined that he would spring up behind, but Gareth casually dismissed him.

The yellow-bodied curricle bowled off down the gravel drive at a swift pace, and Thea asked where they were going.

'I have business at the parsonage.' Gareth flicked a glance in her direction. 'You will like John Morgan. He was my first schoolmaster.' He chuckled. 'A more patient man you'd be hard pressed to discover.'

Thea sat back to enjoy the drive.

It was a fine morning, sunny and less windy than it had been the day before. The road wound along the coast, affording picturesque views at every turn, and Thea let out a tiny exclamation of delight.

'You never told me how beautiful it was.'

'You don't mind living out in the wilds?'

'Not in the least.' There was a slightly quizzical lift to his thick eyebrows that made her add, 'You think I shall miss city life, don't you?'

He acknowledged it.

'I don't think I will,' she protested. 'But in any case, Swansea is only an hour away.'

'You are free to visit there whenever you wish, but I'm afraid I won't always be on hand to offer you my escort.'

Thea hid her disappointment. She was being foolish. She had always known he was a busy man, with many claims on him.

'I suppose your tenants and the villagers must be practically self-sufficient,' she said, deliberately choosing a safer topic of conversation.

He nodded, and she continued in the same light tone, 'There are a great many sheep hereabouts. Is that how most people make their living?'

Gratified by her sensible behaviour, Gareth explained that any spare yarn left over once the villagers had made their own clothes was sold to a factor from Swansea.

'And there's the fishing, of course. Not that it brings in much money.' Gareth shook his dark head.

The road demanded his full attention for a moment and then he said, 'I've decided to suggest to my bailiff that we try planting potatoes. One of my neighbours, Colonel Secombe, our local magistrate, has had considerable success with them. The war has led to an increased demand for foodstuffs, and they don't spoil on their way to market.'

'It sounds a good idea.'

He shrugged. 'Unfortunately my father took no interest in farming, except to wring profit whenever he could. Our methods have remained sadly old-fashioned and Davis is suspicious of change.'

'I'm sure you can win him over if you try.' Impulsively Thea reached out to touch his arm. 'You have a very persuasive tongue, my lord.'

For an instant, Gareth wondered if she mocked him, but her clear eyes were innocent. Then, realising that she wanted to reassure him of her support, he experienced an unexpected glow of pleasure.

They were almost there.

'Don't expect a model village on a tidy English pattern,' he warned hastily. 'Llanrhayadar has more than its fair share of tumbledown cottages, I'm afraid.'

Hardly were the words out of his mouth than they swept round the last bend and Thea got her first sight of the village.

Framed by a high hill which rose behind the tiny settlement, Llanrhayadar nestled by a small bay. The sunlit sea gleamed blue like a jewel, and Thea caught her breath in admiration.

Unfortunately this first impression was quickly spoilt once they reached the row of cottages that formed the main street. Everywhere she looked Thea could see broken window panes, drunken chimney-pots and missing slates. Some of the houses looked about to fall down!

She had heard Gareth talk of the need for repairs, but she hadn't imagined such neglect.

The sound of the carriage wheels brought people out into the street. When they saw that it was the Viscount with his new bride they let out a loud cheer.

Blushing, Thea allowed Gareth to hand her down to acknowledge this lusty welcome.

The crowd comprised a few old men and young boys, but mostly women and children. Everyone was dressed simply in dark homespun, with little concession to fashion, though Thea did notice several of the women were wearing handsome shawls. Some even appeared to have gold earrings, so perhaps not all the villagers were as poor as Gareth had led her to believe.

Not that there was time to speculate. Gareth was already explaining that they were due at the parsonage.

The crowd parted to allow them to return to the carriage.

'I hope you didn't find that too much of an ordeal,' Gareth remarked, giving his horses the office to start once more.

'I hadn't expected quite such a public welcome,' Thea admitted.

The women, at least, had been frankly assessing her. She thought her elegant appearance had won their approval, although no doubt they wished Gareth had chosen a Welshwoman.

'Welsh folk aren't shy of showing their emotions.'

She cast him a sharp look. Was he hinting that he wanted her to show her feelings? She wished she had the courage to ask.

The parsonage was set in a large garden behind a white-painted fence on the edge of the village. A servant came running to attend to the carriage.

Gareth stepped aside to speak to the man about the care of his greys, leaving Thea at leisure to admire the profusion of blooms that graced the Reverend Morgan's abode.

'You like flowers, my lady?'

The cracked thin voice made Thea swing round.

An elderly man dressed in clerical black was surveying her. He bowed.

'John Morgan at your service, ma'am. I *do* have the honour of addressing Gareth's bride?'

Thea curtsied. 'You are correct, sir.'

Gareth came up to join them.

'I was just admiring Mr Morgan's violas.' Thea gestured to the display. 'They are very colourful.'

'My wife wants to restore the flower garden at the *castell*,' Gareth remarked as the minister led them indoors.

'A praiseworthy ambition.' The old man gave her a smile, and Thea was struck by the kindness in his expression.

The house was small and plainly furnished, but the drawing-room faced south and was filled with sunshine. They had barely sat down before the housekeeper came bustling in to offer fresh-baked cakes and wine.

After they had finished their refreshment, Thea asked if she might see the church.

'Of course.'

In spite of his civility, Thea had a sudden feeling that the minister was anxious to speak to Gareth in private.

However, it was too late to to retract her request, and she dismissed her unease as they all strolled across the short-cropped grass to the small church.

Inside it felt cool, and the light was soothingly dim. Gareth pointed out the memorial tablet to his grandfather, and Thea complimented Mr Morgan on the church's well-cared-for appearance.

'I am lucky in my parishioners.' A spark of genuine enthusiasm lit up his faded eyes. 'So many people have been persuaded to join the Methodists that the church is in a poor state here in Wales. Many of my fellow clergymen have lost touch with the people and failed to give them proper spiritual guidance. Some are more interested in their stipends than in tending souls!'

He shook his white-haired head at such folly.

'I'm told that the sermons are often splendid at these Methodist meetings,' Gareth remarked.

'Passionate oratory appeals to our countrymen, my lord. Your father was not a religious man, but he understood the power of the pulpit. He liked to attend church on Sunday, whenever he was in residence at the castle, to set an example to his tenants.'

'It might have done more good if he'd spent money on repairs.' Gareth's tone was dry.

'I fear you may be right. They have a hard life, and prayer alone cannot mend a leaking roof.' John Morgan nodded, looking distressed.

'I used to assist our local vicar's wife with charitable work in Bristol,' Thea said hastily. 'Perhaps I could help in some way here?'

She shot a look of enquiry at her husband. 'Do I have your permission, my lord?'

Something in her crisp tone cautioned Gareth that she would brook no refusal, but he felt compelled to try.

'It won't be easy,' he warned. 'Are you sure you want to get involved?'

'Of course.' Thea's tone was impatient. 'I'm not afraid of hard work, sir. I know what dreadful conditions the poor frequently live in, but dirt and squalour are no reason to hold back if we can give help.'

Gareth eyed her with fresh respect. *Duw*, her compassion was a sharp contrast to his mother's indifference!

The Dowager rarely visited the village. At Christmas she might send down a hamper of food, but she took little interest in the sick or needy.

'I shouldn't let such work interfere with my other duties.' Thea wondered why he was looking at her so strangely.

Gareth nodded silently. He hadn't been thinking of Cati.

Most of the women of rank he knew—with the

exception of his sister—avoided contact with their social inferiors. They cared more for their gowns than the plight of the poor. Pleasure was all they lived for, and be damned to any thought of morality or conscience.

He had learnt the hard way that a sweet smile was no guarantee of honesty or loyal affection.

Dared he hope that his wife was different?

'If you are certain you wish to help John, I have no objection,' he declared, his smile betraying nothing of his troubled inner thoughts.

'Thank you.' Thea swept him a graceful curtsy.

The matter settled, they returned to the drawing-room.

'If I may, I should like a word in private with your husband before you leave?'

Startled to be reminded of her earlier premonition, Thea murmured a rather confused acquiescence.

'I won't keep you above a moment,' Gareth promised.

'I shall wait for you in the garden.' Declining the minister's offer to see her out, Thea marshalled her wits and left them.

She had barely reached the front door when she realised she had left her gloves behind.

After a moment's indecision, Thea turned to retrace her steps. They were an expensive pair, and Gareth would probably never notice them on the side-table.

The door to the drawing-room was ajar, just as she had left it.

'Damn it all to hell!'

The sound of Gareth's voice raised in anger stopped her in her tracks.

'I'm sorry to give you such bad news, my boy, but I thought you ought to know he was back.'

'Are you sure it was Y Cadno's ship?'

Gareth's tone was so curt that Thea hesitated, not wishing to interrupt them.

'Iolo swore it was the *Llwyinoges*, and he has good

eyesight.' The thin old voice was sorrowful. 'I suppose we should have expected that devil to return one day. He must have heard you were home.'

'And he thinks to bait me.' Gareth sounded bitter.

Thea decided she had heard enough. She had no business eavesdropping on their private conversation!

Silently she fled back down the narrow corridor and out into the garden.

It wasn't until she took a big gulp of fresh air that she realised she had been holding her breath.

Who on earth was Y Cadno, and what had he done to make her husband so angry?

Cati had already taken her place for luncheon when Gareth and Thea walked into the dining-room.

'You are late. Where have you been?' she asked.

To Thea's surprise, her narrow little face lost its usual hostile expression when her brother explained.

'And John Morgan was pleased to accept Thea's offer of help,' Gareth finished.

'You will enjoy getting to know the people of Llanrhayadar, Thea,' Cati said, in the friendliest voice Thea had ever heard her use. 'You must meet everyone. All the villagers and the tenants, of course. I'll come too. We can start tomorrow.'

'Hold fast, Cati. I've already warned Thea that I might be too busy to escort her.' Gareth's tone was a marked contrast to his sister's enthusiasm.

'Oh, there's no need to worry.' Cati blithely reached out and took another helping of fresh bakestone bread. 'We can walk or take the servant's gig.' She flashed a smile at Thea. 'I am safe with horses.'

'Thank you, Cati. It is very kind of you.'

Hope flared in Thea. This was the first time her sister-in-law had said a pleasant word to her since her arrival.

Thea glanced at her husband, expecting to see her excitement mirrored in his dark eyes, but his expression was grim.

Puzzled, she took another spoonful of *cawl*, the nourishing meat and vegetable soup of Wales.

Did Gareth have some objection to his sister hob-nobbing with his tenants? But why?

Perhaps the Dowager disapproved? Thea was suddenly glad that her mother-in-law rarely partook of luncheon. She had never seen Cati so animated.

Deciding to take advantge of this good mood, she asked Cati if she would like to take a walk with her after they had finished their meal.

Cati agreed, and went off to fetch a wrap.

Thea turned to her husband and said, 'You don't mind, do you, Gareth? Only you did say that you had to concur with your bailiff.'

His preoccupied frown vanished. 'Of course not. Go ahead—enjoy your stroll.'

Scorning to walk in the gardens, Cati set off at a fierce pace for the clifftop. Panting a little, Thea managed to keep up with her until at last Cati slowed down.

'Out of breath?' Cati gave Thea a mocking glance.

'A little, but I dare say this sea-breeze will soon cure me.' Thea was determined not to show any weakness.

Cati grinned.

They continued in silence for a few moments, and then unexpectedly Cati halted and pointed at the marvellous view of the bay.

'This is one of my favourite spots in the whole world.'

'It is very beautiful,' Thea agreed.

'Then you must see why I cannot bear the idea of being sent away.' Cati swung round, her expression urgent. 'Can't you intercede for me with Gareth?'

'I'm sorry. There is nothing I can do.' Thea closed her ears to the coaxing note in her sister-in-law's lilting voice.

'Cannot, or will not?'

'Cannot,' Thea affirmed, adding quietly, 'It will only

be for a short while, and then you can come home again.'

'I suppose so,' Cati sighed.

There was a short silence, and then Cati tossed back her long untidy hair and lifted her face to the sky. 'I love the sun. Summer is my favourite season. Which is yours?'

'Early spring, when the earth starts to bloom again and you know that winter is finally over,' Thea replied, quick to accept this tacit truce.

'But it is still too cold to swim then.'

Thea laughed, a shade ruefully. 'I wouldn't know.'

Cati's mouth dropped open. 'You can't swim?'

Hiding her amusement, Thea shook her head.

'I'll teach you, if you want.' Cati made the offer in an offhand tone, but Thea caught a glimpse of the eagerness in her eyes.

She is lonely!

The realisation strengthened Thea's conviction that a few months away from Castell Mynach would be to Cati's benefit. The girl needed company of her own age.

'I should like that very much.'

They turned back, and so skilful was Thea's handling of the conversation that when they arrived back at the castle much of Cati's initial hostility had faded.

Cati headed automatically for the kitchen door.

'I see you care for formality as little as your brother,' Thea said in a teasing tone.

Cati returned her grin. 'I loathe ceremony.'

Thea had a feeling that the Dowager would criticise them for forgetting what was due to their position, but this thought went straight out of her head as they entered the kitchen.

A strong smell of burning filled the room.

She stared in amazement at the sight of the capable Mrs Jones seated in the rocking-chair awash with tears. Her two daughters were trying in vain to soothe her while the little scullery-maid bawled in sympathy.

'What's the matter?' Cati demanded.
Megan looked, up her rosy cheeks drained of colour. 'The Llwynoges is back.'
Cati whistled soundlessly.
'But Geraint is missing.' Blodwen began to sob. 'He was washed overboard in a storm.'
'Dead!' Mrs Jones lifted her ravaged face out of her apron. 'My son. My Geraint. Drowned!' Her voice rose in a shriek of lamentation.
Thea decided that it was time to take a hand. The tragedy which had befallen was plainly connected to the arrival of the mysterious Y Cadno, but there was no time to indulge in curiosity now.
Tactfully despatching the scullery-maid to fetch more vegetables, she said, 'Megan, help your mother upstairs and see to it that she lies down. Stay with her until she settles.'
She turned to Blodwen. 'Dry your eyes, my dear. I want you to help me brew a tisane to soothe your mother.'
Recognising the voice of authority, they all obeyed.
'What shall I do?' Cati asked with a hint of amusement in her voice, when Megan had led the weeping cook away.
'You can lift that saucepan off the fire for a start,' Thea ordered. 'No! Use a cloth or you'll injure your hand!'
'It's burnt,' Cati observed, peering at the contents of the pan.
'You surprise me,' Thea answerd drily. 'Do you think you could put it in some water to soak?'
Cati obediently carried the pan out into the scullery.
'Where does your mother keep the household herbs, Blodwen?' Thea asked in her gentlest voice.
Blodwen found the items Thea wanted and Thea quickly made an infusion of dried cowslip roots and camomile flowers.
'Why are you using those? What good will they do?' Cati asked curiously.

'Cowslip acts to calm the nerves and camomile will help Mrs Jones sleep.'

'How do you know?' Cati asked in surprise.

'My grandmother was insistent that my sister and I were taught housewifery.' Thea smiled faintly. 'She said that we would never know when we were being cheated by the servants if we didn't learn how things should be done ourselves. Most of it was deadly dull stuff, but I found the use of herbs interesting and decided to learn more about the subject.'

'You seem to know a great deal.' There was a hint of admiration in Cati's tone.

Handing a tray containing a cup of her brew to Blodwen, Thea laughingly denied it. 'I'm no expert, but I do enjoy making useful potions and lotions!'

Instructing Blodwen to go to her room and rest after she had delivered the tisane, Thea fixed Cati with her gaze and continued lightly, 'You might discover a similar interest for yourself one day. Schooling can provide unexpected benefits, you know.'

Leaving her sister-in-law to digest this pointed observation, Thea turned her attention to the fire, where a meal had obviously been in the process of being cooked.

'This, presumably, was meant to be our dinner,' she murmured ruefully, examining the congealed contents of another of the pans.

'Mother will throw a fit,' Cati remarked, coming up to stare at the ruined sauce. 'She will blame poor Mrs Jones. She is always saying that she is a bad cook and that her family are a feckless lot.'

Thea lifted her eyebrows at her in enquiry.

'Geraint, the boy they were talking about, served as a groom here until Mother claimed he had stolen some money. My father found the missing purse later. It had become wedged down one of the barouche squabs, but by then it was too late.' Cati sighed. 'My mother never apologised to Mrs Jones for causing Geraint to run off.'

'But why does your mother dislike Mrs Jones? She seems an admirable woman.' Cati's story had not improved Thea's opinion of her mother-in-law.

'She is! She was my nurse, you know, and Gareth's too. When I was a child I loved being down here in the kitchen. It was so warm and cosy. She would let me help her bake, and there was always something delicious to eat.'

Cati's reminiscent smile faded.

'But Mother never wanted her at Castell Mynach. She had chosen someone else to look after Gareth, but Father overruled her. She never forgave him for it. When I was eight years old she insisted I no longer needed a nurse and hired a governess for me. But Father refused to let her dismiss Mrs Jones.'

A flush stained Cati's thin cheeks. 'He wanted to keep her here because she was his mistress.'

'Cati! You shouldn't listen to gossip.'

'It's true! I overheard my parents arguing about it.' She gave an angry shrug. 'They often quarrelled about Father's women.'

'You mustn't talk about such things.' Cati's surmise was probably correct, but the whole business was a most unsuitable subject for a girl of her years.

'Oh, don't worry, I shan't sully your prim ears any longer,' Cati retorted, and stalked out.

Thea sighed, hoping she hadn't lost all the headway she had made with her prickly sister-in-law.

An hour later Gareth walked into the kitchen to find her up to her elbows in flour. A huge white apron protected her dress, but strands had escaped from her carefully dressed hair and clung damply to her pink face.

'*Duw*!' he exclaimed, laughing. 'What on earth are you doing, *cariad*?'

'Cooking dinner,' Thea replied grimly. 'And a devil of a job I'm having of it, Gareth Rhayadar, so don't you dare laugh at me!'

She glared with distaste at the contents of her mixing-bowl. 'I swear I never dreamt it could be so hard to make pastry!'

Gareth composed his expression. 'Why are you trying to make pastry?' he enquired mildly.

Thea was not deceived by the innocence of his tone.

'Because, my dear husband, tonight's dessert was to have been a cherry pie, and I have already stoned what seems to be a hundredweight of the wretched things!'

Gareth's eyes twinkled. 'Did you know you had a smut of soot on your nose?'

Thea's hand flew automatically to her face. Before she had realised what she was doing she had touched the offending mark with her floury finger. 'Oh, no!'

'Never mind. It looks quite colourful,' Gareth consoled her.

'You beast, Gareth!' Laughing, Thea flung the nearest dishcloth at him.

He caught it in mid-air, and deftly set it aside.

'Saucy wench! Don't you realise I am lord of this castle?' he growled with mock rage.

He strode towards her with a threatening scowl, and Thea giggled.

'I demand a forfeit for such *lèse-majesté*,' he declared, and made a grab for her.

With a shriek of laughter, Thea dodged his outstretched hands and fled.

Gareth chased her round and round the big pine table until they were both breathless with laughter.

'Enough! Enough! I beg for mercy, kind sir!'

Thea collapsed against the end of the table, leaning on the edge to support herself as she shook with mirth.

Gareth positioned himself in front of her. He bent forward and placed his hands on the table either side of her slight figure, so that she was imprisoned.

'Will you pay my forfeit, lady?'

The laughter died in Thea's throat as she looked up into his dark face.

She swallowed hard. There was no need to ask what the forfeit was to be. It was written in his eyes.

'Oh, Gareth,' she whispered huskily.

'Is that a yes?' Gareth's voice shook.

In answer Thea reached up and wound her arms around his neck.

His raven head dipped and their lips met.

Gently, tenderly, Gareth caressed her mouth with his. Thea clung to him, dazzling explosions of pleasure tingling in each and every nerve.

Behind her closed eyelids, rainbows sparkled. His lips felt so warm and soft. She had never imagined a kiss could be so wonderful!

Eager for more, she pressed closer to him.

Coming to his senses, Gareth broke off the embrace and released her.

'Consider your debt paid, my lady,' he said lightly.

Thea forced a smile. Her stomach was churning and she ached with a new strange frustration, but pride came to her aid.

'In that case, I shall get on with cooking dinner.'

'Is there anything I can do to help?'

Thea shook her glossy head.

'Then I'll take my leave.' Distinct reluctance filled Gareth, and he was tempted to ignore the inner voice which advised caution.

Thea turned away, pretending to busy herself with sifting more flour into her china bowl.

'Until later, *cariad*.' He could not stay. Honour demanded he treat her with the greatest respect.

Thea heard him leave. A desire to weep swept over her but she ignored it, and, plunging her hands into the bowl, she vented her feelings on the unlucky pastry mixture.

CHAPTER SIX

THEA soon realised that her instinctive desire to help Mrs Jones and avert the Dowager's wrath had brought about an unexpected benefit. Without meaning to, she had won the approval of the entire staff.

Over the next two days, while Mrs Jones was incapacitated by grief, she took over running the household. It was hard work but Thea was glad to have something to distract herself from her own problems.

Why had Gareth drawn back? His touch had detonated an explosion of sensation in her untutored body. She had *wanted* him to continue! Surely he must have known?

The only solution she could come up with was that he wished their peculiar *status quo* to remain. He might enjoy flirting with her, but he wasn't ready to commit himself.

This conclusion was as depressing as the grey rainy weather, and she decided to seek solace in one of the package of new books which had just been delivered to the castle.

Gareth found her curled up in a chair in the shabby but comfortable library.

'What have you got there?' he asked, coming to sit down near her and stretching out his long legs.

'It is called *Childe Harold's Pilgrimage*.' Thea lifted shining eyes to his. 'It is wonderful.'

'I remember now. My mother ordered it. It is by that new poet, Byron. Apparently it's all the rage in London.'

'I hope she won't be offended. I would have chosen another volume if I had known she was particularly interested in this one.'

'Don't fret. I doubt if she will ever actually bother

to open it. She just likes to be in fashion.' Gareth gave her a wry grin.

Discomfited by her mistake, Thea set the book aside.

'I suppose I ought to go and check on how dinner is coming along.'

'No need. I've just seen Mrs Jones. She has everything in hand and she tells me she is ready to resume her duties. She was very grateful.' Gareth smiled. 'May I add my thanks to hers? Without your sterling efforts the place would have collapsed into chaos.'

Delighted by his praise, Thea returned his smile.

'At least I didn't poison anyone,' she joked, to hide her embarrassment.

'I expect you are tired of being cooped up indoors?'

'A little,' she admitted.

'Look, the rain is stopping at last.' Gareth pointed to the window. 'Why don't we enjoy a breath of air? I know it is late, but Trebor swears it will pour down again tomorrow.'

'You have convinced me, sir.' When he smiled at her like that it was impossible to remember her intentions of keeping a clear head.

Collecting her hat, and a warm shawl to throw around her shoulders, Thea rejoined him in the courtyard.

To her surprise, his curricle was drawn up.

'I thought we were going for a stroll?'

Gareth shook his head. 'There's just time for me to show you one of our local landmarks if we hurry,' he remarked, handing her up into her seat.

'Where are we going?'

'Correct me if I am wrong, but you are interested in stone circles, are you not?'

Thea nodded. 'I remember. You told me there was a monument close to Castell Mynach.'

She let out a gasp of awe when the curricle stopped.

Ahead of them, quietly dreaming in the last of the afternoon sunlight, stood an ancient ring of tall stones. Short-cropped grass filled the inner circle, testimony to the action of sheep in this flat meadow, but the landscape was empty of all signs of life. There were no trees, only the blue-grey menhirs framed against the clear sky, and, in the distance, the sound of the sea.

It was so quiet that Thea could hear herself breathing. Hesitantly she approached the stones, and laid her hand on the rough surface of the nearest one.

'It feels warm. Almost as if it were alive,' she said with a little sigh.

'That's the sunlight.' Gareth was amused.

Thea shook her head at his prosaic explanation. She couldn't explain it but she sensed a presence lingering there—a faint echo of some dim, unimaginable past.

'Do you know how old these stones are?' she asked. 'Or the reason why they were erected here?'

'Locally it is know as the Druid's Circle, but I suspect its origins are far older.' He shrugged lightly. 'As to its purpose, your guess is as good as mine, *cariad*.'

'I think it must have been a place of worship.' Thea patted the menhir beneath her hand. 'A temple of love in stone.'

The dreamy note in her voice surprised Gareth. He had always thought she was so practical, but there was a streak of romantic mysticism in her character.

'You should have been born Welsh,' he said to her softly.

Suspecting that he was teasing her, Thea none the less could not resist demanding to know why.

'Because you have a passionate nature beneath that cool façade of yours, my *lili'r môr*.'

Thea coloured.

Unable to meet his gaze, she swung round and rather frantically began to count the stones aloud.

'There are only twelve. Strange, I thought there were more.' Now that her first sense of awe had lessened, she saw that in fact the ring was smaller than she had supposed. It was also badly-weathered, and a few of the stones leant sideways at drunken angles.

But there was no mistaking its sense of power.

'Thank you for bringing me here,' she said.

He acknowledged her remark with one of his charming smiles, but his expression changed to dismay as she stepped forward to enter the circle.

'No!' He lunged forward and made a grab for her arm.

Thea let out a squeak of alarm and he rapidly released her.

Brushing aside his apologies, Thea demanded to know why he had stopped her.

'It is considered bad luck to enter the ring except at certain times of the year,' he explained in a faintly embarrassed manner. 'Forgive me—old superstitions die hard.' He waved a hand towards the centre of the circle. 'Enter by all means, if you wish to do so.'

Thea shook her head. 'I have no desire to infringe local customs,' she replied, but there was a tinge of regret in her expression.

'You can enter it soon,' Gareth consoled her. 'On May Day everyone comes up here at sunset. A big bonfire is lit and there is feasting and dancing.' He chuckled. 'Don't ask me why. I think it has something to do with pagan rites. At any rate, it happens every year without fail.'

'A sort of Welsh dancing round the maypole?' Thea suggested, with a twinkle in her eyes.

'Something similar, anyway.'

In actual fact, the celebrations could get distinctly bawdy once the light had gone and the drink was in, but he decided that it would only spoil her romantic imaginings if he mentioned it.

Firmly curbing the tormenting voice in his head that said it might be very enjoyable to dance in the firelight with his bride, Gareth resolved that if they did attend he would make sure he whisked her away before things got too uncomfortably pagan.

On the drive home Thea asked him if anyone else knew more about the origins of the May Day celebrations.

'John Morgan used to have an interest in antiquities. He might be able to help—or you could try old Trebor. He knows a host of stories and legends—*if* you can persuade him to talk.'

Thea had made the acquaintance of the taciturn gardener yesterday. Escaping from the rigours of attempting to cook dinner with Cati's inept help, she had wandered into the kitchen garden for a breath of cool air.

Intent on trying to think of a suitable stuffing for the duck that was to grace the dining-table, she had almost stumbled over the figure crouched at the side of the path.

Her startled exclamation had been drowned out by a string of what had sounded suspiciously like Welsh curses as the little old man had dropped his trowel and jumped to his feet.

Thea had stared at him in fascination.

Bald, and brown as old seamed leather, he seemed to have grown out of the soil. Even his clothes were earth-coloured, and patchy with grass-stains.

At first he had been suspicious, but then, sensing her genuine interest, he had taken her on a tour of the garden. In spite of his limited English they had quickly established a rapport, and when she had regretfully left he had bestowed a handful of herbs and tiny mushrooms on her.

Cati had been astounded.

'Trebor gave you those for the duck? Wonders will never cease!'

Thea smiled at the memory and, glancing across at her, Gareth felt his heart twist.

Part of her charm, of course, was that she was so unconscious of her effect on him.

Brought up with a dazzlingly beautiful sister, she had never become vain. But it wasn't only her looks he found attractive. Day by day he was learning how her kindness matched her delicious sense of humour.

He had been afraid that she would find life at Castell

Mynach daunting, but beneath her quiet exterior there lay a core of steel. She had already made her mark on the castle. The servants respected her and even Cati was beginning to respond to her gentle but firm handling.

Admit it, *bach*, you may have asked her to marry you on impulse but you don't regret it. You no longer have any intention of asking for an annulment. You *want* her to stay!

This reflection was so unsettling that it caused Gareth to drop his hands and his team shot forward.

Thea let out a squeak as they headed at terrific speed towards a sharp bend.

'Sorry!' Gareth steadied his horses. 'I was thinking about something else.'

His tone was so curt that Thea was startled.

A moment ago he had been smiling. Now his expression was grim.

Could his sudden black mood have something to do with the conversation he'd had with John Morgan two days ago?

One glance at her husband's face warned Thea that now was not the time to tax him with questions, but as soon as a suitable opportunity presented itself she was going to ask him about this mysterious Y Cadno!

The next day was a Sunday, and Thea expressed the desire to attend Divine Worship.

'If I don't, Mr Morgan will think I mean to neglect my duties!' she laughed.

'I doubt it,' Gareth replied. It hadn't escaped his notice that she had already begun to visit the more needy cases in the village.

'I shall accompany you since the rain has now stopped,' the Dowager announced, when Gareth went to tell her where they were going.

She took so long over her toilette that they were almost late. It put Gareth in such a bad temper that

Cati cried off and escaped, leaving Thea to play peacemaker.

Honestly, I swear she is enough to try the patience of a saint, Thea thought as her mother-in-law fussed all the way into Llanrhayadar. It is no wonder that she and Gareth do not get on!

Once they were settled in the family pew Thea was able to relax, and she decided that the excellent sermon more than compensated for all the earlier aggravation.

'Come, I see Colonel and Mrs Secombe. I must introduce you to them.'

The Dowager bore Thea off the minute they emerged from the church. Involved in a flurry of meetings and small talk with several of Castell Mynach's more notable neighbours, she didn't notice that Gareth had become separated from them.

When she looked for him, she saw that he was talking to John Morgan. With a sudden flare of apprehension she saw him begin to frown.

She was standing too far away to catch what was being said, but she was willing to lay odds that the elderly parson was passing on bad news!

Were they talking about Y Cadno again?

It wasn't until the following morning that she found the right moment to discover if her suspicions were right.

She was weeding a sadly neglected bed when Gareth came striding into the flower garden.

'I am going into Swansea. Do you wish to come?'

Thea hesitated, glancing down at her old dress and stained hands. 'It might take me rather longer than you would like to get ready,' she murmured.

He laughed. 'Am I so impatient? I swear not to complain.'

'I should like to come, but I did promise your mother I would begin Cati's music lessons this morning,' she continued regretfully, hoping that he wouldn't think she was trying to avoid his company.

'Don't worry. It was just a thought.' Gareth shrugged

with assumed carelessness, thrusting aside his disappointment. 'In point of fact, you'd probably have found it boring. I'm going to confer with Griffiths.'

Thea remembered that this was the name of his man of business.

'Have you any commissions for me to execute once I'm finished with him?'

Thea shook her head absently, too busy trying to pluck up her courage to think of frivolities like shopping.

'Then I must take my leave, *cariad*.' Gareth turned to go.

'Wait.'

He halted. 'Is something wrong?'

'I. . .no. Or at least, I'm not sure.' Thea could feel her tongue begin to tie itself in knots.

To cover her confusion, she gestured towards the wooden seat that graced the garden's finest viewpoint.

'May we sit down for a moment? There is something I wish to ask you.'

With a casual disregard for his pale fawn pantaloons, the Viscount sat on the ancient bench. 'Well, what is it?'

His tone was slightly impatient so Thea came straight to the point.

'Who is Y Cadno?'

Beneath his tan, Gareth paled. 'Where did you hear that name?'

'Someone. . .someone in the village mentioned it,' Thea replied evasively.

Gareth bit off an expletive, and Thea recoiled from the sudden fury in his eyes.

'I asked Cati. All she would tell me was that the name meant the Fox, but she said I must apply to you for further information.' Thea was beginning to regret her curiosity.

Gareth took a deep breath. 'Y Cadno is a smuggler.'

'I see.' She had been expecting him to say something of the sort. 'Then the *Llwynoges* is his ship?'

He nodded, his expression hard. 'The *Vixen*, crewed by rogues and scoundrels.'

It was a little unnerving to have her suspicions confirmed.

'Don't worry. He'll not trouble you. He keeps away from the castle.'

'Are any of the villagers involved in his operations?'

Thea knew that smuggling provided an easy source of income. In Bristol, the vicar's wife had had a brother who was a Preventive Officer, and she had told Thea several stories concerning his escapades. Smugglers bought luxury items such as tea and brandy cheaply in Holland and France, and then sold them on to people anxious to avoid the heavy taxes imposed on these goods. Anyone who succeeded made an enormous profit.

The authorities could do little to stop this illicit trade. According to the vicar's brother-in-law, their forces were too thinly spread. The coast around Llanrhayadar was full of deserted coves and Thea suspected that if this Y Cadno was clever he could easily evade the revenue patrols.

'Unfortunately, some of them help him land cargoes and distribute the goods.' Gareth frowned. 'His gang have a reputation for cruelty, so even the unwilling give way to his demands. It takes a brave man to withstand Y Cadno.'

'It is dreadful to have such lawlessness on our doorstep,' Thea agreed, but before she could press him for further details he stood up.

'If that is all, *cariad*, I must go or I will be late,' he declared, with a firmness that bordered on impatience.

With a faint sigh Thea returned to her task when he had gone. Picking up her hoe, she tried to dismiss her doubts. Perhaps she was letting her imagination run away with her. But an inner voice told her that Gareth was hiding something from her. Something important.

* * *

It was the Dowager who had given Thea the idea of suggesting music lessons to Cati. Bemoaning her daughter's lack of ladylike accomplishments, she had complained that Cati never touched the splendid pianoforte in the music-room.

Thea had visited this room on her initial tour of the castle. It made a splendid setting for any musician, with its walls covered in exquisite frescos of the Nine Muses sitting enthroned upon Olympus while Apollo played his lyre for them.

Each figure had been delicately executed in spring-like colours and with great attention to detail, and it was equally obvious that a connoisseur's eye had also been applied to the selection of instruments that the room housed, all in good condition. Given the state of the rest of the castle, Thea had been amazed, until Gareth, who had been acting as her guide, had wryly explained that his father had been very fond of music.

'May I?' she had asked, raising the lid of the pianoforte.

'I believe it has been kept in tune.' Gareth had waved her to continue.

Thea had sat down, and from memory selected a Mozart sonata.

The notes rippled with delicate precision from her fingers, and when she had finished Gareth had said gruffly, not quite concealing how the music had affected him, 'You play very well.'

Hoping she might repeat this earlier success, Thea hurried now to meet Cati.

As usual, her sister-in-law was late.

'I consider this a waste of time,' she muttered as Thea opened the pianoforte, but Thea sensed her interest and put every effort into her playing.

'That was very pretty.' Cati's tone was begrudging, but her dark eyes betrayed her.

'I could teach you to play it,' Thea coaxed.

Cati hesitated, and then, abandoning her reserve, nodded eagerly.

Thea smiled. 'It will take time, of course,' she warned. 'We shall have to start at the beginning.'

'I don't mind.'

'Then come and join me.' Thea patted the stool invitingly.

Thea was astonished by her new pupil's aptitude. Cati played the harp, which helped explain her ear for music, of course, but her quick understanding made her a joy to teach.

'Thank you, Thea,' she said shyly as she got to her feet. 'I enjoyed that.'

'We can have another lesson tomorrow. If you wish?'

Cati agreed with an eagerness that gave Thea fresh confidence. At last she had found a means to breach her sister-in-law's stubborn dislike of all things she considered boringly ladylike.

Thea felt a glow of satisfaction. Gareth would be delighted. Not liking to examine too closely the real reason why she wanted to please him—the real reason why his approval mattered—Thea told herself that she merely wanted to to prove his faith in her had not been misplaced.

She might only be a tradesman's daughter, but she was worthy to be his wife!

The following day the Dowager surprised her family by appearing for luncheon.

She seemed in such a good mood that Gareth eventually asked her the reason for her high spirits.

'I had a letter this morning from London. From Cousin Mary. She had news she thought I might like to know.'

Thea, who was trying to decide between a luscious-looking lemon cheese pudding or some fruit for dessert, glanced up in surprise. Unless she was sadly mistaken, there was malicious amusement in her mother-in-law's tone.

'Guess who is to return to Llanrhayadar?'

Cati looked blankly at her. 'We don't know anyone who is in London at present.'

'Well, I must admit it has been a visit of long duration,' the Dowager purred.

Seated at his side, Thea caught Gareth's sudden intake of breath.

'But Nerys always said she would return to the Gower one day.'

'*She* is coming back?' Gareth's voice was ice.

'And soon.' The Dowager nodded. 'Apparently she intends to live at the Cwrt.'

A muscle twitched by her son's well-cut mouth. 'I hope you do not plan to receive her.'

'Don't be stupid, Gareth. Of course I shall receive her. To refuse to do so would merely revive unpleasant rumours we would all prefer to forget.'

Completely baffled, Thea was about to interrupt, but Cati beat her to it.

'Well, I agree with Gareth!' she burst out. 'I don't want her here. Nerys Parry is a vile creature and I think it is stupid of you to even consider——'

'Hold your tongue, Cati!'

Cati swung round to face him, the colour draining from her face. 'I am trying to take your side,' she gasped.

'Thank you, *chwaer*, but you must mind your manners.' Gareth's voice softened, but, recognising inflexibility in his expression, Cati collapsed into silence.

His gaze hard, Gareth turned back to the Dowager. 'Pray reconsider, ma'am.'

'No!' A stubborn frown puckered Angharad's brow. 'Not unless you mean to forbid me from choosing my own guests?'

'I beg you will not be absurd, Mother! This is your home. You must do as you will. But do not expect me to be present when she calls.'

He rose abruptly from the table. 'Please excuse me.'

Thea watched him leave, stiff-backed with the anger

filial duty had forced him to contain, and longed to run after him.

Common sense intervened. He was so furious that he would probably snap her head off if she tried to offer him comfort!

'I suppose you think I am being unreasonable,' the Dowager announced provocatively.

Thea laid down her dessert fork. 'It is not my business to question your reasons, ma'am. However, I think it regrettable you should quarrel with your son.'

Angharad gave a harsh laugh. 'I wonder if you will still mouth such prim sentiments when you discover why Gareth objects to Nerys coming here.'

She opened her dark eyes wide at Thea. 'I take it he *has* told you who she is?' she enquired in dulcet tones.

Thea glanced uneasily at Cati, who was glaring at her mother as if she longed to tell her to be quiet but didn't dare.

'I know Lady Parry is the owner of Parry Cwrt, which makes her a near neighbour.' Thea was unable to control a slight tremor in her voice. It made her nervous when Angharad wore that malicious smile! 'And I believe her late husband was Gareth's godfather?'

'Oh, indeed. Sir Owen was the hero and mentor of Gareth's youth. A better father to him than his own, if the truth be known—which, of course, is why what happened later was so unfortunate.'

'Mother!'

Thea tensed.

'You see,' Angharad Rhayadar continued, her smile deepening, 'Gareth betrayed him.'

Cati let out an inarticulate cry of denial.

The Dowager ignored the interruption.

'It is guilt which makes my son so angry. Nerys Parry was his mistress. He was mad with love for her!'

Clinging desperately to her self-control, Thea forced herself to reply with assumed calm, 'Perhaps so, ma'am, but it was a long time ago.'

'Yet a first passion always dies hard.' The Dowager laughed sweetly. 'And she was so very beautiful! Do you know, I think he might still be in love with her beneath all that furious bluster?'

Thea stood up as abruptly as her husband had done a few moments ago, red flags of temper flying in her cheeks.

'I fail to understand your motive in telling me all this, ma'am, unless it is from sheer pleasure in causing mischief,' she said hotly, her patience at an end. 'But let me tell *you* something! You are living proof that high birth is no guarantee of good manners! In fact, ma'am, your behaviour is atrocious!'

The Dowager's mouth fell open in astonishment, and before she could recover Thea swept out of the room and banged the door shut behind her.

Thea took a walk to cool her temper. She wasn't in the least bit sorry that she had told Angharad what she thought of her devious little games, but she already knew it had been a mistake.

She would have to apologise, or the Dowager would make life at Castell Mynach unbearable for everyone.

But not yet!

Finding the gardens too tame to suit her present mood, she decided to walk on the beach below the castle.

The wind was strong, whipping up wild waves that flung spray high into the air as they dashed themselves against the outer cliffs which guarded the entrance to the bay. It snatched at her silk shawl as she scrambled down to the sands, theatening to tear it from her shoulders.

One end came loose and it ballooned out like a sail. Quickly Thea grabbed it, and as she whirled round to use her back as a windbreak while she wrapped it more closely around herself she became aware that she was not alone.

Gareth was sitting on one of the flat rocks that

littered the back of the beach. He was staring out to sea, an abstracted look on his handsome face, and for a moment she wasn't sure if he had even seen her.

Before she could decide whether she wanted him to, he stood up.

'Did you follow me?'

His deep voice was unusually bleak, and Thea's heart turned over. In an instant, a wave of fierce protectiveness swept over her, and all her anger drained away as the myriad doubts which had plagued her dissolved like so much foam on the sea.

Dear God, what a ridiculous moment to realise that she was in love with him!

'No.' To Thea's infinite relief, she managed to keep her voice steady. 'I think my reason for coming down here was the same as yours. I just wanted to get away from everyone for a while.'

He nodded.

'Would you like me to leave?'

'There's no need.' A slow smile dawned on Gareth's face as he realised that she wasn't going to badger him with questions. 'You have never been a nuisance, *cariad*.'

Thea's pulse hammered. When he smiled at her like that her insides began to melt! Swallowing hard, she strove for composure.

'May I join you?'

'Please do.'

Once they were seated, of necessity so close that Thea could feel the warmth emanating from his body, Gareth spoke again.

'I was watching the tide come in.' He paused, almost as if he hated to admit it. 'I needed some peace in which to think.'

Her nerves still quivering with the shock of her discovery, Thea struggled to think of a rational answer.

But she couldn't. She couldn't think of anything at all but how much she wanted to kiss him as her whole body flooded with a raging surge of emotion in response to his nearness. She felt giddy and breathless, and knew with a little choke of inward laughter that it was fortunate she was sitting down because her legs were too weak and boneless to support her.

The silence stretched on and, attempting to gather her wits, Thea forced herself to break it.

'Watching the sea is very soothing,' she murmured inanely.

He cocked his dark head in enquiry. 'Are your nerves in need of solace?'

Thea cursed her careless tongue. She was in too much of a bedazzled state to remember how quick he was to catch her thoughts!

'You are very acute, sir,' she said with a rueful shrug. 'I didn't mean to speak of it, but I suppose you would hear soon enough. Your mother and I have quarrelled.'

'I'm only surprised you have been patient with her for so long.' For an instant Gareth grinned at her, and Thea felt a spurt of relief. 'My mother quarrels with everyone. Frequently.' His expression sobered. 'Dare I ask why?'

Thea hesitated.

'Then it was about Nerys,' Gareth declared, in an oddly flat tone.

'She claimed that Lady Parry was your mistress.'

'And you believed her?'

'I told her that it was none of my business!' Thea's eyes flashed at the memory.

Gareth barely restrained a whistle of surprise.

When he had seen her coming towards him, he had braced himself for an awkward scene. He would have laid odds that his mother had been mischief-making—it was one of her chief amusements—and he expected Thea to reproach him. She would cry, or even work herself up into a state of hysterical rage, the way his mother had always done when confronted with his father's misdemeanours.

Most women he'd known had used tears and tantrums to achieve their purpose.

His wife, it appeared, was different!

'What you did before we were married is your concern,' Thea said, pinkening. 'I have no right to question your past behaviour.'

Which wasn't to say that she didn't long to do so! A fierce curiosity burned in her breast, but her instincts warned her that he would brook no questions. Whatever had happened, it was still a sore subject!

'You are very magnanimous, *cariad*.'

Her blush deepening, Thea shook her head. 'I am merely practical, sir.'

Only a complete ninny would fail to realise that a man of almost thirty was bound to have had affairs. All she could do was hope that his past was not going to impinge upon their future.

But with Nerys Parry's return to Wales imminent, it seemed a forlorn hope!

A cold prickle of anxiety feathered down Thea's spine. Angharad had said that she was very beautiful!

Was she going to lose Gareth before she'd even had time to find a way to tell him how much she loved him?

'Moreover, since we married for convenience, you are hardly bound to consider my feelings in the same way you would your real bride's,' she continued with apparent calm, desperately crushing her fears. 'You do not owe me explanations, sir, for I am not entitled to them.'

To her consternation, he lifted her left hand from her lap.

'You wear my ring,' he said softly. 'It entitles you to my loyalty.' He raised her hand to his lips and kissed it. 'I have no intention of being unfaithful.'

'Thank you.' Thea's voice shook. He was still holding her hand and she could feel her skin burning. 'However, I can hardly expect you to give up your friends.'

'Nerys Parry is no friend of mine!' Gareth gave a growl of rage, his fingers unconsciously tightening on hers.

Thea gave an involuntary gasp, her eyes watering, and he instantly released her.

'*Duw*, I'm sorry, *fy merch fach*.' The endearment slipped out before Gareth had time to think.

Thea's expressive little face revealed her longing to ask him what he had just said, but she stoutly resisted the temptation.

Gareth smiled. 'It is a term of affection. You could translate it as my dear girl.' He paused. 'You don't mind if I call you that?'

Speechless, Thea shook her head.

'I'm glad.' Impulsively Gareth bent to kiss her cheek.

Unable to prevent herself, Thea moved her head so that his lips found hers instead.

For one infinitesimal second Gareth held back, and then slowly he deepened the kiss.

Obeying the pressure of his mouth, Thea opened her lips. To her surprise, his tongue slipped inside to caress hers. After a moment the sense of strangeness was replaced by a vibrant excitement, and she clung to him more tightly, pressing herself against his lean body in her eagerness.

'*Lili'r môr*!' Gareth growled the endearment, his voice hoarse. He began to kiss her throat, his lips scorching her skin.

Thea felt as if she had caught a fever. She felt hot and shivery, and her legs were trembling. If he hadn't been holding her so tightly she was sure she would have fallen from her rocky seat.

'Gareth. Oh, Gareth!' Murmuring his name, she buried her fingers into the thick black curls that clustered on his nape. His hair felt so soft and warm, just as she had always imagined it would.

Gareth experienced a fierce explosion of joy. He lifted his head and stared down into her small face. Her expression was dazed, the pupils of her lovely eyes dilated with desire.

With a groan, he tightened his arms about her waist. 'Thea. *Annwyl Crist*, but you are lovely!'

His hand slid upwards and he began to caress her breast.

A shiver of pleasure shot through Thea. His fingers seem to burn her through the thin muslin she wore. She could feel her nipple hardening at his touch, and the dizzying excitement coursing through her veins made her catch her breath.

Gareth felt her arousal and the blood pounded in his head, deafening him, overcoming his good resolutions.

He kissed her again, harder this time, letting his hands roam over her slender body. Stroking her neck, he ran his hands over the delicate line of her shoulders and down the length of her spine, to find the fascinating curves of her hips.

Giddily Thea wondered if it was possible to faint from sheer pleasure. Surrendering herself to the delicious sensations his skilful hands were evoking, she sighed against his mouth, arching her back in enjoyment when his hands moved back to to fondle her breasts.

Her abandoned response destroyed the last of Gareth's will-power.

Forgetful of everything but the marvellous gift of her unexpected surrender, he caught her up in his arms and pulled her onto his lap.

'*Cariad*, you are so desirable!' he whispered hoarsely, kissing her again with a wild passion that left Thea totally breathless.

Before she had time to recover, he'd pushed up her skirts and his hand was caressing her knee.

'Your skin is like silk,' he muttered feverishly, his fingers moving to burn circles of pleasure into her bare thigh. He buried his face into her bosom, kissing the exposed tops of her breasts while his hand slid higher. . .and higher. . .

Thea shuddered violently and opened her eyes.

'*Cariad*?' Gareth stopped.

Thea was unable to answer him. Lost in the realms

of pleasure, she had been brought abruptly, painfully, to her senses.

In a state of shock, she regarded her disordered dress with disbelief. Another few moments and it would have been too late for any annulment!

Taking a deep breath, Gareth forced his passion aside. 'Would you like me to stop?'

The hoarse whispered words made Thea feel even more confused. She could feel him trembling, and instinct told her how desperately difficult he was finding it to restrain himself.

'I'm sorry,' Frantically she dragged her skirts into place and scrambled to her feet. 'I... I don't know what came over me.'

She wouldn't have blamed him if he had shouted and raged at her, but to her relief he shook his head and got to his feet.

'There's no need to apologise.' His tone was wry.

She couldn't meet his eyes. 'It is too soon,' she whispered, desperately longing to tell him the truth but afraid to do so.

She loved him, but he had given no indication that he returned her feelings. In fact, she suspected that he didn't want love! Passion, yes, and he enjoyed her company, but not emotional involvement.

With every day that had passed since their arrival at Castell Mynach, she had found it harder to ignore the truth. She had agreed to marry him because she had fallen in love with him, not for any other reason! Now that she had finally admitted it to herself, it was going to be even more difficult to conceal her feelings. If she surrendered to desire it might be impossible!

For the sake of her own sanity she had to hold back, until she was sure that she could bear to be his real wife knowing that he didn't love her. For surely desire without love would prove a bitter enchantment in the end?

Gareth waited to see if she would say more, but as

her silence continued a tide of disappointment flooded him.

He inclined his dark head. 'As you wish.'

For one mad impulsive moment he had been on the point of forgetting the past. It was so tempting to think that she was different from the rest—the one he had always been looking for in his dreams.

Striving to recover her composure, Thea attempted a smile. 'Look at me. I must resemble a perfect scarecrow,' she announced with brittle gaiety, raising her hands in a vain attempt to tidy her wind-ruffled hair. 'I wonder that you should want to kiss me, sir!'

'Right now I can think of nothing I would rather do than kiss you. . . Unless it is to take you to bed.'

His honesty brought a blush to Thea's cheeks.

'You mustn't say such things to me,' she murmured in utter confusion. Heavens, if he didn't stop she would fling herself into his arms and to the devil with the consequences!

'Don't worry. I'm not about to renege on our bargain.' There was a bitter amusement in his tone.

Thea glanced at him sharply. What she saw in his face reassured her, and gave her the courage to ask, 'Are we still friends, Gareth?'

'Of course.' He gave her a crooked smile. 'For now, at least. But one day, *cariad*, I think we'll be more than that.'

Thea's pulse began to hammer once more as she listened to his deep, hypnotic voice.

'One day soon, my lady, I think we will be lovers.'

Looking into his darkly blazing eyes, Thea had no option but to believe him.

CHAPTER SEVEN

'SIT down, Mother.' The Viscount waved dismissal to his valet and indicated a chair that he had placed in readiness before the fire in his study.

'I cannot think what has got into you, Gareth. Sending your man to drag me here in this manner. It is very high-handed of you,' the Dowager declared, the instant the door had closed.

Gareth ignored her outburst. 'Please be seated.'

She threw him a darkling look, but prudently obeyed when she saw his mouth tighten.

He waited politely until she had settled herself to her satisfaction.

'I am sorry if Jenkins exceeded his instructions,' he said with icy formality. 'However, you have only yourself to blame. For two days you've been hiding in your rooms and telling Williams not to admit me.'

His bluntness made her bridle. 'I have been ill!'

'Ill—or worried that I might have something harsh to say about your deliberate attempt to upset my wife?' There was an edge of anger to Gareth's tone.

Angharad flushed. 'I meant no harm.'

Gareth's black brows rose. 'I shall do you the courtesy of believing you, Mother, but I want you to understand this: I won't have Thea made unhappy.'

'I wish you hadn't married a tradesman's daughter. It isn't even as if she brought a large dowry with her!'

Gareth bit back a curse. 'Please do not make such remarks, Mother. I mean you no disrespect, but I will not tolerate criticism of my wife.'

Gazing into his angry eyes, Angharad knew she had gone too far. 'Oh, very well. I shall endeavour to be pleasant to her.' She began to rise.

'One moment, if you please. There was another

reason for asking you here.' Gareth picked up a sheaf of documents from the polished walnut surface of his large pedestal desk. 'I've been going through the accounts—'

'Good gracious, what on earth for? Surely Griffiths can handle such matters? It is hardly the business of a gentleman!'

Gareth caught the note of fear underlying her hasty interruption. His heart sank.

'It was Griffiths who brought my attention to the discrepancies, Mother. Several large sums of money appear to have gone missing.'

She paled so that her rouge stood out on her cheeks in bright circles. 'I. . .I hope you are not implying that I know anything about this unfortunate occurrence!'

Gareth slammed the papers back on to the desk.

'For God's sake, Mother! Let's stop all this pretence! We both know you've been bleeding the estate dry. What I want to know is why.'

Struggling to maintain his temper, he ran a hand through his thick locks and tried again in a quieter voice. 'Please, I promise not to be angry with you. Won't you tell me the truth?'

She glared at him. 'The truth? You want the truth? Very well, you shall have it—but you won't like it!'

'I dare say not.' Gareth leant back against the edge of the desk and waited.

'I did take that money, but it was for your sake.'

Baffled, Gareth stared at her.

'It began soon after your father died.' The Dowager's voice dropped to a whisper. 'Believe me, it went against the grain, but what else could I do? You were no help! You refused to leave the Navy and come home, in spite of all my pleas.'

The hair at the back of his neck prickling, Gareth said slowly, 'I was on blockade duty, guarding the channel. You knew I could not abandon my station.'

'And what of your duty to me?' Angharad's voice rose in a shrill shriek. 'I had no one to turn to—no one! I was the innocent victims of Emrys's crime! I thought his death would release me, but it brought worse torment!'

Swiftly Gareth moved to pour a glass of sherry from the decanter kept on the lowboy to oil his estate meetings and hand it to her.

'Drink this and calm yourself, Mother. You know it does you no good to get upset.'

She took a large gulp. 'You think me hysterical,' she said bitterly. 'I'm not. But, by God, I've cause!'

There was a tiny silence.

'I'm afraid you are talking in riddles.'

She sighed. 'That money went to Vaughn.'

'What?' Gareth's fists clenched involuntarily. 'He has dared to threaten you?'

'He's been blackmailing me for months.' Angharad shuddered. 'You see, somehow he found out the truth.'

She lifted her head and met his puzzled gaze.

'Vaughn Y Cadno is the real heir to Castell Mynach.'

The cave was ill-lit and damp. Gareth could hear the sound of water trickling down the walls, and the thought came to him that it was a cheerless place in which to decide his whole future.

A wry smile twisted his mouth. He was hardly in a position to cavil at the lack of comfort. Where else could he hold a secret meeting? Too many listening ears abounded ashore, and the whole of Llanrhayadar would have known within minutes if he'd gone aboard the *Llwynoges*!

As it was, the uncannily accurate village grapevine would soon be whispering that he had held discussions with Y Cadno.

A cold sweat broke out down his spine, and he was almost glad to hear the heavy tread of booted footsteps approaching the entrance to the cave.

'Hello, *brawd*. It's glad I am to see you after all this time.'

The man who came towards him, squinting against

the gloom after the brighter light outside, was much of the same height and colouring as himself.

'Vaughn.' Gareth greeted him tersely, his stomach muscles tightening. It was almost fifteen years since they had met like this, face to face, but the hatred still remained.

In spite of the amiable smile on Vaughn's lips, Gareth knew that he felt it too. 'Are you alone?'

'I've two men waiting on the path.'

'Out of earshot?'

'Aye, unless I yell for them.' A wolfish grin split Vaughn's face. 'I see you came armed.'

'Naturally.' Gareth's tone remained ice-cold.

'Well, well.' Vaughn Y Cadno gave a sneering laugh. 'You've grown up, lad.'

Gareth forced down the surge of rage that threatened to overwhelm him. It had always been Vaughn's way to provoke him to anger with insults and taunts, knowing that his greater size and strength would inevitably decide the fight that automatically followed.

With an odd sense of detachment, Gareth noted that time had added to Vaughn's girth. He had always been stockily built, but now he carried a little too much extra weight. Along with the lines of dissipation on his face it made him seem older and slower. An impression which was probably dangerously false!

'Let's dispense with the insults, Vaughn. We are no longer children.' Gareth wasn't going to make the mistake of underestimating him. 'I asked you here for a specific purpose.'

Vaughn shrugged. 'I didn't think it was for the pleasure of my company.'

He moved closer, towards the lantern which Gareth had hung from one of the iron wall-sconces. Its light revealed evidence of a makeshift hearth—a ring of flat stones blackened by previous fires—with a few upturned small barrels placed round it to serve as rough seats.

'*Duw*, it's cold in here. Why didn't you light a fire?'

'We won't be here long enough to need one.'

'Well, what is it, *brawd*? Why did you want to see me? Or shall I guess?' Vaughn gave a short bark of laughter. 'If you think I'll agree to meekly leave Llanrhayadar, you're out of luck. I'm staying, and there's damn all you can do about it.'

Gareth lifted his brows. 'I shouldn't be so sure about that,' he retorted. 'However, I didn't ask you here to discuss smuggling.'

Vaughn stiffened. 'So that's it,' he said softly. 'I wondered how long she would be able to keep it a secret once you got home.'

Gareth jerked his head in assent.

Vaughn sauntered over to one of the barrels and sat down. 'And you are wanting to know if it's true, I suppose?' he enquired, his tone deliberately offensive.

'I want proof,' Gareth replied calmly. 'You may have bamboozled my mother, but you needn't think to deceive me with your lies.'

With a leap of hope Gareth watch how the older man's eyes narrowed. His reponse had hit home!

'Oh, but there is proof, *brawd.* I've got my mother's marriage-lines and a witness who attended the wedding.'

Gareth stared at him, his elation fading. 'You are lying.' He spat the words with ferocious contempt.

'Am I, now?' Vaughn chuckled mirthlessly. 'Not this time. Emrys Rhayadar married my mother. In May 1780, four months before I was born.'

'She was a serving-wench in a London tavern. He would never have married her!'

'Not stone-cold sober, no. Still, in spite of the brandy he'd consumed, I have it on authority that Emrys was fully aware of what he was doing.' Vaughn crossed one knee over the other and smiled with smug satisfaction.

'What authority?' Gareth was scornful.

'My uncle's. He was still living at the same address in Holborn. He was glad to see me again.'

Vaughn laughed, but his eyes never left Gareth's face.

'Said it was funny to hear me sound like a Welshman. "I'd have hardly recognised you, lad, but for the fact you've got my sister's smile."'

'Come to the point.' Gareth could feel his patience slipping.

'The point, my noble lord Viscount, is that my Uncle Frank attended the wedding. He was the one to whom my mother entrusted her marriage-lines when she lay dying. Emrys had threatened her into silence, but at the end she wanted me to know that I wasn't a bastard.'

'She died years ago.' Gareth rapped the words out. 'Why didn't you come forward until now?'

'I didn't know myself. I found out by chance, when I was in London and decided to pay a visit to my old haunts. *Duw*, I didn't even know the old fellow was still alive!' Vaughn gave a bellow of mocking laughter. 'Proof, don't you agree, that the devil looks after his own?'

Gareth remained tight-lipped.

Seeing he would not be drawn, Vaughn shrugged and continued. 'Frank had kept the paper safe, but he'd been too afraid to try and find me. He remembered, you see, what a ruthless swine Emrys could be.'

Gareth's memory involuntarily hurtled back to a day when he had been six years old. His father had come home from London on one of his rare visits. He had rushed out to greet him, but the Viscount hadn't been alone.

A tousled-haired and rather grimy boy had climbed out of the coach after him, to stand gazing with open-mouthed awe at the castle.

Vaughn. His father's bastard.

Gareth could still remember the arguments, and his mother screaming furious refusals. But in the end his father's will had prevailed, and Vaughn had come to live with them.

'I don't blame Uncle Frank.' Vaughn's voice broke into Gareth's uneasy thoughts. 'He couldn't afford to take on Emrys. Who would support him, a poor labouring-man, against a peer of the realm?'

This simple observation held a ring of truth. It echoed in Gareth's head like a death-knell.

Until this moment he hadn't been sure. Vaughn was acquainted with any number of rogues. It would have been easy for him to find a good forger, and with both principles conveniently dead. . .

'So you intend to claim he committed bigamy?' To his relief, Gareth heard his voice emerge with a cool and steady clarity.

'Of course he did!' Vaughn's tone lost a little of its satisfaction and turned bitter. 'You cannot have forgotten how fond he was of getting his own way! He wanted Angharad, and her price was marriage.'

Vaughn made a crude gesture with his fingers and spat on the floor. '*Crist*, I don't suppose he even hesitated, but the fact remains he wasn't free. For all the pomp and fancy celebrations, that second wedding ceremony in January 1781 was a bogus sham.'

His wolfish grin reappeared.

'Which means, of course, my dear half-brother, that you are the bastard, not me. You are no more the Viscount Rhayadar than old Trebor is!'

Gareth clenched his jaw. 'I want to see this document. Did you bring it with you?'

'Do you take me for a fool?' Vaughn let out a snort of derision. 'What's to stop you trying to destroy it?'

'Don't judge me by your standards, Vaughn!' Gareth took a deep breath, and successfully regained his icy self-control. 'I've no intention of stooping to dirty tricks.'

'Aren't you going to fight me for the title, then, *brawd*?'

Gareth ignored this mocking taunt. '*If* this document is genuine, then you may have a claim, but I doubt it.'

'What do you mean?' Of course I have the better

claim!' Vaughn jumped to his feet, a sudden unease mingling with the anger in his voice.

'Perhaps. We shall have to let the lawyers decide.' Gareth smiled for the first time. 'Honour forbids me to blow a hole in you, Vaughn. Whatever else you are, you are my brother—and I have no wish to commit fratricide. But you needn't think I am going to hand you Castell Mynach on a plate.'

'You'll bring the case to court?' Vaughn blanched, and lost some of his blustering swagger.

Gareth nodded curtly.

'Why bother? You will lose anyway. The courts might sneer at my mother, but I am the real heir. There's nothing you can do about that!' Vaughn regained a little of his colour with each boast. 'And, unlike my uncle, I'm a rich man. I've enough money to bribe a whole tribe of judges if need be!'

'Money you've accumulated through crime, violence and terror.' Gareth gazed at him with contempt. 'You always were a bully, Vaughn.'

It took a moment to quell the surge of revulsion that twisted his stomach as he remembered all the vicious tricks Vaughn had pulled to try and humiliate him. Unfortunately it seemed as though this latest attempt might have some basis other than jealous spite.

'However, *if* the lawyers decide in your favour, I'll abide by their decision, but until that moment as far as I am concerned you remain nothing more than one of my father's many bastards.'

A look of angry frustration crossed Vaughn's face. 'I never thought that the title mattered so much to you!'

'By itself, it doesn't,' Gareth replied crisply, effectively silencing him. 'But the estate and the people do. I know you, Vaughn. You are greedy. You would strip the place bare and care nothing for the consequences.' He gave a faint smile. 'You don't deserve Castell Mynach. You would only ruin it.'

'You'll drag your mother's name through the gutter for the sake of a principle and a few miserable peasants? You fool, the scandal will rock the whole of Wales!'

A snort of laughter escaped Vaughn as he saw how a muscle twitched by Gareth's mouth, and he shook his head mockingly.

'*Crist*, I don't think you have the nerve for it.'

'You are mistaken, Vaughn.' Gareth quickly recovered himself. 'I'd dare anything to keep you from getting your filthy hands on Castell Mynach.' His smile deepened. 'I'm going to find a way to stop you, and that, *brawd*, is a promise!'

'Take off my dress? Surely you are joking? I never heard of such a thing!'

The indignant look on her sister-in-law's face made Cati giggle.

'How do you expect to learn to swim in all those yards of French crêpe? You'll sink. Anyway, the sea-water will only spoil it.'

Cati was busy stripping off her own gown as she spoke. An instant later she stood revealed in her shift, and, unhampered by petticoats or stockings, ran down to where the waves were curling up on to the beach.

'Oh, come on, Thea! Don't be a spoilsport. Who can see you?'

Thea watched her for a moment. The water looked so tempting!

'All right!' she called, conquering her notions of propriety. 'You win, but don't you dare tell anyone you persuaded me into this, Cati Rhayadar.' Thea was laughing as she took off her shoes. 'Your mother would never forgive me!'

The damp sand felt cool between her bare toes once she had removed her stockings. A delightful sense of freedom filled her, and with a bold movement she pulled her petticoat over her head and tossed it to join Cati's discarded garments.

It was a glorious morning, unusually warm for the end of April, and dazzlingly bright with sunshine. The perfect day to learn how to swim, Cati had announced, marching into the library.

'I'm too old to be playing in the water,' Thea had protested.

'We'll go down to the next cove. It's always deserted; no one will see us there.'

In the end, Thea had put aside her book and given in.

She strolled down to the water's edge. It felt strange to wear so little in the open air. The sunlight was hot on her bare legs and arms and she had to shade her eyes from the dazzle as she gazed out to sea.

Cati had plunged straight in, and was now swimming with a swift strong stroke that Thea couldn't help envying. She made it seem so easy!

Tentatively Thea stepped into the water.

'Merciful heavens!' She leapt backwards. 'Cati, you could have warned me! It is like ice!'

Cati waded towards the shore. 'You'll soon get used to it,' she promised, grinning. 'Come on. I'll show you how to begin.'

Thea hesitated, eyeing the waves dubiously. 'I'm not sure I want to learn to swim after all,' she muttered.

'Coward!' Cati laughed, and began to splash water at her.

Giggling, Thea splashed back, and within seconds was as thoroughly soaked as her sister-in-law.

'There, you see. It's not so cold, is it?' Cati declared triumphantly.

Thea allowed herself to be drawn into deeper water.

'Copy me,' Cati said, demonstrating the correct movements.

Thea had hoped that swimming lessons might cement the friendship that had begun to grow between them during their sessions in the music-room. Cati still disappeared for hours on end, refusing to say where she was going, and she still sulked when she did not get her own way, but her hostility had faded.

'Oh, I am exhausted,' she declared with a giggle as

she staggered ashore when Cati prounounced the lesson at an end.

Cati handed her a towel and took one for herself from the basket they had brought with them.

'You made real progress,' she said, drying herself vigorously. 'If this weather holds, you'll soon be able to astonish Gareth with your competence.'

'If I do, it will be due to your patience,' Thea answered warmly. 'I didn't expect it to be so much fun.'

Cati flushed, and shrugged the compliment aside, but Thea could tell that she was pleased.

'Does swimming always make one hungry? I am ravenous,' Thea exclaimed, squeezing water out of her hair and towelling it dry. She reached for her petticoat. 'I hope Mrs Jones gives us some of those flat currant cakes for lunch. I could eat a dozen of them right now.'

Cati looked puzzled for a moment. 'Oh, you mean *pice ar y maen*.'

'They are delicious whatever they are called.' Thea held her hands over her stomach in a mock-dramatic gesture. 'I feel positively hollow!'

'Take care, Thea, or you'll end up fat,' Cati warned her with a grin. 'And then Gareth will look for a new wife.'

Thea smiled, but some of her enjoyment in the bright day vanished, and she finished dressing in silence.

Cati, of course, had been joking. She knew nothing of her strange bargain with Gareth, but Thea was beginning to wonder if he now regretted his quixotic generosity. Perhaps he did wish he were free to find another wife!

He is deliberately avoiding me, she thought to herself with a frisson of despair.

It had begun a few days ago, and at first Thea had been able to convince herself that she was mistaken, but now she knew that she wasn't imagining it.

That lovely sense of camaraderie which they had shared had completely vanished.

'Come on.' Thea shook her head to clear it and leapt to her feet. 'I'll race you up to the clifftop.'

Cati laughed, and accepted her impulsive challenge.

Thea won, but her sense of foreboding remained. She couldn't chase anxiety away so easily, and she knew it.

Gareth did not appear for lunch. The two girls ate on their own, and then after her music lesson was over Cati disappeared without a word of explanation. No amount of scolding seemed to cure her of this exasperating habit, so, rather than waste time and energy in wondering what unladylike behaviour Cati was indulging in, Thea decided to visit the village.

Evening was drawing in when she returned.

'Where the devil have you been?' Gareth was in the courtyard and he strode towards her, his expression thunderous. 'I was just about to come looking for you.'

Thea's happy smile faded. 'I'm sorry. I was visiting Gwen Evans. Her youngest child is sick. I didn't realise you would be anxious.'

Gareth folded his arms across his chest. 'Then think more carefully next time,' he snapped. 'I don't enjoy being kept waiting.'

Thea's temper began to fray. 'Nor do I,' she retorted, thinking of how often he had been absent lately.

Gareth paused. He knew he was being unreasonable. *Duw*, he shouldn't take his foul mood out on Thea!

'I don't like you being out on your own,' he said in a quieter tone. 'Particularly when it is getting dark.'

Thea stared at him in astonishment.

'Gareth, it is barely dusk. Anyway, what possible harm could I come to?'

Gareth's fists clenched at his sides. There was no way he could begin to explain his anxiety for her safety!

Thea let out a weary sigh. 'Oh, Gareth, why do we no longer talk?'

'I've been busy.'

'So busy that you rarely appear even for meals?'

There was an edge of sarcasm to Thea's tone. 'I've hardly seen you for days, and when you do come home your mood is invariably bad!'

He flushed beneath his tan and Thea's annoyance died.

'Need you work quite so hard?' she asked, attempting a smile. 'I know your father left a lot of problems behind him for you to solve, but——'

A muscle flickered at the corner of his well-cut mouth and she broke off in alarm at the sudden fury in his eyes.

There was a strained silence for an instant.

'Is there something else bothering you?'

Gareth hesitated. He was tempted to confide in her, but how could he? She might turn from him in disgust!

'No. Nothing.'

'But, Gareth——'

'*Crist*, must you harp on? I don't want to hear another word!'

Thea paled. 'If you are just going to be unpleasant, I see no point in remaining!'

Whirling on her heel, she stalked off into the house.

Gareth bit back an expletive and watched her go, his expression bleak.

Inside the hallway Thea slowed to a halt and pressed her hands to her hot cheeks.

Her desire to throttle her husband had fled, leaving her feeling sick and cold.

Why had he spoken to her so harshly? She was certain that he was hiding something. Why would he not tell her? Did he not trust her?

'Oh, there you are, my lady.' Mrs Jones came bustling into the hallway. 'I've been looking for you. His lordship's mother wishes to see you.'

Thea hastily straightened and composed her features into a semblance of repose. 'What, now? I was just about to go and change my gown for dinner.'

'Right away, she said, my lady.'

Thanking her, Thea made her way to her mother-in-law's lavish apartments.

'Ah, Thea! At last.' The Dowager greeted her impatiently. 'Do stop dawdling by the door and come and sit down. We haven't much time.'

Crushing her irritation, Thea obeyed this imperious summons.

'I wanted to discuss how we are to celebrate your marriage to my son.' Angharad's dark eyes held a strange determination. 'We must do something soon.'

Thea wondered what had inspired this urgency. Really, Angharad seemed to be behaving as oddly as Gareth lately!

'I think we should hold a formal ball.'

'But Gareth has already said we cannot afford such extravagance, ma'am.'

The Dowager tapped her fan irritably against her knee. 'Nonsense. You must tell him you want a ball in your honour.'

'But I don't.' Thea smiled, but her tone was inflexible. 'Gareth thinks it unnecessary, and I am sure he is right,' she continued, wondering why she was bothering to defend her husband.

'Oh, very well! Perhaps a full-scale ball would be too costly.' Angharad's beringed fingers beat an angry tattoo upon the arm of the Hepplewhite satinwood chair. 'But some sort of evening party we must have! I will not have everyone gossiping and whispering that Gareth has married beneath himself!'

Thea winced. Tact was not her mother-in-law's strong point!

They had mended their earlier quarrel, but Thea knew that they would never be friends. Their characters were too dissimilar.

Her mother-in-law had a sharp intelligence, but rarely chose to exercise it. She preferred to gossip or complain of boredom. Her health was poor, but Thea suspected that she often exaggerated her symptoms, particularly when she desired an excuse for her shrewish behaviour. Immensely proud and snobbish, she could be charming when she wanted—but only if it suited her purposes.

But Thea couldn't think why Angharad was so anxious now. After all, the Rhayadars were the leading family in the neighbourhood. Why should public opinion suddenly be of such importance to her?

'The marriage must be creditably established. It is vital to scotch any gossip.' Angharad fixed Thea with a look that brooked no argument. 'I shall draw up a list and you may write out the invitations. The fifteenth of May will give us a clear two weeks to make all the necessary preparations.'

'It is quite short notice, ma'am.' Thea decided with a touch of wry amusement that she might as well enter into the spirit of the thing if she was to be cast in the role of secretary. 'Your guests may have prior engagements.'

'Possibly, but you will have been married over a full month by then.' The Dowager frowned. 'If we delay much longer we might as well wait to celebrate the first christening!'

Thea, to her great annoyance, blushed.

Her mother-in-law laughed rather unkindly. 'You really must try to rid yourself of that habit, my dear. It is so desperately bourgeois. Now, let me see. . .'

She began to reel off a list of names. Some, like John Morgan and Colonel Secombe and his wife, Thea had already met, but many were unknown to her.

'Do you think we ought to invite such numbers?' she asked uneasily, when her mother-in-law paused for breath.

'Any less and it will hardly be worthwhile opening up the crimson salon.'

Thea barely managed to refrain from giving vent to a vulgar whistle of astonishment. If Angharad was planning to use that formal entertaining room, now under holland covers, she must have an elaborate affair in mind after all.

'Moreover, we shall serve only the finest champagne,' Angharad added pointedly, and Thea realised that her face must have betrayed her thoughts. 'I have never yet given a shabby party and I don't intend to start now. I abhor penny-pinching. It is a habit fit only for tradesmen.'

'Extravagance is all very well for those who can afford it, ma'am,' Thea replied, nettled by this sly barb.

Angharad shrugged, and then in a more conciliatory tone continued, 'Do not let us come to cuffs, my dear. Heaven knows, it is dull here. We must use this opportunity to enjoy ourselves.'

'I don't find Castell Mynach dull,' Thea mumured.

'Wait until you have experienced a winter in the depths of the country.' The Dowager shuddered expressively.

'I'm surprised you do not remove to town.'

'My health does not permit it.' Angharad's expression became secretive.

Thea decided that a tactful silence was the best answer to this strange claim!

'By and by, I hear you have been visiting the sick with your herbal remedies.'

Thea was stung by the note of disdain in her voice. 'I've also given out blankets and food, ma'am,' she snapped.

'I applaud your generosity, but take care not be to deceived by too many tales of misery.'

'The poverty in Llanrhayadar seems real enough,' Thea retorted shortly.

The Dowager smoothed her expensive silk skirts.

'Possibly. However, it is not a fit subject for a lady's drawing-room, and you would do well to remember it. A modest display of charity is quite acceptable, but anything more will be considered eccentric.'

She gave Thea a mocking look.

'You already labour under too many disadvantages to run that risk, my dear.'

Thea bit back a sharp reply, and silently counted to ten.

Angharad launched into further plans.

'I shall instruct Howell to check his cellar-book at once, in case we need to send to Swansea for further supplies, and we will certainly have to hire more servants.' She began to tick items off on her fingers. 'Several women from the village to come and clean everything in readiness. Additional staff for the actual night. Extra help for the kitchen—that woman has no notion how to cater for a large party.'

'I think Mrs Jones an excellent cook,' Thea protested.

The big dark eyes, so disconcertingly like Gareth's opened very wide. 'Do you? How very odd of you, to be sure, Thea. But then no doubt your palate is provincial.'

Sensing that to defend Mrs Jones further would only provoke an unpleasant scene, Thea rose swiftly to her feet.

'When you let me have your list, ma'am, I shall write out the invitations for you,' she said, in a tightly controlled voice. 'But now I'm afraid you must excuse me.'

'Oh, but I wanted to discuss my ideas on decorating the salon with fresh flowers.' A petulant note crept into the Dowager's tone.

'I am sure whatever you decide must be acceptable, ma'am,' Thea answered with rigid politeness.

Once outside the room she took to her heels and fled to seek refuge in the flower garden.

One of the kitchen cats was sunning itself on the rustic bench, and Thea plumped down beside it.

'That woman is impossible!' she told her companion. 'The whole family is impossible!'

The cat opened one lazy eye at her.

'I must be mad. Only an idiot would have fallen in love with a man who clearly wants nothing to do with her!'

Tears pricked at her eyelids, and angrily Thea blinked them away.

'Oh, damn him to hell!' she exclaimed, and thumped the arm of the bench.

With a yowl of alarm that drowned out Thea's yelp of pain the cat sprang from his comfortable seat and stalked off, throwing a look of reproach over his shoulder at her as he went.

Thea began to laugh, but it was a bitter sound. Even to her ears, it sounded almost like weeping.

The last day of April dawned overcast, and Thea declined Cati's suggestion of swimming.

'It is too cold, and anyway I must finish this list.' She indicated the pile of invitation cards on the writing-table that still awaited her attention.

'How boring!' Cati exclaimed. 'Surely you don't intend to spend the whole morning acting as my mother's unpaid secretary?'

Thea shook her head. 'I shall ask Owen to drive me into Swansea later. I want to pay a visit to the dressmaker's.'

'Oh, if you are going into town I shall come too.' Cati glanced out of the library window. 'Look, there's Gareth. Why don't we ask him to take us? He said something about going to see our lawyer this morning.'

'No!'

Cati glanced at her in startled surprise.

'I'm sure he is too busy to be bothered.'

'Don't be silly,' Cati laughed.

She flung open the window before Thea could stop her.

'Gareth!'

Drawn to the window by a force she could not resist, Thea saw her husband turn and look up.

He was particularly handsome this morning, in a smart dark olive-green coat and pale lemon pantaloons, and Thea's heart turned over with longing.

'Can I come into Swansea with you?' Cati shouted.

'If you are quick. I'm leaving in a few minutes.'

Cati grabbed Thea by the hand. 'Come on. It will be more fun driving with Gareth.'

Thea hung back. 'There is so little room for three,' she murmured.

'Oh, Thea, it isn't like you to be feeble!' Cati gazed at her with reproachful eyes. 'Don't you want to go?'

There was no denial that Thea could sensibly make.

Hurrying up to her room to fetch her bonnet, Thea tried to tell herself that she was worrying needlessly. Perhaps Gareth's black mood was to do with the estate. He had been perfectly polite to her since his outburst yesterday.

'Thea. I didn't realise you wished to join us.'

Thea watched his smile disappear, and her confidence evaporated. He *didn't* want her company!

Pride came to her rescue. 'I was to have a fitting for my riding-habit at Madame Duroc's today, but I dare say she will come out to the castle if I send her a message. You two go ahead. I shall see you later.' She turned to leave.

'Please.' Gareth gestured to his curricle. 'I shall be happy to escort you both.'

Cati glanced from one to the other, her mouth forming a circle of astonishment.

'Is something wrong? Have you quarrelled?' she whispered as they took their places in the carriage.

'Shush!'

They drove in silence for a while, and then Gareth said, 'I hear my mother has dragooned you into helping her arrange this party.'

'It is no trouble,' Thea replied politely.

'What gown are you going to wear, Thea?' Her puzzlement diverted, Cati broke into the conversation.

'My eau-de-nil silk, I think,' Thea replied at random, trying to sneak a glance at her husband's classical profile.

'Mother says I must have a new dress.' Cati sighed.

'Don't you want to be fashionable, *chwaer*?'

Cati glowered at him. 'I look stupid in frilly pastels,' she muttered.

'Something plain would suit you better. With your dark colouring you would look good in a warmer colour,' Thea remarked, forcing herself to concentrate. 'It would be a departure from convention, I know, for a girl of your age to abandon white, but perhaps I can persuade your mother to let me choose something else for you.'

She received her reward when Gareth flashed her a look of gratitude.

'That beauty lotion you made up for me to soothe my windburn worked,' Cati said thoughtfully, her expression reflective. 'Very well. I will heed your advice, Thea. You are very clever about such matters.'

Thea's cheeks glowed with pleasure at this compliment, and when she glanced at Gareth she saw that he was smiling.

A tiny ray of hope illuminated her gloom, and she was able to bid him farewell with at least the appearance of composure when he dropped them at the dressmaker's.

Madame Duroc was an *émigrée* from the days of the Terror, and she had an abundance of style and grace. Her workmanship was equally fine, and Thea was very pleased with the way her riding-habit was progressing.

When the fitting was over, they spent an agreeable hour poring over Madame's copies of Heideloff's *Gallery of Fashion* and found a gown both Thea and the elderly Frenchwoman agreed was perfect for Mademoiselle Catari.

'There are some particularly fine gauzes in that shop on Castle Street,' Madame advised. 'You might like to look there.'

'If we find anything, I shall send it directly to you,' Thea replied.

They had agreed to meet Gareth at the Golden Harp, but there was just time to do some shopping first.

A helpful assistant at the expensive emporium Madame had recommended produced bolt after bolt of material, until they found the one Thea had been looking for.

She held a length of the fine coral-pink jaconet up against Cati's shoulder.

'This shade suits you,' Thea declared, and promptly bought it.

They moved on to purchase some silk stockings, a gold net reticule and a pair of long white gloves.

'I think that will have to do,' said Thea. 'If we don't hurry we will be late.'

'And my brother hates to be kept waiting,' Cati laughed.

They spotted Gareth's greys being led away as they entered the inn.

'Good. I'm glad you are on time. I took the liberty of ordering some luncheon.'

Cati let out a squeal of delight. 'I am starving!' she exclaimed.

They were shown into the same private parlour that Thea and Gareth had briefly occupied on their wedding night, and Thea couldn't help remembering her happy optimism.

What had gone wrong between them since then? Listening to herself making polite small talk, it occurred to her that they sounded like strangers.

Her appetite deserted her, and she declined the dish of buttered cabbage that the waiter proffered.

'Thank you. We can serve ourselves from now on.' Gareth dismissed him.

'Did your morning go well?' Cati enquired, spearing a piece of chicken with her fork.

'Tolerably.' Gareth had no intention of revealing why he had been to see his lawyers.

'We had an excellent time.' Cati launched into an account of her proposed gown.

Watching Gareth closely, Thea noticed how tense

his shoulders seemed. He won't admit it, but something is worrying him, she thought.

'Look, it's started to rain!' Cati had finished extolling her proposed finery. 'I hope the weather is better tomorrow. It would be awful if it spoilt the bonfire.'

An expression of puzzlement crossed Thea's face.

'What do you mean?' she asked, putting down her knife and fork.

'Traditionally there are celebrations at the Druid's circle. To mark May Day.' Gareth answered her query.

'Oh, yes, I remember now.' Thea nodded.

'It is great fun, and I expect you will find the music fascinating,' Cati declared.

Abruptly Gareth put his wine glass down. The movement was so fierce that the slender stem snapped and the claret flowed over the white tablecloth, spreading like a pool of blood.

'I don't wish either of you to attend the bonfire this year.'

'But we always go!'

'Unfortunately I'm afraid you will have to stay at home this time.'

'Gareth! That's not fair!'

Cati's cry of protest echoed in the silent room.

'May I ask why?' Thea kept her voice calm. 'Do you have any special reason for forbidding us to go?'

'I have a very good reason,' Gareth retorted. 'However, I have no intention of entering into a discussion on the subject.'

He rose from the table.

'If you have both finished, I will go and tell them to put the horses to.'

'Mean beast!' Cati muttered the words in a rebellious undertone as he quit the room.

Thea heard her, but for once she hadn't the heart to issue a rebuke.

CHAPTER EIGHT

THEA stared at Gareth's dressing-room door. Taking a deep breath to quell her nervousness, she knocked.

There was no answer so she knocked again, harder.

The door opened.

'Thea! What is it?'

He was in his shirtsleeves, his waistcoat and neck-cloth off, and with his black hair so untidy that she knew he had been running his hand through it.

She swallowed hard. She had always seen him formally clad, and she was disturbingly aware of the inverted triangle of broad chest revealed by the open neck of his shirt. She could hardly tear her eyes away from the tangle of dark hair which hazed his sun-bronzed skin.

'What do you want, Thea? It is after midnight.'

The impatience in his tone recalled her to her senses.

'I want to talk to you.'

'At this hour?' He raised his brows at her.

'You made sure I didn't get a chance to speak to you in private.' Thea's eyes flashed angrily. 'You have been avoiding me since we got back from Swansea.'

Gareth leant his shoulders back against the frame of the door and folded his arms over his chest.

'Have I really?' he drawled.

'Don't pretend! You know what I am talking about!' Thea quivered with indignation.

'You'll have to explain it to me, *cariad*.'

'Gareth!' Why was he behaving in this provoking manner? 'Do you think I will just go away if you make me angry enough?'

The telltale muscle flickered by his well-cut mouth and she knew she had scored a direct hit.

'Please, don't let's quarrel.' Thea curbed her temper.

'You know why I'm here. I want to know why you have forbidden us to go to the Druid's Circle. You said you didn't want to discuss your reasons, but——'

'I don't,' Gareth interrupted her, so bluntly that she gasped.

'Surely I am entitled to an explanation?'

'May I remind you of your recent vows?' Gareth's expression remained coolly distant. 'You promised to obey me, ma'am, not to question my orders.'

'I am your wife, not your slave!'

Gareth abandoned his pose and straightened to his full height.

'This conversation is pointless. Believe me, I have no wish to upset you, but you must understand that my mind is made up. Neither you nor Cati may attend the bonfire.'

'Has this. . .this edict got something to do with Y Cadno?'

Gareth shot her an intent look from beneath his dark brows.

'Why do you ask?' he said evenly.

Thea bit her lower lip. 'I don't really know,' she admitted. 'It was just a guess.'

'A mistaken one.' Gareth smoothed back a lock of hair which had fallen over his forehead. 'It is getting very late. I suggest you go back to bed and forget about the Fox.'

'Must I forget about Lady Parry too?' The words sprang from Thea's lips before she had time to think.

'Nerys Parry means nothing to me.' Gareth's expression became grim.

'Your mother told me she'd had a note from her today. She is back at the Cwrt,' Thea persisted, unable to resist discovering what his reaction might be. 'Your mother is going to pay a call there tomorrow. She wants me to accompany her.'

'If you wish to make Lady Parry's acquaintance, I won't stop you.' He frowned savagely. 'However, I will not discuss that woman.'

'Why?' Thea's patience snapped. 'You won't talk about her. You won't talk about Y Cadno. What is going on?'

'Nothing! You are letting your imagination run away with you.'

She shook her head. She would not let him fob her off so easily. 'Then why have you changed, Gareth? You were happy when we first came here, but your mood has been dreadful for almost a full week now.' She paused, and then added hesitantly, 'Is it something I have done?'

'*Annwyl Crist*, no!'

'Yet you've barely said a word to me since. . .since that day on the beach.' Thea swallowed hard and forced herself to go on. 'I. . . I thought we were starting to grow closer together.'

His dark eyes flashed, and she knew that he too was remembering the passionate kiss they had shared, but to her disappointment he remained silent.

'I *know* there is something troubling you.'

'I appreciate your concern, but there is nothing for you to worry about.' Gareth's voice was reassuring, but Thea caught a swift glimpse of bleak misery in his eyes before his expression became shuttered once more.

Impulsively she stretched out her hand and laid it upon his arm. 'Oh, Gareth, I want to help you.'

To her utter consternation, he flinched from her touch.

She withdrew her hand on the instant, a hot tide of mortification flooding her cheeks.

Gareth stared down at her and inwardly cursed his involuntary reaction.

'I'm sorry. I did not mean to offend you,' he said gruffly, knowing further explanation was impossible.

'Pray, think nothing of it, sir.' Thea adopted a sparkling smile to disguise the bitter hurt his rejection had dealt her. 'It was presumptuous of me to think myself entitled to your trust. After all, we both know I am not your real wife.'

A savage little laugh escaped her.

'Perhaps if I had allowed you to lie with me you might have been more willing to share your secrets, but you must forgive me if I deem it too high a price to pay.'

Gareth winced. '*Duw*, but you've a sharp tongue on you, woman!'

'Or maybe you've a guilty conscience,' Thea retorted. 'The other day you positively encouraged me to think that we would enjoy the May Day celebrations together.'

Unable to deny it, Gareth said, 'Circumstances have changed since then.' He gave a coolly dismissive shrug.

It was the last straw for Thea.

'You were quite correct, my lord. This conversation is pointless. Allow me to bid you goodnight!'

Gareth bowed with formal civility. 'Sleep well.'

She looked so bewildered and unhappy as she turned away that it took all of his determination to walk back into his room and close the door behind him.

Sleep eluded Thea, and when her eyes finally closed horrid dreams pursued her. Waking late, she rang for Blodwen.

'I shan't go down to breakfast this morning. Please bring me a tray of tea and toast.'

Blodwen's round face creased in surprise at this unusual request.

She bustled off, leaving Thea to wonder if she had noticed the tearstains on her cheeks.

The hot tea revived her spirits a little, and after donning her prettiest morning-gown to give herself courage she went downstairs, where she encountered Howell.

It came as no surprise to find that Gareth had already left the castle.

Coward! You deliberately hid in your room until you thought he had gone!

Ignoring this inner voice, Thea thanked the elderly butler for the information and went into the morning-room. Picking up the embroidery she had previously left on a rosewood Pembroke table, she began to set stitches at a furious rate.

Cati came bounding into the room. 'Oh, good, you are up at last.'

'If one more person expresses surprise that I overslept I shall throw that vase there on the mantelpiece at them,' Thea declared grimly.

Cati let out a hoot of laughter. 'How famous! I'd like to see you lose your temper. You are always so cool and collected.'

'You may get your wish today.' Thea tossed her needlework aside with an impatient frown. 'I slept badly and I'm in a vile mood, I'm afraid.'

'*Duw annwyl*, you needn't apologise to me.' Cati grinned. 'You've had to put up with my sulks often enough.'

Thea shrugged.

'Tell you what, why don't I ring for Howell and ask him to bring you a bottle of brandy to restore you?'

Thea began to laugh. 'You will do no such thing, you abominable girl!'

She stood up.

'Let's go and see how that pianoforte exercise I set you is progressing.'

An hour in the music-room helped soothe Thea's nerves, and she was in a much happier frame of mind when they returned to the morning-room.

'Shall I ring for a pot of coffee?' Cati moved towards the bell-pull, but as she did so her mother swept into the room dressed in a smart pelisse and a very fashionable hat trimmed with a lace veil.

Angharad's plucked brows ascended in annoyance. 'I thought you would be ready.'

Thea suddenly remembered the morning call Angharad wished to pay at Parry Cwrt.

'I'm not sure I should accompany you, ma'am,' she murmured. 'Gareth was not best pleased by the idea.'

'Fiddlesticks! You cannot restrict your social life to suit his gothic notions!'

'I think Thea is right, Mother.'

'No one asked for your opinion, Cati.' The Dowager turned a glacial frown upon her daughter before continuing to press her argument.

'My son may regard Nerys as a pariah, but he forgets she is received everywhere. It would be foolish to slight her. People will wonder at it, and they might begin to remember old rumours.'

Thea hesitated. She could see sense in what Angharad said. 'No doubt you are right, ma'am. However, I do not wish to disoblige my husband.'

'I am not suggesting you befriend Lady Parry. All I ask is that you act in a manner befitting your position. Don't ignore the proper courtesies. It will do more harm than good in the long run.'

It struck Thea had she had heard the same note of urgency in Angharad's voice before, when her mother-in-law had spoken of the necessity of holding a party to scotch any gossip about their hasty marriage.

Really, it was very strange that she had such a bee in her bonnet. Thea would have laid odds that she was too proud to give a damn what the rest of the Gower thought, let alone to wish to cultivate their good opinion!

Cati's angry voice broke into Thea's musing.

'Don't expect me to come!' She glared at her mother. 'I detest that woman, and I don't care who knows it.'

'Go to your room, Catari. At once!'

For an instant Thea thought Cati might defy this order, but then she whirled and ran from the room.

There was an awkward silence.

'I ordered Owen to bring the barouche round ten

minutes ago.' Angharad broke it, a note of appeal underlying her voice. 'It won't do to keep the horses standing.'

'Very well, ma'am.' Thea nodded briskly. 'I shall come with you and pay my respects to Lady Parry.'

She tried to tell herself that her capitulation was not inspired by mere curiosity!

Parry Cwrt was as modern inside as it looked from the outside. Thea stared about her with appreciation as the smartly liveried footman led them up to the first floor drawing-room. Everything was of the very best quality, but with an air of discreet restraint which spoke of good taste.

'My husband advised Sir Owen. He wanted the house redecorated to welcome home his bride,' the Dowager murmured in response to Thea's interest.

The late Viscount might have been a dreadful landlord, but he had certainly known how to spend money to effect! Thea was in the middle of wishing that her grandmother might have taken a hint from his master hand when the footman flung open the door and announced them.

The sole occupant of the room raised her red-gold head and rose lazily to her feet to greet them.

All coherent thought fled Thea's head. They had said Nerys Parry was beautiful, but she hadn't expected her to be quite so stunning!

Tall, she had perfect classical features and a voluptuous figure clad in an expensive gown of Italian crêpe. The colour exactly matched her huge hazel eyes.

'Do come and sit down, Lady Rhayadar.'

Nerys indicated the chair placed next to her own.

They settled themselves and she rang for refreshments.

'Did you enjoy a good journey from London, Lady Parry?' Thea enquired politely.

'Excellent, thank you.'

Her voice was low-pitched and somewhat husky. It had a seductive quality that Thea immediately detested.

Angharad proceeded to make enquiries regarding several of their mutual acquaintance in London.

'I think we must stop,' Nerys remarked after a few moment. 'We are boring your daughter-in-law.'

'Not at all, ma'am.' Thea smiled politely.

She hadn't been listening. She had been discreetly surveying her opulent surroundings and concluding that her hostess must know what a wonderful frame the white and gold decoration of the room made for her beauty.

'Oh, please, need we be so formal? You are out of the schoolroom after all. You may call me Nerys.'

The smile on her perfect oval face was sweet, but Thea heard the patronising note behind this invitation.

'Thank you. And you may call me Thea.'

Her brisk reply seemed to surprise Lady Parry, but she recovered rapidly. 'I hope you will visit often. Gareth was my best friend when I used to live here before.'

She fluttered her impossibly long eyelashes.

'I hope you don't mind my mentioning it? You may hear absurd rumours, and I shouldn't like you to be upset.'

The Dowager coughed, and directed an urgent look at Thea.

Thea responded to this mute appeal, but could not resist saying, 'I don't mind at all. I shall welcome the chance to get to know my husband's godmother.'

Nerys lost her honeyed smile.

'That honour, alas, is not mine. It belonged to my predecessor. I was Sir Owen's second wife.'

Thea opened her eyes wide. 'Of course! How silly of me! You wouldn't have been quite old enough at the time to stand as Gareth's godmother,' she said innocently.

The Dowager hastily suppressed a titter.

'Actually, Gareth is a year older than I am,' Nerys

snapped, a furious look coming into her magnificent eyes.

A knock at the door interrupted them, heralding the arrival of their refreshments, and there was a lull in the conversation while the ratafia was poured and a plate of sweet biscuits handed round.

'I was surprised to hear that Gareth was married,' Nerys announced as the door closed behind her footman. 'He was always such a determined bachelor.' She smiled at Thea. 'You married in haste, I believe?'

Thea nodded silently, determined not to satisfy her obvious curiosity.

Nerys gave a tinkling little laugh. 'Then I shall pray you do not repent at leisure, as the saying goes.'

Thea gritted her teeth. 'You are too kind.'

'Actually, you are not in the least how I imagined.' Nerys took a delicate sip from her wine glass. 'To be honest, I thought he must have fallen victim to some great beauty. But then, I suppose, beauty isn't everything, is it?'

'Such lovely weather we are having today. Do you think we may hope the rest of the month will stay as fine?'

Thea barely heard her mother-in-law's desperate intervention.

Such venom could not be accidental!

She doesn't like me any better than I like her. But why? What can she have against me? Only look at the pair of us! Apart from the superiority of my title, she has every advantage!

The title. . .or the man?

Thea could feel the blood drain from her face. Oh, no, surely she *must* be wrong!

'Are you quite well, my dear?'

The sugary but false sympathy in her hostess's enquiry restored Thea's wits.

'Perfectly, thank you.' Thea smiled back. 'I was merely thinking how pleasant it would be if beauty and goodness marched hand in hand.'

The Dowager stiffened warily at the blandness of her tone.

Thea looked full into Nerys's eyes. 'But appearances can be deceptive, can they not?'

Lady Parry's full red lips compressed to a tight line.

It was, Thea suddenly realised, a rather hard mouth, even in repose. In fact, seen close to, there were other tiny imperfections in what first appeared to be a flawless beauty. The diamonds in Nerys's ears could not conceal their over-large thick lobes, while beneath that exquisite *maquillage* there were several fine lines around her magnificent hazel eyes, as if she had indulged a little too freely in life's dissipations.

And her hair is coarse and lacking in shine, for all its lovely colour! A stab of pleasure shot through Thea. She knew it was mean-spirited to notice, but she couldn't bring herself to be ashamed.

Nerys pointedly turned away, and directed her remarks at the Dowager.

'Do you intend to visit the bonfire this evening, Angharad? It is still held each May Day, I assume?'

'Indeed. But I will not attend.'

'What a pity. I thought of making up a picnic party.'

'I'm sorry. My health is too frail these days.' The Dowager set down her glass. 'Speaking of which, I am a little tired. We ought to be going. Thea, are you ready?'

Thea promptly stood up and shook out her skirts.

'Thank you for your hospitality, Lady Parry,' she said crisply.

Nerys inclined her red-gold head. 'It was most interesting to meet you, Lady Rhayadar,' she replied with conventional politeness, but there was a waspish edge to her husky voice.

She did not come to the door with them.

'What were you thinking of, Thea?' The Dowager settled herself into her seat with much fussing of cambric skirts. 'I was never so embarrassed!'

Thea lifted her chin in a militant fashion. 'The fault

was not mine alone. Pray do not expect me to apologise.'

Angharad nodded. 'Nerys behaved badly,' she admitted. 'She has taken you in dislike, I'm afraid.'

Thea's irritation was somewhat mollified by this unexpected reply.

Angharad sighed. 'I do hope she isn't going to cause trouble!'

Thea smoothed the fringe on her silk shawl. 'Forgive me, but I do not understand why you wish to be friends with her. Surely it cannot be just because you do not want unpleasant gossip?'

For a moment she thought Angharad would not answer.

'I suppose it is out of habit,' she said at last. 'When she first came here to the Gower I lacked lively company. She can be very amusing when she wants, and we shared the same interests. After a while I realised she regretted marrying Owen. He was too old for her and she hated country life. I sympathised, which is why I understood about that. . .that business with Gareth.'

Thea could feel her fingers curling into claws. Horrified by the effect Nerys was having on her, she hastily straightened them.

'Naturally I was angry at the time, but she begged to continue our friendship and in the end I forgave her. When they settled in London she used to write to me. On the rare occasions Emrys permitted me to visit him in Grosvenor Square, she went out of her way to entertain me and introduce me to her friends.'

'I wish she hadn't come back!' Thea exclaimed.

'I think she is on a repairing-lease. Her tastes were always expensive. Owen left her a very handsome fortune, but I've heard she is deep in debt.' Angharad sighed. 'It is all so very awkward!'

Her gaze avoided Thea's and she looked embarrassed as she continued. 'In spite of what I told you the other day, I thought the past was over and done with. But now I'm not so sure.'

Thea swallowed hard. She too had a feeling that the real reason behind Nerys's return was the fact that Gareth had come home.

They reached the end of the park that surrounded the Cwrt and emerged on to the public road leading back to the village and Castell Mynach.

Thea pretended an interest in the passing scenery, but it was no use.

'Do you think she is still in love with him?'

'I don't know.' Angharad was loath to answer this bald question. 'However, I suspect she resents you. *If* she had any hope of becoming the next Viscountess Rhayadar, *you* have ruined it!'

Thea came to a decision. 'I won't visit the Cwrt again.'

'You won't cut her in public?' Angharad looked alarmed. 'Please! I don't want any scandal!'

Thea was so busy reassuring her that she almost missed seeing the rider in the distance. He was coming towards them from the direction of the village. Something about his broad shoulders clad in a smart dark green coat looked familiar.

Thea stopped talking, and her pulse began to beat in an uneven rhythm. He was riding a piebald roan. It could have been a twin to the one her husband often rode.

They reached the crossroads first.

The man was still too far away to see his face clearly, but with a sickening lurch of her stomach Thea realised that he had jet-black curly hair.

The barouche took the fork that led to Castell Mynach, and gathered speed as the horses sensed their own stable ahead.

Twisting in her seat, Thea glanced back, but it was too late. The rider had turned off, taking the road they had just left. The road that lead to Parry Cwrt.

Thea slowly sat back in her seat.

After a moment she looked up, and discovered Angharad's eyes fixed on her. For once there was none of the usual malice in her mother-in-law's expression, only an odd kind of pity.

Gareth held up his hand for silence.

'Is it agreed?'

The crowd of men standing in the church all began talking at once.

Gareth glanced at John Morgan, who smiled encouragingly.

'Iolo.' After a few moments Gareth decided that it was time to put an end to the discussion. 'You be spokesman.'

The middle-aged fisherman stepped forward. 'We are with you, my lord. It's time we stood up for ourselves.'

Gareth nodded. 'Good. Now, does everyone understand what they have to do?'

'Aye, it's clear.' Iolo answered. 'We'll meet here on the appointed night and bring our weapons.'

Gareth permitted himself a smile. 'Then away with you and enjoy yourselves.'

They started to file towards the door, but Gareth halted them with one last instruction.

'Remember, no talking! If Y Cadno gets wind of our plan we lose the element of surprise.'

When they had gone he stepped away from the altar-rail and joined the parson, who had waited for him.

They walked back to the house.

'Will you stay and have a glass of wine before you leave?'

'Thank you.' Gareth accepted the invitation, knowing that the older man felt the lack of company, but inside his head a tormenting voice called him coward.

You are looking for an excuse to avoid her!

Over a bottle of fine Canary John Morgan raised the subject of the bonfire.

'Are you going to light it, my boy?'

Gareth nodded. By tradition that task fell to the lord of the castle, if he was in residence.

'I shall go straight to the Druid's Circle when I have finished this,' he said, lifting his glass to his lips. 'It isn't worth my while returning home. Dinner will be half-over by now. It is always served early on May Day, to allow the servants to get away.'

The parson glanced at the marble and gilt clock which graced his mantelpiece and nodded.

'Can I offer you some supper?'

Gareth refused. 'I'll get something there.' He stood up. 'Are you sure you won't come?'

John Morgan shook his silvery head.

'Not tonight, my boy. I'm beginning to feel my age and I want to save my strength to help you fight off Y Cadno.'

His blue eyes were faded but his vision was still sharp, and he spotted the slight involuntary clenching of Gareth's jaw.

'What is it? Has Vaughn come up with some new delivery?'

'No more than usual.' Gareth laughed, and deftly changed the subject.

Riding away from the parsonage, Gareth was aware of a growing tension. For all his denial just now, he was uneasy.

Calling Vaughn's bluff had been necessary but, knowing him, he would strike out in retaliation. He'd wager all Lombard Street to a china orange that Vaughn would seek revenge, and where better than in the noise and confusion of the Druid's Circle?

An assassin was much cheaper than a law-suit!

Not that he intended to forgo the celebrations. If he stayed away it would only occasion talk, and in any event he'd be damned before he'd give Vaughn the satisfaction!

All he could do was keep his wits about him and take consolation from the fact that both Cati and Thea were safely out of it.

* * *

'I shall say goodnight. This warm weather makes me feel fatigued.' The Dowager announced her intention of retiring as dinner ended.

In the drawing-room Thea picked up her embroidery, but she could not concentrate.

A growing anger was taking possession of her. Gareth had been absent all day!

'I think I shall go to bed early too,' Cati said after a while, laying aside her book and getting up from her chair.

Thea nodded, concealing her surprise. She had expected Cati to kick up a fuss and refuse to obey her brother's command.

It seemed very quiet when Cati had gone, and Thea was thinking of taking a turn about the gardens in the hope that the fresh air might soothe her restlessness when Blodwen knocked.

'Do you want me to bring the teatray in, ma'am?'

Thea shook her head.

'Then, if there's nothing else, my lady, may I go?' There was an eagerness in the little maid's voice. 'The others have left already, but I might catch them up if I hurry.'

'But how?' Thea was curious. 'They took the gig.'

Blodwen laughed. 'There's a short cut, ma'am. When the tide is out you can cross the sands. The Druid's Circle is not far over the fields, look you.'

Thea nodded slowly, an idea forming in her brain.

'Can I come with you?'

Blodwen goggled at her. 'My lady?'

Rebellion flared in Thea's heart. 'I would like to watch. Trebor says that the festival is very old. He told me that once it was called Beltane and the bonfires were part of a fire-cleansing ritual.'

Blodwen shrugged helplessly.

'I wouldn't be any trouble.'

Her maid relented. 'You'd best change your gown,' she giggled.

Rushing to put on one of the plain, serviceable dark

gowns which had formed the basis of her wardrobe in Bath, Thea crushed the guilt which reared its head. Why should she miss out on all the fun? Gareth had refused to give her any reason, and the way he was behaving he didn't deserve to be obeyed without question!

Tying the ribbons of her bonnet beneath her chin, she stared at her reflection in the mirror. Her eyes were feverishly bright but she was very pale. Finding it disturbing to see her nervousness so plainly revealed, she snatched up her shawl and fled to meet Blodwen.

It was a fine evening, although there were patches of cloud obscuring the moon from time to time, and they had no trouble in climbing down the path and crossing the sands.

They didn't catch up with the gig, but within what seemed a very short space of time Thea saw flames brightening the darkness ahead of them.

'That's it, ma'am!' Blodwen grinned at Thea, who, catching her excitement, quickened her pace.

The Druid's Circle was so brightly lit that it could almost have been day. In addition to the enormous bonfire blazing away in the centre of the ring several smaller fires had been lit outside, and meat was roasting on spits over some of them.

'Lady Thea! Come and have a drink!'

One of the women called to her as they crossed the meadow and Thea recognised Gwen Evans, the mother of the sick child she had tended.

'Thank you.' Thea accepted the tin mug held out to her and took a cautious sip. It was metheglin—a herb-flavoured mead, sweet and strong.

Someone called out to Blodwen in Welsh, and she giggled and shouted to them in the same language before turning to Thea with a hopeful expression.

'Megan and the others are here, ma'am,' she said.

'Off you go. I will be all right.' Thea smiled at her. 'Oh, and Blodwen, don't worry about waiting for me. I can find my own way home if need be.'

After a few moments Thea handed back the tin mug and excused herself. 'I must go and say hello to some of the others.'

She walked away, towards the ring, exchanging greetings as she went. After a little while she stopped feeling nervous and was able to appreciate the noisy scene spread before her.

It was an extraordinary sight.

Dozens and dozens of people were dancing in a long chain that wound slowly between the stones while singing filled the air. Clouds of blue-tinged smoke coming from a wide shallow dish set atop a large copper tripod in front of the main bonfire imparted a strange dreamlike quality to the crowd. Faces came and went with brief, startling clarity, only to dissolve back into the haze.

Drawn by an irresistible curiosity, Thea moved closer. A nagging bittersweet perfume filled the air, and she wished she knew what herbs they were burning. The heavy odoour seemed to cloud the senses.

The music was equallly strange. Thea couldn't understand a word of the song, but the wild notes of the harp and flute were accompanied by a drum. It had a simple, insistent beat. Her foot began to tap in time to the compelling lively rhythm which surged through her veins, gradually dispelling all her earlier tension.

'Will you try a piece of this roast lamb, my lady?' Old Trebor appeared out of the darkness and held out his offering. 'Taste it. It's good.'

Thea accepted. He was right. The meat was sweet and succulent, with a hint of smoky crispiness that lingered on the tongue.

Wiping her fingers on her handkerchief, Thea thanked him.

Thea watched the dancers and, despite her underlying guilt, it wasn't long before she began to enjoy herself.

The undulating chain of dancers came to a halt on the opposite side of the clearing from Thea, and one of the young men stepped forward. With a strange ululating cry, he swept his arms up above his head and made a dramatic leap high into the air, straight through the narrow gap between the two biggest bonfires.

Applause for his feat crashed out, with wild whoops of approval. Still bemused by his daring, Thea saw one of the girls break away from the rest and come running forward.

'Cati!'

The girl leapt through the flames to safety and was caught by the young man, who whirled her round and round in his arms. Amid loud cheering he kissed her soundly, and then they melted back into the other dancers, who swung away back into the shadows.

Thea blinked. She must have been mistaken. The light was poor, and so many of these girls were small and dark-haired. It couldn't have been her sister-in-law. Cati was home safe in bed.

Thea shook her head, hoping to clear it, but she found it difficult to think. It was impossible to ignore the insistent music, which had grown louder and wilder until it seemed only natural that she should start to sway in time to the drumbeat.

The chain of dancers threaded its way past her and several strong hands reached out to draw her into their midst. Thea did not resist. Laughing, she allowed herself to be swept along by the pulsating rhythm. They wove in and out of the stones, going faster and faster until she was breathless and dizzy.

Thea felt her bonnet slip off. There was no chance of retrieving it at the pace they were going. Filled with a strange recklessness, she found that she didn't care and danced on.

Finally, after what seemed a very long time, the chain slowed, and with a gesture to excuse herself to her companions Thea pulled free. She felt dizzy and her feet were sore—to say nothing of the fact that her hair was tumbling around her shoulders.

'It's time you went home,' she scolded herself in a

muttered undertone, and turned to walk back across the meadow.

It was dark here, beyond the ring of stones, and the very ground seemed to be dipping and swaying beneath her. Fearing she was about to stumble, she paused to catch her breath.

A tall body loomed up and Thea stepped back instinctively. Her heel caught in the hem of her gown and she staggered off balance.

'Thank you,' she exclaimed with automatic politeness as a steadying hand reached to help her.

The man didn't answer, but instead to her shocked dismay he tried to put his arms around her.

'Let me go! What do you think you are doing?'

'Your ladyship!' Tomos, the second footman, jumped back, his expression ludicrously horrified. 'I'm. . . I'm sorry. I didn't know it was you.'

He backed away as he spoke, and with one last mumbled apology fled, leaving her standing alone in the darkness.

Torn between amusement and fright, Thea's eyes grew wide as she stared after him. Scattered in the shadows, several couples were lying entwined in the long grass, apparently oblivious to everything but the passion which had seized them.

Blushing furiously, Thea carefully picked her way towards the light, clossing her ears to the amorous murmuring all around her.

Why had no one warned her? Far from resembling the innocent May Day celebrations she had imagined, the goings-on at the Druid's Circle were much more akin to ancient fertility rites!

She hurried on. The large crowds had thinned and most of the smaller bonfires had burnt out, leaving the meadow much darker than it had been previously. The dance had ended and the singing had stopped too, although the wild notes of a lone harpist still rang through the air.

A girl ran past, her bodice open to the waist. She

was laughing and waving a bottle high in the air. Thea watched in shocked fascination as a man darted after her and they both disappeared into the shadows.

Deciding that she could not linger any longer, Thea turned, and almost let out a shriek of alarm as a burly male figure suddenly materialised in front of her.

She didn't recognise him but it was clear that he was drunk.

'Let me pass.'

'Nay, not so fast, m'dear.' He waved the bottle he held. 'Let's have a drink first.'

Frightened by his manner, Thea tried to push past him.

He reeled back and dropped the bottle, which rolled away into the darkness. 'Hey!' His leering expression turned ugly. 'Why, you stupid little. . .'

Thea took to her heels.

She would have escaped if it hadn't have been for the bottle. Tripping over it, she went sprawling on to her hands and knees and screamed as he grabbed her.

'C'mon, don't be shy!' He dragged her upright. 'Just one little kiss.'

Thea jerked her head away in disgust, but he clung to her with the tenacity of an octopus, unremitting in his efforts to force a kiss upon her unwilling lips.

'Oh, thank God!'

Thea suddenly found herself free, but her relief quickly changed to dismay as she recognised her rescuer.

With a cry of rage Gareth spun Thea's assailant round. One blow sent him crashing to the ground.

He lay there unmoving, and Gareth's fist dropped back to his side. Much as he wished to pound the man into the earth, it was obvious that he was in no fit state to defend himself.

With an angry oath, he hauled him to his feet. The sour fumes of his breath almost asphyxiated him.

Thea's fingers clenched convulsively upon her skirts. 'Gareth, what do you mean to do with—?'

'Be silent, ma'am. I shall deal with you in a moment.'

She shrank back, terrified by the fury in his black eyes.

A snap of his fingers and two men materialised out of the shadows.

'Huw. Alun. Take this fool away.'

They nodded assent and, supporting their charge between them, hauled him off.

Thea forced herself to meet her husband's gaze, trying to appear coolly unconcerned.

'Well? What the devil do you mean by disobeying me? I told you to stay at home.'

'I wanted to watch.' Thea's expression was mutinous. 'I didn't see why you should have all the fun!'

He laughed—a bitter, harsh sound. 'And I suppose you were enjoying yourself a moment ago?'

'I did not encourage that. . .that oaf to behave in that abominable fashion, if that is what you are insinuating.' Thea began to shake. 'How was I to know that these celebrations would turn into an. . .an orgy?'

Gareth ran a distracted hand through his hair and strove to curb his temper. At least she was safe!

'Where's Cati? Is she here?'

'She is at home.'

'At least one of you showed some sense.'

Goaded by this remark, Thea snapped, 'I would never have been driven to disobedience if you had bothered to explain. But you never talk to me any more.' She pushed back a stray curl from her hot forehead. 'I dare say you are tired of me.'

'That's nonsense and you know it!' Gareth could feel his self-control slipping. How could she think such a thing, when desire had tormented him almost into insanity?

'If it isn't true, why have you been avoiding me?' Thea could feel a lump forming in her throat, and gazed up at him with utter misery. 'Oh, Gareth, why did you go to the Cwrt this afternoon?'

'What?' Gareth stared at her in astonishment. 'I haven't been near the place in years!'

'I saw you!' Rage exploded in Thea's chest. 'Why won't you tell me the truth? I am sick of your secrets!'

'I have never lied to you.' Gareth turned pale beneath his tan.

Thea laughed wildly. 'I don't believe you!'

Gareth grabbed her by the shoulders, forgetting his resolve not to touch her. 'Stop it, Thea. You are becoming hysterical.'

He was breathing hard and his voice was unsteady as he continued roughly, 'I haven't set eyes on Nerys Parry for years, and I don't want to. No matter what else you might doubt, you must believe that!'

His grip was hard, almost bruisingly tight, but Thea scarcely noticed the discomfort. It was impossible to concentrate on what he was saying. A fierce wave of giddiness assailed her and her pulse began to race.

They were so close that she could trace the faint network of lines that crinkled the corners of his dark eyes, and smell the heady masculine scent of his body. The sudden longing to feel his lips on hers was devastating in its intensity. It overwhelmed her, drowning out all sense and reason.

He stopped speaking and Thea was achingly aware of the silence wrapping itself around them. Even the harp had stilled, and the only sound left in the universe was Gareth's ragged breathing.

He stiffened, and Thea saw from his expression that he too had suddenly become conscious of the fact that they were alone in the starlit darkness.

Alone in the pagan magic of this special night, when the ancient stones seemed to whisper a spell of desire.

'Thea! *Annwyl Crist*! Thea!'

She heard him murmur her name in a desperate whisper, and her hands clutched wildly at his broad shoulders as she swayed towards him, her eyes closed.

An instant later his mouth came down hard on hers.

It was a long kiss, deep and exciting, and Thea pressed herself urgently against him, revelling in the feel of his strong hard body against hers. Obeying the pressure of his demanding lips, her own parted. His tongue sought entrance into the secret warmth of her mouth and a fresh wave of desire swept over Thea.

Growing bold, his hand sought her breast, and Thea did not shrink from his touch but welcomed him, thrusting against him until his eager fingers wrenched her gown aside to lay bare her naked flesh.

'Oh, Gareth!' In an ecstasy of delight Thea's head fell back as his lips left hers and blazed a trail of fiery kisses down her throat until they found her exposed breast.

A sharp gasp of pleasure exploded from her when his teeth gently grazed her nipple. It immediately hardened into a tight crest, sending a voluptuous shock tingling throughout her entire body.

With a low growl of satisfaction, Gareth circled it with his tongue, alternating a light butterfly kiss with a hot, demanding, rasping suckle.

The caress was so arousing that Thea began to feel almost faint. The blood drumming in her ears, she began to tremble.

'Don't stop.' she whispered huskily, burying her fingers into his hair. 'Oh, please, don't stop!'

A throaty chuckle escaped him, and he redoubled his attentions until Thea let out little sobs of pleasure.

'*Lili'r môr.*' Gareth lifted his head and gazed down into her eyes. '*Crist*, but I want you!'

In answer Thea threw her arms around his neck and drew his head down to hers.

They began to kiss again, with a passion that left them both breathless, and then suddenly, in the midst of the desire which gripped him, Gareth suddenly heard a faint sound behind them.

Instinctively he spun round and flung himself to one

side, pulling Thea with him in lightening-swift response.

The knife went whistling past, slicing the air where he had stood a moment ago. It flew on, to clang harmlessly against one of the outer menhirs.

Her knees giving way with fright, Thea would have fallen had he not caught her and held her safe against the broad wall of his chest.

'What. . .what was that?' she gasped, the fever which had been raging in her blood abruptly cooling.

Gareth managed to summon up a wry smile.

'That, *cariad*, was one of the reasons why I wanted you to stay at home.'

CHAPTER NINE

AFTER all that had happened Thea was astonished to find that it still wanted twenty minutes to midnight when they arrived back at the castle.

Mrs Jones, who was dozing over her knitting, came alert at their entrance.

'Master Gareth.' She bobbed a curtsy, her kind face anxious. 'I heard what happened. Jenkins brought the girls home a little while ago. Are you both all right?'

'Perfectly. Thank you.' Gareth acknowledged her concern with a nod of his head.

He ushered Thea towards a chair. 'Sit down.'

'There is no need to treat me like an invalid,' Thea protested, but she knew that her shocked horror must still be written on her face.

'I'll mull you a tankard of ale, my lady. It'll put a bit of heart into you.' Mrs Jones became busy at the kitchen range.

Thea listened to the quiet ticking of the longcase clock which occupied one corner of the kitchen, and tried to will her brain to function normally.

It was no use. All she could think of was that knife flashing past them, and the dreadful terror she'd felt when she realised what had happened.

'Thea, I must go back. The search may have yielded some success by now.' Gareth laid a gentle hand on her shoulder. 'You look exhausted. Get some rest.'

Thea clutched his hands. 'Someone tried to kill you!'

Gareth shook his head. 'You're exaggerating, *cariad*. I've already given you the most likely explanation. That fellow you repulsed came back. I dare say he wanted revenge for the blow I dealt him. He saw we were. . .too occupied to notice him, and seized his chance. Luckily he was too drunk to aim straight.'

'I suppose you are right.' Thea sighed.

'Of course I am,' Gareth replied briskly. 'You mustn't refine too much upon it.' He smiled at her. 'I don't want you spoiling those lovely eyes with sleepless shadows.'

Thea ignored this pretty compliment. 'You'll take care, won't you?' she begged.

He touched his free hand to her cheek. 'It is good of you to worry.' His smile grew warm. 'But, truly, there is no need. It was nothing more than a drunken prank.'

Thea doubted it. All her instincts screamed that it had been a deliberate, premeditated attack, even though she had no evidence to prove her theory.

Leaving her in the capable hands of Gwen and Iolo Evans, Gareth had rounded up a couple of the villagers and immediately mounted a search of the area, but the man who had tried to kiss Thea had not been found.

Once it had become clear that the search would be prolonged, Gareth had decided to bring Thea home. She had protested, wanting to stay and help, but she had soon given way, realising that she would have been nothing but a hindrance. She didn't know the area, and in her shocked state she would barely have been capable of thinking straight.

'Ah, here is your ale.' Gareth took the tankard from Mrs Jones and handed it to her. 'Drink it while it is hot and then go to bed, *cariad*. I'll see you in the morning.'

Thea watched him go and longed to call him back.

'Shall I call Blodwen, my lady?'

Thea shook her head. 'There is no need to distrub her. I can see myself to bed.'

Mrs Jones tut-tutted disapproval and insisted on accompanying Thea to the tower. Only when Thea was undressed and tucked up between sheets she had personally heated with the warming-pan did she consent to leave.

'Please pass me that book on the table,' Thea requested. 'I think it might help me get to sleep.'

'Don't read too long though, my lady,' Mrs Jones admonished, handing it to her. 'You'll ruin your eyes.'

Thea had found a copy of Scott's *Lady of the Lake* in the castle's library. It was a poem she enjoyed, but now the words danced on the page until at last she abandoned the attempt and lay back against her pillows.

How could she concentrate on poetry when the man she loved had almost been killed before her eyes?

Every instinct told her that the drunk who had molested her was not the same man who had thrown the knife.

'There were two of them, I'm sure of it. What's more, I think Gareth knows it.'

The sound of her own voice seemed unnaturally loud in the silence, and Thea shuddered.

She felt utterly exhausted but knew that there was no use in trying to go to sleep. She was too tense to close her eyes.

Suddenly she sat up straight.

Why hadn't she realised it before? That man had spoken English to her, which meant he had either recognised who she was or—more likely in view of his subsequent behaviour—he himself had been English.

No wonder she hadn't known who he was. He wasn't from the village at all. He was a stranger. But what had a stranger been doing at the Druid's Circle?

There was only one logical explanation. He had to be one of Y Cadno's men.

Had the notorious smuggler been present tonight? Thea shivered at the thought.

Ever since she had heard that man's name, a shadow seemed to have fallen over the castle. Why would no one discuss him? Angharad had almost fainted when Thea had asked about him, and even in the village her shy questions had been met with blank stares and apologetic shrugs.

Who was he? And what was his connection with the Rhayadars? For some connection there must surely be!

It was a most tantalising, irritating puzzle!

Unable to sit still a moment longer, Thea got out of bed and pulled on her wrapper. She began to pace up and down, ruefully reflecting that she was acquiring one of her husband's habits.

Unfortunately the exercise did not help clear her mind.

The memory of Gareth's passionate kiss and the wonderful embrace they had shared kept intruding upon her thoughts, destroying her attempt to consider the problem logically. Even the terror she had felt afterwards couldn't tarnish its delight, and she couldn't help wondering what would have happened if that knife hadn't put an abrupt end to desire.

An hour later she was no nearer a solution, and sheer weariness made sleep seem imperative.

'What you need is a glass of warm milk,' she told herself firmly.

A glance at the mahogany bracket clock near her bed reminded her just how late the hour was. Deciding it wasn't fair to ring for one of the servants, she pulled on a warm pelisse over her wrapper and picked up the candlestick by her bed.

The winding stairs were blackly forbidding. Thea hesitated. Telling herself to stop being foolish, she began to descend. Then, suddenly, her ears caught the sound of footsteps.

'Who is there?'

The slight figure creeping up the stairs froze to a halt.

'Cati?' Thea held up her candlestick. 'Is that you?'

Her sister-in-law's dark head whipped up at the sound of her name, and Thea saw a tide of guilt colour her narrow face.

Thea stared at her. She was carrying a lantern and was dressed like one of the village girls, in a shorter-skirted country costume. Suddenly there was no need to ask where she had been at this ungodly hour.

'You were at the Druid's Circle!'

'So were you.' Cati tossed her long black curls in a defiant gesture. 'I saw you.'

Thea nodded slowly. 'But I never intended to try and hide the fact,' she pointed out.

'More fool you,' Cati retorted.

Thea ignored the childish gibe. 'How did you manage to leave the castle without anyone seeing you?'

Cati shrugged. 'Do you mean to tell Gareth?' she demanded.

Thea recognised a note of fear underlying her defiant tone. 'I think *you* should tell him,' she said gently. 'It is your secret.'

Cati stiffened. 'I don't know what you are talking about.'

'Who is he? The young man who helped you leap the Beltane fire?'

'It's none of your business!'

'In that case I shall let your mother deal with it,' Thea retorted briskly. 'Shall we go and wake her?'

'No!' Cati took a long breath. 'Oh, very well. I suppose I shall have to tell you the whole.'

Thea gestured to her room. 'We might as well make ourselves comfortable.'

Cati shook her head. 'Since I am to confess, I will show you how I got out. There's a hidden tunnel under the tower, you know.' She turned and began to descend the steps again. 'Come on.'

Thea followed the bobbing lantern. 'Do you mean to tell me that there is a secret exit?' She wondered why she was surprised. After all, the castle had been built in desperate times.

Cati nodded. 'Gareth discovered it by accident one day. It was just before he left for Oxford, so I suppose I must have been about four years old.' A smile flashed briefly over her thin features. 'He was playing hide and seek with me to amuse me.'

Thea was too busy concentrating to answer. It seemed a very long way down to the base of the tower.

'The secret door is over here, concealed behind this

panelling.' Cati held up her lantern and pointed to an upper border of carved flowers. 'Can you see the catch?'

Thea examined it but shook her head. 'It must be well hidden,' she murmured.

She had never been down here before. Gareth had informed her that the tower's small, heavy door to the outside world hadn't been opened in his lifetime, and she had assumed that the entrance hall would be as empty and stark as the rest of the stone stairway. However, at some point in the past, one of Gareth's forebears had tried to impress his neighbours by cladding the walls with oak up to the height of a man's shoulder. This panelling and the matching carved chest which stood opposite the door were now dull and scratched, but they remained impressively intact.

'Watch!' Cati reached up to press the centre of a carved daisy, and a tiny, seemingly solid section of wall swung inwards.

Even though she had been expecting it, Thea let out a gasp. 'Where does it lead?' She peered into the yawning darkness but could see nothing.

'Down to a cave just above the beach. Do you want to take a look?'

Thea hastily shook her head. 'Not just now, thank you.'

'It's quite safe. Gareth had the tunnel cleared of all the accumulated rubbish and fallen rock when he came home on leave after Trafalgar.'

Thea started. It was the first time she had heard that her husband had taken part in that famous battle.

Another secret!

'Didn't he tell you?' Cati sounded surprised. 'He was a midshipman on the *Royal Sovereign*. He received a commendation for bravery but his right leg was badly injured and he was ordered home to rest until it healed.'

Thea remembered that the *Royal Sovereign* had

been Admiral Collingwood's ship. It had taken a fearful battering.

'He was quite ill for a time,' Cati continued, sending a strange twist of dismay shooting through Thea's stomach. 'But when he started to get better he grew bored. Mrs Jones suggested he explore the tunnel to amuse himself.'

'Then all the servants know about this secret?' Thea's voice was sharp.

'Of course.' Cati let out a laugh. 'We call it a secret tunnel out of habit, but I dare say half of Llanrhayadar could work the trick of opening this door, since many of them helped to clear the passage and make it safe.'

Thea felt both annoyed and extremely foolish.

Why hadn't anyone bothered to tell her? Perhaps for the same reason that no one had mentioned the bawdy aspect inherent in the May Day revels. It was such common knowledge that they hadn't thought she might be in ignorance!

'This is all very interesting, Cati, but it doesn't excuse your recent conduct,' she said abruptly. 'You had no business creeping out, and you still haven't told me your reason for so doing.'

Cati pressed the catch and the door swung back into place. 'What do you want to know?' she muttered, moving out of the light to perch upon the edge of the carved chest.

'The name of that young man for a start,' Thea answered tartly.

'Glyn. His name is Glyn Edwards.'

'Edwards?' Thea thought for an instant. 'The boy from the Home Farm?'

'Yes! Now do you see why I don't want my mother to know?'

Thea nodded silently. Angharad would throw a fit of the vapours if she heard that Cati's sweetheart was the son of their farm manager!

'I have known him from childhood.' Cati spoke in a low, rapid voice, keeping her face averted. 'Then about six months ago things changed between us. He loves me, Thea, and I love him!'

Thea gazed at her in dismay. 'But Cati, you are both so young——'

'I won't go away and leave Glyn,' Cati rushed on, heedless of this interruption. 'I shall die without him!'

Thea curbed the urge to laugh. Cati would never have forgiven her! But the dramatic declaration merely strengthened her conviction that her sister-in-law was too immature to understand fully what she was saying.

'You don't believe me, do you? You think I'm too young to know my own mind. Well, I'm not! I mean to marry Glyn.'

'Cati, there is more to marriage then admiring a handsome face.' Thea tried hard to keep the exasperation from her voice. 'Your Glyn may be a very good sort, but surely you must realise what a vast gulf exists between the pair of you?'

'You are a fine one to preach! What of the difference between you and my brother?'

Thea winced. 'For all my connections with trade, I was brought up in a genteel manner,' she replied. 'In fact, my grandmother made sure I was trained to marry outside my station. Can you say as much for Glyn? Would he know what was expected of him if by some miracle your family agreed to the match?'

Cati glowered at her. 'You can argue all you like, Thea, but neither you nor Gareth will stop me from loving him!'

'Does Gareth already know of your feelings for this boy?' Thea demanded incredulously.

Cati gave a sulky shrug. 'I think he suspects. Before he left for Bath he ordered me to stop seeing him.'

A wave of annoyance crashed over Thea. Yet another secret! How dared Gareth make no mention of such a vital fact? He had asked her to curb Cati's unladylike habits but had neglected to tell her that the girl fancied herself in love. No wonder she objected so fiercely to leaving Castell Mynach!

'Did he give you any reason?' Thea strove to sound calm.

'He said that I was too old to romp with the village lads and that Glyn was a bad influence.'

Thea remembered how the boy had laughed as he had leapt the Beltane need-fires, and how eagerly Cati had followed him.

There was a little silence.

'Is that all?' Thea had a feeling that her sister-in-law was hiding something.

Cati hung her head and regarded the toes of her boots. 'He doesn't like the fact that Glyn has been helping Y Cadno.'

Thea sucked in her breath. 'But, Cati, he's right. Smuggling is evil and——'

'Oh, don't start being sanctimonious! Half the village is involved in smuggling. How do you imagine the women got those gold earrings and silk shawls?'

Thea bit her lip. 'I'm not pretending that I have any right to judge Glyn or anyone else,' she said slowly. 'I have seen the poverty here. But Y Cadno seems a dangerous man.'

'He is,' Cati replied flatly.

Thea stared at her. There was an odd edge to the younger girl's tone.

'I've asked Glyn to stay away from him,' Cati continued quickly, giving Thea no chance to question her. 'But he says smuggling is a good way to get the money we need.'

'You. . .you aren't thinking of doing anything silly, are you?' Thea faltered.

'Glyn has asked me to elope,' Cati admitted. 'But I won't. I know Gareth would only drag me back, and then we should be worse off than ever.'

She sighed and suddenly rubbed her eyes.

'*Duw annwyl*, but I'm tired. Is there anything else you wish to know?'

A dozen questions hovered on Thea's lips but she

shook her head. 'I am too exhausted to think clearly. I suggest we both go to bed.'

With a murmur of thankful agreement Cati stood up, and they moved towards the stairs.

'You won't tell Gareth that I disobeyed him, will you?' Cati came to a halt, her foot on the first step. 'He will be furious with me. I was out meeting Glyn on the night you arrived, and he made me promise not to do it again.'

Thea hesitated, torn by conflicting loyalties.

Anxiety clouded her sister-in-law's dark eyes. 'It wasn't fair,' she blurted. 'He bullied me into promising!'

'He is your legal guardian—I ought to inform him,' Thea murmured. 'But, no, I won't say anything. At least, not yet.'

Cati's expression brightened and Thea quickly added, 'However, you must give me your solemn word to stay away from Glyn. No more private meetings!'

A mutinous frown creased Cati's brow and then reluctantly she nodded. 'All right. I give you my word.'

'See that you keep it,' Thea said sternly. 'Whatever your feelings for him, you know such behaviour is wrong.'

Even in the poor light she saw Cati flush.

'We have only exchanged a few kisses,' she muttered awkwardly. 'He isn't my lover.'

'Heavens, I should hope not.' Thea deliberately injected a note of light-hearted amazement into her reply. It wouldn't do to let Cati realise how worried she had been!

Cheekily Cati grinned back at her. 'Not that I haven't been tempted! Don't you think he is handsome, Thea?'

'Very. But there are plenty of other handsome boys in the world beyond Llanrhayadar.'

Thea's pointed remark wiped away Cati's smile.

'Perhaps there are,' she said coldly. 'But I want Glyn.'

The stubborn set of her chin put Thea in mind of Gareth, and her tone was sharp as she replied, 'At the risk of sounding like a dry old stick, let me remind you, Cati Rhayadar, that we don't always get what we want!'

'Gareth. I must speak to you.'

The Viscount turned at the sound of his mother's voice.

'I was about to go and see if Thea is awake,' he replied. 'Can it wait?'

Angharad shook her head violently, and, concealing his impatience, Gareth followed her into her boudoir.

'I've received another demand from Vaughn.' the Dowager announced.

A savage frown creased Gareth's handsome face.

'What does he want?'

'The ruby. He is demanding the ruby as the price of his silence.'

'*Annwyl Crist!*' The oath was turn from Gareth.

'Will you let him have it?'

'Never!'

'But think of the scandal——'

'I will not give in to blackmail.' Gareth took a long breath. 'I'm not blaming you, Mother, but there will be no more pandering to his threats.'

'You think I should have ignored him——but what else could I do?' Angharad sank wearily into a chair in a flurry of Italian crêpe, her elegant long fingers pleating together in a nervous gesture. 'I paid to protect our name.'

'It was the wrong choice, Mother.' Gareth knew he had to be blunt. It was time she understood the reality of the situation. 'Vaughn won't rest now he has those marriage-lines. No matter what we pay him, one day he will attempt to claim the title. Distasteful as it must seem to you, we shall have to fight him. I have already spoken to our lawyers and put in train certain investigations——'

'Don't!' Angharad shuddered. 'I cannot bear to think of it!'

Gareth fell silent.

'Please promise me you won't discuss his claim with anyone else until it is certain that the case will go ahead,' she begged, her expression so anguished that Gareth agreed.

'He hates us both and longs to see us brought low.' She gave a little sob of fright.

'Then I shall take care not to let him win, Mother.' Gareth smiled at her with convincing confidence. 'Now, why don't you rest and let me worry about Vaughn?'

Seeing her safely settled under the capable aegis of her personal maid, Gareth headed for the tower.

Thea's sleepy voice answered his knock.

'Good morning. May I come in?' Gareth strolled into the room.

Thea, who had been expecting Blodwen, sat up in bed with a start of surprise.

'My. . .my lord.' She strove to appear composed, subduing the excitement his appearance had sent fizzing through her veins.

'I came to see if you had recovered. Did you sleep well?'

'I am feeling rested,' she answered, hoping that he wouldn't notice her slight evasion.

'Good.' He gave her one of his warm smiles.

Thea felt her spirits soar, and then sternly told herself not to be foolish. She could not let herself be dazzled by his charm or the memory of his kisses. There were several important points which needed to be cleared up before she could allow herself to think of her own feelings!

'May I sit down?'

'Of course.' Aware of a ridiculous shyness, Thea waved him to a chair beside the bed. It felt strange to talk to him dressed in her nightgown, although in point of fact it was a very decorous garment!

Suddenly she wished she had purchased the frothy

lace-trimmed creation she had seen but rejected as unsuitable when shopping for her trousseau!

Flustered by her wanton thoughts, she watched him stretch out his long legs and tried to will her brain to function, but before she could collect her wits Gareth pulled out a letter from his coat and handed it to her.

'This came for you,' he said.

'It is from Grandmama!' Thea exclaimed on a note of surprise. 'I recognise her writing.'

She quickly scanned the contents.

'Good news, I trust?'

'Mostly gossip.' Thea read on and a sudden smile of delight split her face. 'There is an enclosure from Georgy.'

Gareth watched her peruse the sheet carefully.

'She has written to apologise for her behaviour.' She glanced up at him. 'Would you like to read it?'

He shook his head, sensing that she wanted to keep the letter to herself and had only made the offer out of politeness. 'Will you write back?' he asked.

'Of course.' Thea nodded vigorously. 'She is my sister. Oh, I know she behaved badly, but she has a good heart. It is not her fault that Grandmama has always spoilt her.'

Gareth, whose estimation of Georgy's character was less charitable, was impressed by her tolerance. 'You are very understanding.'

Thea looked up and met his dark eyes. 'I deem it necessary, my lord,' she replied, slowly folding her letter.

Gareth winced. 'Does that mean you have found out about Glyn Edwards?' he asked ruefully.

'Cati told me last night.' Thea was grateful for his usual perspicacity.

He was silent for a moment. 'I should have warned you,' he admitted.

Enlightenment dawned on Thea. 'Did you think I wouldn't come with you to Wales if I knew?'

'Her infatuation was one more reason for you to refuse.'

Thea's heart began to beat faster. Had he *really* wanted her to accept his offer?

'Gareth.' She breathed his name, her voice suddenly unsteady. 'About Nerys Parry—'

'Please, *cariad*.' Gareth leant forward and gently laid a finger against her lips. 'Don't let's talk about that woman.' His hands slid down to enfold her shoulders. 'I promise you, she no longer means anything to me.'

At his touch Thea began to tremble. Looking up into his dark eyes, she saw her own passion reflected there.

Clinging to sanity, she said hoarsely, 'And Y Cadno? What of him?'

He stiffened and released her. 'I don't know what you mean.'

Despair swept over Thea. 'You are keeping secrets from me again!'

Unable to ignore her distress, Gareth abandoned his resolve and pulled her back into his arms.

'Thea, I can't tell you,' he muttered, holding her tight. 'Not yet.'

A shiver ran through her slight frame. 'Why not?' she whispered. 'Don't you trust me?'

'Of course I trust you,' Gareth declared, and discovered that it was the truth. She possessed more integrity than any woman he had known!

Thea's hopes rose, but were crushed as he continued slowly, 'Unfortunately, the secret is not mine alone to reveal.'

Another excuse—or the truth this time?

Gareth read the indecision in her face.

'*Cariad*, I swear I will tell you everything as soon as I can.'

With a sense of shock, he realised how vitally important it was that she believed him! He *wanted* her good opinion!

'Very well. I shall try to wait until you are ready.'

Her answer lessened the tension shimmering between them.

'Thank you.'

A knock came at the door. Gareth released her and sat back in his chair.

It was Blodwen, with hot water for washing and the information that Madame Duroc waited below.

'She's here for the final fitting of your riding-habit, my lady.'

'I will leave you.' Gareth rose smoothly to his feet with the fluid grace that always made Thea think of some great predatory cat.

Her eyes followed him to the door.

He turned and smiled at her.

'Until later, *cariad*.'

Happiness bubbled up in Thea's breast. Everything was going to be all right! Gareth had given her his word. All she needed to do was to be patient.

The next week was one of the happiest Thea had ever known, in spite of the fact that both she and Gareth were extremely busy. Gareth was implementing his new ideas to improve the estate while preparations for the Dowager's party and an outbreak of feverish colds in the village created much work for Thea, but in the evenings there was time to talk.

Sitting before the log fire in the drawing-room, they discussed everything—from the latest novels to the increasing threat of war with the former American colonies or the best way of transporting potatoes to market. However, by a common if unspoken consent, they avoided the thorny questions of Y Cadno and their own tangled relationship, even when the Dowager and Cati had gone to bed and left them alone.

Instead they played cards, or laughed together over Gareth's attempts to teach her Welsh. He liked to have her play the pianoforte for him, and in return would agree to her request that he sing something for her. He had a marvellous voice and knew dozens of songs, from old Welsh ballads to rousing sea-shanties.

There was only one flaw in her happiness. He was scrupulously careful not to touch her. It puzzled Thea, but in the end she decided that she was being foolish to let his restraint worry her. The spark of desire still smouldered between them, and she knew that one day it would burst into consuming flame and burn down all the barriers between them.

In the meantime she was content to have his friendship and enjoy the simple warmth and affection which was growing deeper between them with each passing day.

One morning, a week after the revels at the Druid's Circle, Cati marched into tne kitchen, where Thea was brewing up yet another batch of cough medicine.

'Come on. It is a beautiful day. We are going swimming,' she announced.

'But, Cati, I'm too busy.'

'You said that yesterday.'

Cati grinned at Mrs Jones, who was unashamedly listening to this dispute. 'You'll finish stirring this disgusting concoction, won't you?'

The cook nodded. 'You go on now, my lady. You could do with some fresh air. You don't want his lordship to think you are looking peaky.'

This master-stroke put paid to Thea's objections and she meekly removed her apron.

They hadn't been gone an hour when Gareth returned home.

'Have you seen her ladyship, Megan?' he asked, encountering the little maid employing her feather duster in the morning-room.

'Mam said Miss Cati took her off for an airing, sir.'

He thanked her, and, guessing that they might be down at the beach, headed in that direction.

Cati was some way off-shore, swimming strongly. To his complete astonishment, Thea was in the water too.

He watched her for a moment, unobserved. Her

technique was somewhat inelegant, but her movements had confidence and carried her along with commendable efficiency.

'Well done, *cariad*,' he called out.

Startled, Thea floundered and swallowed a mouthful of salt-water. Choking, she waded ashore.

'I'm sorry. I didn't mean to disturb your concentration. Your achievement is splendid.'

'For that handsome compliment, I shall accept your apology, sir.' Thea laughed, responding to the twinkle in his eyes, and Gareth caught his breath.

Did she have any idea how lovely she looked? The water had sleeked her hair away from her small face, revealing an unexpected delicacy in her neat features, and her thin shift clung to her slender curves with heart-stopping accuracy.

Hungrily he devoured her with his eyes, until he realised what he was doing. Stifling the urge to pull her into his arms, he handed her a towel.

'Here. Put this around you,' he said hastily. 'You don't want to catch a chill just in time for this damned party.'

She obeyed and he added, 'Why didn't you tell me you were learning to swim?'

'I wanted to surprise you. It was Cati's idea. I would never have managed it without her help and encouragement. She has been so kind to me. Do you know, I even managed to persuade her to play the harp for me after our pianoforte lesson this morning, and she always vowed she was too shy!'

Thea was aware that she was babbling. She felt strangely self-conscious. Just for a moment his eyes had burned with passion, making her desperately aware of how much she wanted him to kiss her.

'I'm pleased you have become friends.' His deep voice was warm. 'I know you have worked hard to improve her manners, and the difference is remarkable. Thank you.'

'She. . .she just needed someone nearer her own age

to confide in,' Thea murmured, turning pink with pleasure.

'Are you sure you ought to be swimming, though? You have been working so hard. I don't want you overtiring yourself.'

Thea laughed. 'I'm not an invalid, sir! A little exercise will not harm me.'

'Good. I'm glad to hear it.' Gareth's eyes glinted with mischief. 'You see, I have a surprise for you.'

Thea's face lit up. 'A surprise? What is it?'

'Come and find out.' He handed her another towel to dry her long hair.

While she quickly finished dressing Gareth shouted to Cati and signalled that they were leaving.

They went to the stables, where Gareth spoke to Owen.

'Oh, Gareth! She is lovely! Thank you!'

Her eyes shining with excitement, Thea stroked the velvety nose of the little bay mare Owen had just brought out for her inspection and smiled brilliantly at her husband.

Dazzled, Gareth watched her make friends with the latest acquisition to the stable-yard.

'As soon as I saw her this morning I thought she would be perfect for you, and couldn't resist buying her,' he confessed.

The exorbitant price old Cadwalladar had demanded was worth it!

Thea stopped murmuring sweet nothings to the mare and glanced up at him, her smile dissolving.

'Was. . .was she very expensive?' she asked apprehensively, voicing the thought that had suddenly occurred to her.

'No more than I could afford,' Gareth replied firmly.

'But, Gareth——'

'Hush, now, it is insulted I shall be if you say another word,' he interrupted gently.

Thea bit her lip. 'I'm sorry. I didn't mean to seem ungrateful.'

'I know.' he grinned at her. 'Our finances are in a shocking state, but I have hopes that we will soon come about. Griffiths has informed me that we may have a buyer for the London house.'

Gareth had spoken of this plan soon after their return to Castell Mynach. It seemed a good idea to Thea. The opulent mansion in Grosvenor Square, which his father had acquired soon after Gareth's birth, was no longer used.

'We can always hire a suitable house if we wish to winter in Town,' Gareth had said. 'But, since I have no intention of ever spending more than a few weeks at a time in London, I deem it a pointless extravagance to continue to maintain that great barracks. It eats money.'

To Thea's surprise the Dowager had raised no objection to the scheme.

'Does Griffiths think you will get the full price?' Thea now asked.

'Aye. And once the sale is confirmed I shall get rid of all the French furniture and *objets d'art* my father installed there. It is, I'm told, a very impressive collection. Not surprising, I suppose, considering that he spent twenty years and half the Rhayadar fortune on acquiring it.'

The ironic note faded from his tone. 'So you see I can well afford to buy you a present.'

He grinned at her. 'Besides, your new habit deserves a beautiful mount!'

Capitulating, Thea laughed. 'Madame Duroc would agree with you.'

To her delight, the dressmaker had finally finished her riding-habit. It fitted Thea to perfection and she had been looking forward to her first ride, but she had never imagined that Gareth would go to such trouble to find her a suitable mount.

Gareth motioned the head groom away.

'Will you come riding with me this afternoon?'

Thea looked up from patting the mare.

'I should like that very much.'

'Good. I shall look forward to it.'

He moved closer and Thea was suddenly aware of the intimacy of his smile. She moistened her dry lips with the tip of her tongue. Was she imagining it?

Only the sound of one of the horses snickering disturbed the warm, still air as Gareth raised her hand to his lips and pressed a kiss against the soft skin of her inner wrist.

'There is something I must tell you,' he said quietly. 'In private, without fear of interruption.'

Thea nodded, her knees beginning to tremble.

Was the time of waiting over at last?

CHAPTER TEN

UNFORTUNATELY for Thea's hopes of a tête-à-tête with her husband, when she arrived in the stable-yard that afternoon Cati was there.

'Thea, tell my brother not to be such a mutton-head! You don't mind if I ride with you, do you?'

Unable to ignore the appeal in her young sister-in-law's face, Thea exchanged a rueful look with Gareth. 'Not at all, Cati,' she lied.

Gareth, who was already mounted, smothered his annoyance. 'Tell Owen to saddle up your filly.'

Cati gave a whoop of triumph and rushed to obey.

'I'm sorry, *cariad*.'

Thea shrugged lightly to convey her understanding, and struggled inwardly to overcome her disappointment.

They rode out of the yard into the spring sunshine and took the road that wound along the headland.

'How does it feel to be back in the saddle?' Gareth asked Thea after a few moments.

'Utterly marvellous,' Thea replied. 'I dare say I shall be feeling stiff tomorrow, but it is worth it.'

'You look at home to a peg,' Cati announced.

Quietly Gareth concurred. His bride had a light pair of hands and rode as gracefully as she danced.

'Thank you.' Thea coloured slightly at their praise. 'But she makes it easy.'

'She moves very well,' said Cati, casting an approving eye over the little mare. 'What are you going to call her?'

'Guinevere,' Thea said unhesitatingly.

'After Arthur's queen?'

Thea met Gareth's enquiring gaze and nodded. 'I have always liked that legend.'

'*Duw Annwyl*, you and my grandfather would have found lots to talk about then—eh, Gareth?' Cari chimed in.

He nodded. 'I think I mentioned he was fond of old stories, which he used to repeat to us. The Arthurian myth was one of his favourites.'

'Tell her about the ruby.'

'Peace, little sister.'

'What ruby?' Thea turned a puzzled face to her husband.

Gareth groaned, and comprehension dawned on Cati's face.

'Oh, were you going to give it to her for this party?'

'That was my intention, dear Catari,' he replied drily.

'What are you two talking about?' Thea demanded, slowing her mount to a walk.

'The family treasure,' Cati said, with an irrepressible giggle.

Thea's glance flew to Gareth's face. 'Another surprise?'

'A ruined one!' Gareth shook his head and began to explain. 'The only thing my father didn't try to sell was the Rhayadar ruby. It is a very old, very fine jewel which by tradition has always been handed down to the title-holder's new bride.' He coughed, his manner suddenly a little diffident. 'I can extract it from the bank vault, if you think you might like to wear it?'

Thea thanked him, touched by his thoughtfulness. 'But what has it to do with King Arthur's wife?' she persisted.

'Legend has it that it once decorated Guinevere's white breast.'

'Set in the middle of a great collar of gold,' Cati added helpfully.

Thea blinked.

'Quiet, brat!' Gareth frowned with mock severity at Cati before shifting in his saddle to face Thea. 'Let me put your mind at rest. My father had it reset.' His tone acquired a faint but unmistakable irony. 'His taste, as ever, was exquisite. I think you'd be hard put to it to find a more lovely pendant.'

'You haven't told her the best part of the story,' Cati accused him. 'It is supposed to bring great happiness to the wearer and her husband provided that the couple truly love each other, but bad luck to both of them if either one is unfaithful.'

'Well, I suppose all old jewels must carry a curse, or their stories would lack romance,' Thea said in a voice carefully devoid of feeling.

'Oh, for shame, Thea! I thought you would be impressed!' Cati giggled.

Thea smiled, but a little of her happiness in the bright afternoon faded. If only she knew whether Gareth really cared for her!

Her heart was full of love for him, but she knew that wasn't enough. True happiness could only exist if he shared her emotions. Without love their marriage would remain only an empty shell, regardless of whether or not they gave way to desire.

'Come on.' Gareth put an abrupt end to the conversation. 'Let's see if Guinevere can gallop.'

He urged his own mount forward and, thankful to escape her disturbing thoughts, Thea sped after him.

After attending church with them the following morning Gareth excused himself, saying that he wished to deal with some urgent paperwork in his study.

The Dowager had been invited to spend the afternoon with the Secombes, and she insisted Cati accompany her.

'Do you mean to come with us, Thea?'

Thea declined. She found the colonel worthy, but rather too bluff and hearty for her tastes. Besides, she wanted to exercise Guinevere.

The little mare delicately took the carrot Thea offered her and Owen laughed.

'She knows you admire her, my lady.'

'Saddle her up for me, please, Owen.'

'Are you sure you wish to ride, my lady? I reckon we are in for rain.'

Thea glanced up at the sky in surprise. Apart from an increase in the wind, the recent good weather seemed to be holding.

'I'll chance it,' she smiled.

'You should take Dai with you.'

'No, thank you.' Thea shook her head decisively.

'Then I shall escort you.'

'No. You are busy, and in any case I prefer to be alone. I won't go far.'

Owen nodded. It wasn't his place to argue, but he wore a slight frown of unease as he watched her ride out of the yard.

Thea decided to follow yesterday's route. She wasn't foolhardy, in spite of what Owen seemed to think, but the only escort she wanted was Gareth. However, he had seemed to think she'd intended to accompany his mother. Thea had not corrected his mistaken impression, recognising that he was preoccupied.

Thea sighed. He had been in an odd withdrawn mood this morning.

A horrid suspicion suddenly occurred to her. Was he behaving in that slightly distant manner because he regretted allowing his feelings to show yesterday?

But why should he be ashamed of wanting to please her? He was not a cold man—the very opposite, in fact! It was almost as if he was holding his emotions on a tight rein. Was he afraid to let go? Afraid to show that he cared? Surely he couldn't think that she would reject him? Not after the way she had returned his kisses!

'Do you know something, Guinevere?' she said to the little mare. 'I wish I knew what had really happened with Nerys Parry!'

She suspected that youthful experience had left Gareth wary, and his life in the Navy could not have helped, since he would have had little contact with women.

'At least not with respectable ladies!' she concluded carefully.

Guinevere snickered daintily.

Thea chuckled. 'I know. I sound like a complete ninny!'

Her smile faded. It wasn't in the least bit amusing to be shut out from Gareth's confidence. He claimed to trust her. If only he would show it!

Lost in thoughts about her husband, she stared absently at the white-capped racing waves. It took several moments before she consciously registered that there was a ship out there—a ship she hadn't seen before.

'It isn't a fishing-boat. It is too big,' she murmured aloud to herself.

She was about to urge the mare on when a new thought struck her.

Could it be Y Cadno's ship?

Thea counted three masts. She couldn't be sure, but she thought it might be a schooner.

A frown furrowed her smooth brow.

Gareth had asked her to wait, but how much longer could she be patient? Her urgent need to learn about the mysteries of his past was destroying her peace of mind.

'I *have* to know, Guinevere,' she whispered, patting the mare's neck. 'How else can I decide whether there is a chance for me?'

There was one person she hadn't spoken to. One person who knew about Nerys and Y Cadno. He might answer her.

She turned the little mare's head round.

'Come on, Guinevere. We are going to pay a call at the parsonage.'

'My dear! What a pleasant surprise!'

John Morgan laid aside his copy of the *Cambrian* newspaper and rose to his feet as Thea was shown into his study.

'You might find the parlour more comfortable.' He glanced ruefully around the untidy book-strewn room. 'Shall we retire there?'

Thea refused this suggestion.

'Then may I least offer you some refreshment?'

Thea shook her head. 'This is not exactly a social call.'

A look of puzzlement crossed his lined face, but he waited with courtesy until she was settled into the most comfortable chair the little room could boast.

'What can I do for you?'

Thea hesitated. Now that the moment had arrived, she didn't know where to begin.

'Is it parish business you wish to discuss?'

She shook her head and, gathering her courage, plunged straight in. 'Will you tell me what connection Y Cadno has with my husband?'

He flinched.

'Well?' Thea twisted her fingers together impatiently. 'Is there something between them or am I imagining things?'

The parson sighed. 'I wish I could deny it,' he said heavily. 'But there is a tie which binds them.'

Thea swallowed hard to moisten her dry throat. 'Can you tell me about it?'

He shook his white head.

'Please! Believe me, I wouldn't ask out of mere curiosity.' Thea paused nervously. 'You see, I have to take a decision about my furure, and I *must* have more information. I know Gareth doesn't want to tell me about his past, although he has promised he will.' She sighed. 'The waiting is driving me mad!'

Seeing that he looked utterly confused, she decided to put her trust in his discretion as a man of the cloth.

'I had no idea!' The faded blue eyes regarded her with a faintly shocked expression when her explanation of their six-month bargain was concluded.

'I know it sounds dreadful, but Gareth has behaved

with the utmost propriety at all times,' Thea declared hotly, and then blushed. 'Well, nearly anyway.'

'My dear, I have no desire to pry into your private life.' His gentle smile soothed away her flustered embarrassment. 'I understand your anxiety, but my answer must remain the same. I am not at liberty to reveal the Fox's true identity. However, if Gareth has told you he will explain, I'm sure he will do so one day. He is a man of integrity.'

Thea bit her lip. 'Then can you at least tell me what happened between him and Nerys Parry? I know he was in love with her.'

John Morgan was silent.

'It is a lot to ask, but I don't know where else to turn for advice!' Tears sprang into Thea's eyes and she wiped them away impatiently with the back of her hand. 'Forgive me! I have no right to badger you like this.' She began to rise to her feet. 'I should not have come.'

The elderly parson waved her back into her seat.

'Sit down, my dear. I know Gareth would not wish you to be upset, and, since he has not forbidden it, I shall try to answer your question.' He smiled. 'But first a glass of wine, perhaps?'

Thea nodded, relief sweeping over her.

When his housekeeper had brought in the Madeira and it had been poured, John Morgan spoke again.

'Let me begin by assuring you that Gareth has no love for that lady. Quite the reverse, in fact.'

His thin voice acquired a reminiscent note. 'When Sir Owen brought Nerys home as his bride Gareth had just finished his studies at Oxford. He was kicking his heels, trying to persuade his father to let him join the Navy.'

'The late Viscount disapproved?' Thea enquired in surprise.

'Emrys Rhayadar had some strange notions! He would have preferred Gareth to become a town fop, but Gareth wanted to serve his country.'

The elderly parson took a fortifying sip of his wine.

'It was only natural that Gareth and Nerys were thrown together. Gareth had always run tame at the Cwrt, and Sir Owen encouraged him to escort Nerys to functions he did not wish to attend himself.'

He paused delicately.

'Sir Owen was, you understand, a widower of long standing when he met Nerys during a visit to some relatives in North Wales. He was almost thirty years her senior and his health was somewhat precarious.'

'I have a horrible feeling I can guess what happened next,' Thea said slowly.

A deep sigh answered her. 'I blame Sir Owen. He had no business letting his wife run wild, but he always indulged Nerys to the top of her bent. When the inevitable happened Gareth was horrified, and came to me for advice.'

A bitter taste filled Thea's mouth. 'I know I have no right to be jealous, but I can't help wishing they hadn't been lovers,' she muttered.

'Ah, I fear I have misled you. Gareth was dazzled by her but he did *not* succumb to temptation—and that, my dear, is the whole point of this sorry tale.'

Thea stared at him. 'You mean he rejected her?'

'He told her that he could not cuckold his godfather, not matter how attractive he found her. If she had known him half so well as she thought she did she would have realised it for herself. Gareth had always regarded Sir Owen with great affection and respect. Such a betrayal was unthinkable!'

'No doubt Nerys, however, felt herself scorned.' Thea spoke the words calmly, but her hand trembled as she raised her wine glass to her mouth.

'Precisely. They quarrelled but she could not change his mind. In the end, when he told her that he would not see her in private again, she took revenge by accusing him of trying to force her against her will. Whatever his private beliefs, Sir Owen chose to support his wife, and the upshot was an ugly rift between him and his godson.'

John Morgan let out another sigh.

'It was all hushed up, of course. It was in no one's interest to have a scandal, and both families possessed the necessary influence—helped by the fact that Sir Owen immediately whisked Nerys off to London.'

'Was the rift ever healed, sir?'

'No. Sir Owen was dead within the twelvemonth. They never met again.' The parson fixed Thea with a direct look. 'I don't think Gareth ever forgave her for that.'

'Part of the blame was his,' Thea asserted, irritated that her thoughts were so transparent. 'If he hadn't fallen for her charms the situation wouldn't have arisen.'

'True, but what young man is wise when confronted with beauty? She was even lovelier when she was nineteen, and Gareth didn't begin to understand her real nature until it was too late.'

He cleared his throat. 'It ill becomes me to criticise one of my parishioners, but she is a shallow, selfish woman, who cares only for her own pleasure. By all accounts she married Sir Owen merely for his money and, I'm told, was frequently unfaithful to him once they were established in London. Moreover, she has apparently squandered the fortune he left her. Her agent here despairs of ever getting her to listen to his pleas.'

Thea's fingers twisted the stem of her wine glass round and round. 'I have only met her the once, but I fear your assessment of her character is correct.'

Lifting her gaze, she met his eyes.

'Angharad thinks she has returned because she wishes to rekindle Gareth's passion. Do you agree?'

He nodded. 'It wouldn't surprise me. She always had a fancy to be a viscountess!'

Thea took a deep breath, remembering the day she had seen Gareth riding towards the Cwrt. Gareth had denied it, but Nerys was so beautiful, with her perfect features and vivid colouring! And, thanks to their strange bargain, Gareth had been forced to live like a monk. . .

'However, I doubt if she actually loves Gareth.' The Reverend Morgan's voice wrenched Thea from her misery. 'I don't think she is capable of loving anyone other than herself.' He shrugged. 'Such selfishness, of course, is dangerous!'

He gave Thea one of his gentle smiles and raised his glass in salute.

'My advice to you, my dear, would be to keep a weather eye on the lady.'

'Oh, I shall,' Thea promised, meaning it.

The afternoon had grown late by the time she left the parsonage. Knowing his love of company, she had allowed John Morgan to keep her talking, but as she mounted Guinevere she wished the sky did not look so threatening. Black clouds had gathered and the wind was even stronger.

'I fear we are in for a storm.' The elderly parson looked anxious. 'Take care, my dear.'

Thea nodded and waved farewell.

The rain began as she climbed out of the village. Within minutes it was falling in wind-driven torrents, and by the time she approached the crossroads Thea was soaked to the skin. Shivering, she urged Guinevere towards Castell Mynach's headland.

A sudden bolt of lightning split the sky and Guinevere reared, whinnying in terror. Taken unawares, Thea was almost flung off and lost her stirrups.

'Easy girl! Easy!' Desperately Thea tried to soothe the little mare, but her efforts were sabotaged by the enormous clap of thunder which rent the air.

Utterly terrified, the bay kicked up her heels and bolted. Unable to maintain her precarious seat, Thea was thrown clear.

'Guinevere! Come back!' Bruised and winded, Thea watched the mare disappear into the curtain of rain. 'Damn!'

Gingerly Thea ran a hand over her limbs and sent up an inward prayer of thanks that nothing appeared to be broken.

She staggered to her feet. It was going to be a long walk home!

Out on the headland the wind was even stronger, whipping the rain into a stinging lash that bit into any exposed skin. Thea dipped her head to try and protect her face.

Still feeling giddy from her fall, Thea struggled on, her vision obscured and her senses confused by the appalling weather. Unwittingly she began to stray closer and closer to the road's edge, where the surface was loose and crumbly.

'No-o-o-o!' The scream was torn from her throat as a section of friable soil, further weakened by the torrential rain, gave way beneath her, pitching her forward over the edge of the cliff.

Gareth was cleaning his pistol in the gun-room ready for the night ahead when Owen came rushing in.

'Her ladyship's mare has just come home. Alone.'

Gareth dropped the pistol on to the table, his colour changing to a deathly pallor.

'No sign of her at all?' he rapped.

Owen shook his head.

Gareth thought furiously for a moment. He could guess what had occurred. His stomach lurched. There was only one answer.

'Send Dai to the village with a message. I am cancelling the attack. Tell Dai to bring any volunteers he can find back here.'

'My. . .my lord?'

'Damn it, you heard me! I need men now! We must mount a search party to find my wife. Y Cadno can wait.'

Owen swallowed his objections. The Viscount knew better than anyone how much effort had gone into tonight's plan. Now it was all to be wasted, just because a slip of a girl had foolishly ignored his advice!

'I'll ride along the headland and see if I can find any trace of her. If I don't have any luck, I'll meet you back here.'

Owen nodded. 'Yes, my lord.'

Gareth threw him a smile over his shoulder as he headed for the door. 'Never fear. We'll break Y Cadno's power next time.' His smile faded and was replaced by an expression of steely determination. 'But for now my wife's safety must come first.'

A feeling of sick dizziness assaulted Thea, and she quickly closed her terrified eyes.

Don't look down! Don't think about falling! Concentrate!

A gorse bush growing just below the edge had saved her. She had grabbed at it as she had begun to fall and now hung suspended against the rocky slope.

Her leather riding-gloves protected her hands but the strain on her arms was intolerable. Cautiously her boots scrabbled to find a toe-hold. With a gasp of relief she discovered a jutting ledge in the sandstone.

Better able to support her weight, she rested for a few moments. The frantic rhythm of her pulse slowed, and as her panic susbsided she realised what she had to do.

Slowly, praying that nothing would shift loose under the strain, she began to pull herself up, bracing her feet against the rock until all of her upper body was supported by the bush and she was free to lift her arms.

She could just reach the broken edge of the cliff. Inch by inch, her outstretched hands searched for a solid purchase on the loose soil.

Tears of frustration mingled with the rain soaking her cheeks. There was nothing!

Then, after what seemed an eternity, her seeking fingers found a knob of rock which didn't move. Hopefully, Thea tugged harder.

It was safe. With a sob of thanksgiving, Thea gripped it tight and, using her feet to give her extra impetus, managed at last to pull herself up.

She lay there for a long time on the sodden turf, shaking with fright and exhaustion. Gradually her breathing slowed to normal and she pushed herself up into a sitting position.

Her luck had held. She had lost her hat but the stout broadcloth of her riding-habit had protected her. Apart from a few scratches she was unhurt!

A second realisation occurred to her. The rainstorm had stopped and the sky was clearing.

What was the time? Thea wondered if anyone knew yet that Guinevere had thrown her.

She couldn't wait here in the hope that someone would come to rescue her. She was wet through, and now that the crisis was over she was aware of how chilled her body was becoming.

She stood up and brushed off her skirts. What she needed was a long hot bath to ward off any ill and a restorative glass of brandy!

As she turned to go she cast an automatic glance out to sea and froze.

The ship she had seen earlier was now anchored in the little cove directly below! What was more, a rowing-boat was rapidly approaching the shore.

Had they seen her? Thea didn't think so, but she dropped down on to her stomach to make herself less visible.

Knowing it was folly to remain, she still couldn't tear herself away. They must be smugglers. Was she going to catch a glimpse of the mysterious Y Cadno?

A man and a woman stepped out on to the sands. They were talking. The sound carried clearly, but Thea could not understand what they were saying.

The words were Welsh, but with a sense of icy shock Thea recognised their voices.

A strange paralysis seemed to grip her limbs.

With all her strength she fought it, and concentrated on straining her eyes to see the pair better.

A tiny, involuntary cry of revulsion escaped her.

Almost as if she had heard it, the woman far below lifted up her head, revealing her glowing hair and perfect features.

Numb, Thea watched her link arms with her broad-shouldered companion and say something.

His rich laughter rang out and he smiled as he bent to kiss her.

There was no mistake!

Even as she whispered his name a roaring darkness swooped down over Thea, snuffing out the hateful sight.

'Thea! *Annwyl Crist*, Thea!'

The sound of his familiar voice was the first thing that impinged upon her consciousness. Almost simultaneously, she realised that she must have fainted.

'Thea, can you hear me?'

Her eyelids fluttered open. She was back in her own room, warm and dry in her own bed, and Gareth was bending over her, a look of anxious concern on his handsome face.

'Thank God. I thought for a moment... Well, never mind what I thought.' Gareth gave a shaky laugh and stretched out a hand to her. 'How do you feel, *cariad*?'

'Don't touch me!' Her scream split the air as she jerked away from his caress.

Gareth gazed at her in alarm. 'Thea?' He withdrew his hand. 'What is the matter?'

'You lying hypocrite!' Thea forced the words out between clenched teeth.

The pain in her heart was even sharper than the stinging of her various cuts and bruises.

'Thea, I don't understand——'

'Don't lie! I saw you!' Thea knew that she was shrieking like a fishwife, but she didn't care. 'I was there. I saw you kiss Nerys Parry.'

'I think your fall from Guinevere must have deranged your wits.' His thunderstruck expression looked so genuine that in other circumstances Thea might have been tempted to believe it.

'No!' She shook her head angrily at him. 'You were in the cove. You got out of a rowing-boat. With her.'

'Thea, I was here at the castle until I went searching for you.' Gareth hid his perturbation at her revealing remarks and willed her to listen to him. 'When I found you I brought you straight back home. I haven't been anywhere near that beach.'

'And I suppose there was no ship in the bay?'

For a fraction of a second he hesitated.

It was enough.

'You must think me a fool,' Thea said in a tight voice. 'Did you really imagine you could persuade me it was all a dream? I know what I saw!' She shivered. 'You were with that woman.'

'I don't know what you are talking about!' Gareth attempted to sound convincing.

She met his uneasy gaze with a look of contempt.

'There is no need to keep on pretending. It doesn't matter any more.' Tears sparkled in her eyes and she dashed them angrily aside with the back of her hand. 'You aren't interested in making a success of our marriage. You are still in love with Nerys Parry.'

'How dare you suggest such a thing, Thea?' Gareth's temper, already exacerbated by anxiety for her well-being and the frustration of his scheme to curb Y Cadno, began to fray.

'I dare because it's the truth. Why else would you meet her in secret?' She gave a wild laugh. 'What irony that you should tie yourself down in a loveless trap when you would have been free to wed her if only you had waited!'

He stared at her. 'Is that what you think? That I

regret marrying you?' He shook his head incredulously. '*Duw*, don't you realise how I feel about you?'

The little remaining colour fled Thea's cheeks.

'Be silent, sir!' she gasped.

'Damn you, woman, I've been silent long enough!' Gareth took a deep, ragged breath. 'I am not at liberty to explain about the Fox, but that doesn't mean I want to marry Nerys Parry!'

'You were in love with her,' Thea accused him.

'Will it make you feel better if I admit it?' Gareth demanded roughly. 'Very well. I was besotted. I made a complete and utter fool of myself over her.'

Thea shuddered, hating to hear John Morgan's words confirmed.

'But that was nine years ago, when I was too young and inexperienced to see beyond a pretty face.' His eyes were bleak. 'I don't like talking about it—not because I still hanker after Nerys, but because I am ashamed of what I did. I hurt a good man with my selfish folly.'

'I see.' Thea's voice wobbled. Could she have been mistaken? She had good eyesight, but the pair had been a long way off.

'I hope so.' Gareth's stiff expression softened, and his tone was as gentle as a caress as he continued. 'I know it is difficult, but please trust me.'

Thea bit her lower lip to still its trembling.

'I don't want her, Thea. I want you. I want you to stay here.'

Thea promptly burst into tears.

Appalled, Gareth sat down on the bed and took her firmly into his arms. '*Paid a llefain*. Don't cry, *cariad*.'

Feebly Thea tried to shake him off, but he refused to let her go.

'Stop this nonsense,' he said, with all the authority at his command. 'You'll make yourself ill.'

'You are detestable,' Thea hiccuped. 'Let go of me. I hate you.'

'No, you don't,' he retorted, and, tipping up her chin with a ruthless hand, kissed her.

Thea wanted to resist, but the touch of his lips set her afire. The leaping flame of desire that burned in her whenever he was near exploded, sending delicious shock waves reverberating throughout her entire body.

She closed her eyes, surrendering herself to the magic, and a thousand rainbows coruscated behind her lids. Her bones melting, she pressed closer to him. Instantly he deepened the kiss, and her lips parted beneath his. Their breath mingled and she felt him shudder.

Aeons later, he raised his dark head.

'*Annwyl Crist*!'

To Thea's dismay, he released her and leapt to his feet.

'Gareth?' Bewildered, Thea stared at him.

Damning his half-brother to hell, Gareth shook his head and moved to a safer distance.

'I should never have brought you here,' he muttered wildly. 'I must have been out of my mind to suggest such a crazy scheme!'

He took a deep, ragged breath and regained control of himself. 'Forgive me. I had no right to. . .to bother you, when you must be longing to rest after your ordeal. I shall call Blodwen. Dr Pugh will be here any moment.'

All of Thea's angry doubts and confusion came rushing back.

He had denied visiting the Cwrt too. But he had never offered her a convincing explanation for that incident either.

'You ask me to trust you, but how can I?' she demanded as he turned to go. 'You won't tell me the truth, and you shut me out if ever we begin to get close. What is it that you are afraid of?'

He halted, trying not to show how much her blunt observation had shaken him. 'If you still doubt my word, you can ask Owen,' he muttered.

'Why? He would lie through his teeth if he thought you wanted him to.'

Her uncharacteristic cynicism made him wince.

Thea shook her head. 'Anyway, this isn't just about today.'

She tried not to remember the sweetness of his kiss. The thought that he might have tried to manipulate her deliberately was unbearable!

'You do not share your thoughts with me, Gareth. You keep secrets, and exclude me from large areas of your life. Husbands and wives are supposed to help each other. I know you are worried about something, but you refuse to let me get close to you.'

'I regret that you feel excluded.' There was a note of barely concealed frustration in Gareth's voice. 'But for the moment all I can do is repeat that I will tell you everything as soon as I am free to do so.'

She stared at him uncertainly, longing to believe him.

'I'm sorry.' His handsome face twisted into a rueful grimace. 'Nothing has turned out how I imagined it would since I proposed to you.'

In the silence which followed this enigmatic remark Thea could hear her pulse hammering.

What should she do?

Gareth watched her, trying to appear cool, but as the silence stretched on his expression grew bleak.

'If you wish to leave Castell Mynach, you must do so. The six months' trial we agreed is not yet up, but that need not make any difference to the terms I promised you.'

Thea was torn. Her mind and her heart seemed to be pulling her in two opposing directions.

'Do you truly wish me to stay?' she whispered at last.

He nodded.

A tiny sigh escaped her. 'Then I shall try to have faith in you for a little longer.'

'Thank you.' His deep voice vibrated with passion.

'But this is the last time I will give you the benefit of the doubt, Gareth Rhayadar. If I find you have been lying to me—'

'You won't,' he asserted.

Looking into the dark eyes which burned into hers, Thea prayed that her decision was the right one.

It was perhaps inevitable, Thea thought, that she should catch a chill after her soaking. Forced to keep to her bed for the next few days, she had plenty of time to mull over all that had occurred since she had arrived at Castell Mynach.

Unfortunately it proved impossible to apply a compress of cold logic to her tangled feelings. All she was sure of was that she loved Gareth, which left her little option but to be patient and hope for the best.

On Thursday, the day before the party, she got up.

'I am perfectly all right,' she told Blodwen, ordering her to lay out the sprigged muslin morning-gown.

Gareth had already breakfasted and left the house, but Cati was delighted to see her.

They spent the morning quietly, enjoying an hour in the music-room before lunch.

'I think I shall go for a swim,' Cati announced, soon after the light meal was over. 'You don't mind, do you, Thea?'

'Of course not!' Thea laughed. 'I know you like plenty of exercise. I don't feel quite up to joining you, but there is no need for you to stay indoors just to keep me company.'

'Actually, it is more a case of wishing to avoid Nerys Parry,' Cati answered, her young face turning grim.

'*She* is coming here?'

Cati nodded. 'Mother told me last night. To be honest, I don't think she was very pleased, but apparently Nerys more or less invited herself.'

Thea was puzzled. 'I thought your mother was keen to ensure her friendship and avoid any possible gossip?'

'I suppose so.' Cati shrugged. 'At least, I know she visited the Cwrt last week, but she doesn't want Nerys to come here.' A wicked little chuckle escaped her. 'She is trying to keep Gareth sweet, you see. He is furious that she has invited Nerys to this party.'

Thea's pretty mouth compressed to a thin line. *She* hadn't written out an invitation to Lady Parry!

Angharad's deviousness was the final spur.

'I shan't stay and entertain her either,' she declared. 'The less I see of that lady the better!'

Thea returned to her room after Cati had gone, but she was too restless to read or settle to her needlework.

She rang for Blodwen and asked her if her riding-habit was fit for use.

'I cleaned it myself.' The little maid nodded. 'And Mam mended that rip in the skirt. It looks like new again.'

'Good. I want to go riding.'

'Do you think you should, my lady?'

Thea smiled reassuringly at her. 'When you fall off a horse, Blodwen, you have to get back on again as soon as you can. Otherwise you risk losing your nerve.'

When Thea was ready Blodwen asked if she would like her to press the eau-de-nil silk.

About to point out that there was no hurry, since the party wasn't until tomorrow night, Thea paused. It would be the first time that her young maid had dressed her for an important occasion.

'What an excellent idea! We don't want to be on the last minute. Thank you, Blodwen.'

Leaving Blodwen cheerfully humming a tune, Thea made her way downstairs and met Gareth in the ancient passageway.

'I didn't know you were home,' she murmured, trying to still the rush of excitement that his presence always induced in her.

'I got back about twenty minutes ago. I was just coming up to see you.' Gareth smiled at her. 'But I fancy there is no need for me to ask you how are feeling. You are looking very well today.'

He suddenly noticed what she was wearing and his expression changed. 'You mean to ride? Is that wise?'

She chuckled at his anxiety. 'Heavens, I'm not ill. I have had enough of moping in my room, thank you!'

'But the doctor said——'

'Come now, from what Cati tells me you never listened to a word of Pugh's advice when you were recuperating after Trafalgar.'

He grinned. '*Touché*!'

Thea began to walk on and he fell in by her side.

'Why did you never tell me you took part in that battle?' she asked, unable to curb her curiosity.

He shrugged, faintly embarrassed. 'The occasion didn't arise.'

Thea raised her brows in polite disbelief.

'All right.' Gareth gave in. 'I thought you might consider it boastful if I talked of how I came by my wound.'

Thea quickly denied it.

'Serving under Lord Nelson was a great honour. I admired him tremendously.'

Thea nodded and then gasped in dismay. 'You must have thought Grandmama most disrespectful!'

He grasped her meaning at once, and laughed.

'Not in the least. I have only admiration for Master Pug. Without his aid I should never have made your acquaintance that day.'

Thea coloured and hastily said, 'I received a letter from Grandmama today. You will never guess! Georgy is to marry Mr Harley.'

Gareth raised his brows. 'Not a duke?'

Thea grinned. 'He is a very pleasant young man. Grandmama wants us to attend the betrothal party. Do you think we can?'

'When is it to be?'

'The sixth of June.'

Gareth nodded. 'I don't see why not.'

With luck, his lawyers would have concluded their enquiries by then, and he would have a better idea of where he stood. In any event, it wasn't fair to deprive Thea of the treat. She asked for so little and he wanted to give her so much!

They had reached the hallway, and Thea reluctantly prepared to say goodbye.

'May I come riding with you?' Gareth swiftly forestalled her. 'You ought not to go alone.'

There was an odd, urgent insistence in his tone, but Thea barely noticed it in the wave of pleasure that swept over her.

'I should like that,' she replied, rejoicing in this proof that he still wanted her company.

During her recent illness they had spent little time together. Thea had wondered if he was being scrupulous in observing the doctor's advice not to tire her or whether it betokened something more sinister.

'I missed our long conversations,' she murmured. Her suspicions had been unnecessary, and the relief made her feel like singing.

Gareth smiled at her with engaging warmth. 'Then let's not waste another moment,' he said, tucking her hand into the crook of his elbow and ushering her out into the mild sunshine.

On her return, Thea went straight to the tower to change out of her riding-habit, and she knew that something was wrong even before she reached her room. Blodwen's lamentations could be heard all the way up the winding stairs.

'Oh, my lady!' The maid let out a wail as she entered, and pointed helplessly towards the bed.

'Dear God!' Blankly Thea stared at the ruin of her favourite dress.

She picked it up. The eau-de-nil gown had been slashed. Great rents had been ripped in the delicate silk. The bodice hung together by a shred and the skirt was scored with a dozen long cuts.

'I left it on the bed after I had ironed it. When I came back a few minutes ago I found it like this,' Blodwen sobbed.

'Please stop crying, Blodwen. I don't blame you,' Thea said, dropping the gown back on to the bed.

Now that the first shock was wearing off, she was aware of a tremendous rage building up inside her.

'Do you have any idea who could have done this?'

'No. . .no, my lady,' the maid stammered, blotting her eyes with the edge of her apron.

'These cuts must have been made with a knife, or perhaps. . .'

Thea's glance strayed to her workbox, which she had left by the window. It was open.

'The perpetrator used these,' she said, picking up her sharp scissors. 'Look, you can still see a few green threads caught in the blades.'

Thoughtfully she replaced the scissors. She had made no secret of her intention to wear this particular gown for the party, but try as she might she couldn't think of anyone who would do such a thing.

'Have you heard anyone complaining about me?'

Blodwen scrubbed her wet face and shook her head in answer to this abrupt demand.

Thea bit her lip. 'I cannot imagine. . .' She paused as a new and unwelcome thought struck her, and then continued hesitantly, 'Did my mother-in-law come upstairs?'

'Not so far as I know. Lady Parry arrived about an hour ago, and her ladyship rang for a bottle of best sherry.' Blodwen's round brown eyes grew even rounder as the significance of Thea's question sank in. 'You don't think Lady Angharad did it?'

'No, no, of course not.' Thea closed the lid of her workbox with a snap.

Angharad disliked her, and she could be petty, but Thea didn't believe she would stoop so low. Besides, it was in her interest for Thea to look smart at this party.

'It is a mystery. One, furthermore, I see no point in

pursuing.' Thea swept the green silk up into a bundle. 'Please dispose of this. Discreetly, mind. I don't want a word of this leaking out.'

Blodwen took it and nodded obediently.

'Good girl.' Thea smiled at her, mentally reviewing her remaining evening-gowns.

None were suitable, and there wasn't time for Madame Duroc to create a new one, but she had seen something in Cati's wardrobe which she might be able to adapt.

Thea gritted her teeth. She wasn't going to let her unknown enemy beat her. She'd had lots of experience in refurbishing old gowns to make them seem new.

Determination filled her. By hook or by crook, she was going to be the belle of the ball and make Gareth proud of her!

CHAPTER ELEVEN

THE knock came at the door just as Blodwen laid down the hairbrush.

'You may answer it,' Thea murmured, admiring the results of her maid's handiwork in the dressing-table mirror. The high knot of upswept curls Blodwen had wrought gave her a look of elegance.

'It is his lordship.' Breathless with importance, Blodwen came hurrying back to report that the master of Castell Mynach desired admittance to his wife's bedchamber.

Excitement welled up inside Thea's chest. 'Let him in.'

She rose to her feet as Blodwen opened the door with a flourish.

'Good evening. I hope I am not intruding——'

Abruptly, Gareth fell silent.

He had been expecting to see her in the pale green dress he liked, but she had on a new gown. It was one he hadn't seen before, but it surpassed all her others. Why it should be so he didn't know, for it was only a simple sheath of white satin, with a band of gold set near the hem to match the fluttering ribbons tied at the high waist.

Perhaps it was the way in which the heavy, supple fabric clung with fluid elegance to her slender curves, or the daringly low round neckline and the tiny puff-sleeves which emphasised her white shoulders and graceful arms. Whatever, it suited her to perfection!

The admiration in his dark eyes was as heady as wine, and Thea felt triumph surge along her veins.

She had ruthlessly stripped a dozen blue lace roses and every inch of trimming from a dress donated by

Cati, who had promised to keep a still tongue in her head.

Thea knew she was taking a gamble, but she did not want Gareth to learn what had happened. He had enough in his dish to worry him. Fortunately her judgement had proved correct. Once the over-fussy decoration was off, an elegant dress had been revealed.

It had, however, been too short. She had overcome that problem by letting down the generous hem and hiding the mark under a band of gold satin ribbon, painstakingly attached with tiny, near-invisible stitches. Matching gold streamers to define the high waist had added the final touch.

It had been a lot of hard work, but Gareth's reaction made it all worthwhile!

Thea nodded dismissal to her maid. 'Thank you, Blodwen. That will be all. You need not wait up for me.'

Blodwen bobbed a curtsy. 'Goodnight, my lady. Goodnight, sir. I hope you enjoy the party.'

They barely noticed her go.

'You look beautiful,' Gareth said, with a directness that brought a swift rush of colour into Thea's cheeks.

She watched him advance towards her and her heart began to hammer against her ribcage. It required considerable effort to speak in her usual calm manner. 'I take it you came to see if I was ready to go downstairs?'

He nodded. 'Also, I wanted to give you this.'

He held out a flat velvet jewel-case to her.

'The Rhayadar ruby, I assume?' She took it from him with a hand that shook slightly.

Again he nodded, and Thea was very conscious of him watching her as she opened the case.

'It is magnificent!' She stared at the pendant in awe. She had never seen a ruby so large. It lay against its bed of white velvet like an enormous blood-red tear-drop, suspended from an intricate web of gold.

Gareth noted that although she wore the pretty pair

of gold earrings which had been her grandmother's wedding gift, she had left her neck bare.

He tore his gaze away from the enticing valley between her breasts, revealed by her daring *décolletage*. 'Will you wear it for me?'

Thea lifted her eyes to meet his and nodded, not trusting herself to speak.

'Then turn around, *cariad*, and I will fasten it for you.'

His fingers were warm, but Thea shivered. She could only hope that he would think she found the metal cold.

Carefully Gareth slipped the pendant around her throat, glad that he didn't have to contend with any loose curls. It was all he could do to stop his hands from shaking! Resisting the almost overwhelming urge to press his lips against the tender skin of her nape, he finally managed to close the fastening.

'There. How does that feel?'

'Quite secure, thank you.' Her voice came out as a faint whisper, and died altogether when his hands slid down to clasp her bare shoulders.

'Thea.' Slowly Gareth turned her round to face him.

He could feel her trembling. With all his heart he longed to kiss her, but he sternly reminded himself of his vow.

Until he knew whether or not Vaughn was lying, he would not touch Thea or reveal his feelings. Should he be declared bastard, he would have nothing to offer her. He had no right to be so selfish!

Instead, he held out his arm to her with courteous formality. 'If you are ready, we had better go down. It won't do to be late for our own celebration.'

Thea hid her disappointment. For an instant, she had been sure. . . But it was foolish of her! She must strive to be more patient!

Taking a deep breath, she touched the ruby pendant for reassurance. 'I am ready.'

She placed her fingers upon his dark-coated sleeve

and smiled a little nervously. 'Or, at least, as ready as I'll ever be!'

The crimson salon was full. Beneath a blaze of wax candles, the mild evening air eddied to the sound of laughter and conversation. Music played gently in the background, provided by the quartet hired from Swansea, and smartly clad servants circulated with Gareth's best champagne.

'A most enjoyable party, Lady Rhayadar.' Colonel Secombe beamed at his hostess. 'And I must congratulate you on the improvement in young Miss Cati.'

'Indeed, my dear, I hardly recognised her.' Mrs Secombe, a plump woman in her fifties, chimed in. 'What a difference a new hairstyle and a pretty dress makes. You must be very proud. Angharad told us it was all your doing.'

She ran an approving eye over Thea's slim figure.

'You have excellent taste, if I may say so. I don't think I have ever seen a more elegant gown than the one you are wearing.'

'Thank you.' Thea hid her amusement.

Another couple came up to them, and Thea concentrated on making pleasant small talk.

She was the focus of attention. Everyone, it seemed, wanted to speak to the Viscount's new bride. Since the purpose of this party had been to introduce her to the cream of local society Thea knew that it was unreasonable of her to resent their interest, but as the evening wore on she found herself longing for them all to go home.

Eventually she achieved a moment's respite, and heaved a sigh of relief. Her jaw was aching from so much smiling!

'Hard going, isn't it?' Cati appeared at her elbow, an enchanting figure in her delicate coral gown. 'Never mind, it will soon be over.'

'Hush! Someone will hear you.' Thea shook her

head reprovingly, but her grey eyes lit up with amusement.

'Look, Mrs Price-Williams has cornered Gareth. She is the biggest gossip in the district. They say she talked her first husband to death.'

Thea gave up. She let Cati's wicked comments flow over her head and tried without success not to follow Gareth's athletic figure with her eyes.

'Catari. You are neglecting our guests. Go and speak to Mrs Pritchard.' The Dowager swept up to them, impressive in dark bronze taffeta and diamonds.

Reluctantly Cati obeyed, and her mother turned to Thea.

'We shall have to order supper to be served. We cannot delay any longer. Where can Nerys have got to?'

Thea, who had been extremely pleased by Lady Parry's dilatoriness, merely shrugged. 'I shan't mind if she doesn't turn up at all.'

'Facetious remarks do not help, Thea!' The Dowager frowned. 'People will notice her absence. I don't want them gossiping.'

Thea forced herself to smooth her mother-in-law's ruffled feathers. She didn't want a quarrel, and it was obvious that Angharad was in one of her difficult moods.

Part of the trouble, Thea suspected, was that the Dowager hadn't liked relinquishing her claim on the Rhayadar ruby. She had given a start of surprise on seeing it clasped around Thea's neck, although Gareth had assured Thea that he had given her fair warning of what he meant to do.

It was equally plain that she didn't enjoy seeing Thea the centre of attention. She was not the kind of woman who was happy to take second place. Until this moment the difficulty had not arisen, since Thea had taken care not to challenge her position, but she guessed that the reaction of their guests had forcibly reminded Angharad that it was Thea, and not herself, who was the mistress of Castle Mynach.

It was a problem Thea did not wish to address tonight, and she was relieved when a stir at the door distracted her mother-in-law's attention.

Turning to see who this late arrival could be, Thea sucked in her breath.

Nerys Parry stood on the threshold, looking utterly magnificent in a gown of jade silk that clung daringly to her lush curves. Emeralds blazed around her neck and in her ears, and her red hair had been dressed in artful curls.

Thea tried not to feel envious, but a sense of depression crept over her. She couldn't compete with such dazzling beauty and she knew it!

The hazel eyes swept the room and found Gareth.

Thea watched her head straight for his side, virtually ignoring the greeting of her acquaintance. Regardless of the fact that his wife stood only a few feet away, Nerys was making it plain that she had time for no one else.

She knows he won't be rude to her—not while she is a guest under his roof! thought Thea.

Thea didn't think she had ever witnessed such shameless behaviour. In spite of his thunderous expression, Nerys was fluttering her long eyelashes and hanging on to Gareth's arm as if she had every right to do so!

Angharad gave a little moan. 'Oh, dear God!'

A spurt of anger gave Thea the strength to shake off the stupefaction which had gripped her. Giving a curt nod to her mother-in-law, she crossed the intervening space and coolly interrupted the tête-à-tête.

'Good evening. I trust my husband is making you welcome, ma'am.'

Lady Parry swung round. 'Ah, Thea!' she smiled. 'What a pretty dress. So sweetly simple!'

'Thank you.' Thea responded with politeness, but

she was not deceived. The husky voice had dripped mockery.

'Do you know, I expected to see you wearing green?' Lady Parry indicated her own gossamer skirts. 'Like myself. I'm sure Angharad said eau-de-nil.'

Thea's eyes narrowed in sudden concentration. The dazzling lights, the music and the hum of conversation all around her faded into the distance as an incredible suspicion swam to the surface of her mind.

Inhaling sharply, she dismissed it. She must not let dislike prejudice her!

'I changed my mind.'

'But white?' Nerys made a little moue of distaste. 'Take my advice, my dear. Next time leave that choice to schoolgirls like Cati. Married ladies ought to wear something a little more sophisticated.'

Thea struggled to think of a suitably cutting reply, but it was Gareth who answered.

'My wife looks attractive whatever she wears,' he said bluntly.

Nerys's bright smile wavered. 'You always did have simple tastes,' she snapped.

Thea flashed her husband a wry look, and received a grin that made her spirits rise.

'I am most impressed by this gathering.' Her smile firmly pinned back in place, Nerys changed the subject, waving one bejewelled hand about her. 'You've managed to lure everyone of any consequence here tonight. A very worthy feat, my dear.'

'I imagine it was achieved through curiosity rather than cleverness,' Thea replied crisply, refusing to acknowledge an undeserved compliment.

Nerys gave a brittle little laugh. 'I don't think your wife likes parties, Gareth.'

'Perhaps she is fussy about the company she keeps.'

His dark gaze met hers with unmistakable hostility, and Thea saw how Nerys paled.

Had she finally realised that he didn't want her here?

A flicker of reluctant sympathy stirred in Thea, only to die as Nerys took up the challenge.

'One should indeed be careful of the company one keeps! So many people of low birth are infiltrating society these days.'

Thea gasped, and Nerys lifted a hand to her mouth in a gesture of mock contrition.

'Oh, I'm sorry! Did you think I was referring to you, Thea? Actually, I had in mind someone else. Someone whose birth is even less respectable than yours.'

She stared straight at Gareth, and her voice acquired a venomous sweetness.

'You do agree that bastards ought to be excluded from a party such as this, don't you, Gareth?'

Thea saw how his broad shoulders tensed, and realised that there were undercurrents here which she did not understand.

Nerys gave a pretty tinkling laugh. 'What a pity you didn't invite Vaughn. He would have made the gathering complete.'

'That's enough!' Gareth flushed with anger.

Before Thea could ask what was wrong he took the titian-haired beauty by the arm.

'Pray excuse us for a few moments, Thea,' he said grimly.

'Gareth! Supper is about to begin!'

To her dismay he ignored her protest and swept out of the room, bearing Nerys off with him.

Numerous pairs of eyes followed their progress, and several heads turned inquisitively in Thea's direction, forcing her to school her expression hastily.

Strolling over to rejoin Angharad, Thea exuded absolute unconcern, but inside her heart was racing with nervous apprehension.

'I know everything!' Nerys screeched. 'Vaughn told me himself. You had better give him what he wants before everyone else learns the truth.'

Secure in the knowledge that the thick library walls

would defeat any chance eavesdropper, Gareth decided to put an end to her interference in his life for once and for all.

'My affairs are none of your concern, but since you are so interested let me tell you that Vaughn will get nothing from me. Nothing. Not the ruby. Not another penny piece.' He smiled grimly. 'I am going to take him to court and force his lies down his throat.'

'You are mad. Don't you know what will happen?' Nerys flung out her hands in a dramatic gesture. 'Those marriage-lines are genuine. I have seen them.'

Gareth shrugged. 'Perhaps.'

'He will destroy you!'

Gareth laughed. 'What a loss the stage suffered when you decided to marry my godfather instead of treading the boards,' he murmured silkily.

Nerys flushed beneath her *maquillage*.

'You will regret that insult,' she grated. 'I have influence over Vaughn. Influence I can use for your good. . .or your downfall!'

'The only thing I regret is that I was ever fool enough to imagine you the innocent you pretended,' he retorted, growing angry in spite of himself.

'What heat, *bach*.' Venom infused her sweet tone. 'Do you know, it makes me wonder if underneath all this spleen you wish you had bedded me when you had the chance?' She tilted her head sideways and surveyed him through narrowed eyes, a provocative smile curving her red mouth.

He said nothing, and, mistaking his silence, she laughed softly—a breathy thread of sound.

'You see. You may profess to dislike me but I know it isn't true.' She glided towards him and held out her arms with sinuous grace. 'You still desire me, my love. Admit it!'

'I hesitate to call you a liar, ma'am,' Gareth replied with exquisite mockery. 'But I wouldn't touch you with a ten-foot oar.'

Nerys came to an abrupt halt, her smile dissolving into an expression of furious incredulity.

'Do you really think I will forget how you falsely accused me of rape? Or how unhappy you made Owen? He deserved better!'

'And you, of course, were totally blameless,' she retorted, her hazel eyes mocking him.

'At least I knew my behaviour was wrong!' For an instant Gareth's flinty calm deserted him. 'I tried to make amends—but you. . .! I've never heard you express one iota of remorse for the heartbreak we caused him.'

'Why should I? For God's sake, he was an old man when he married me! What did he expect?'

'A little loyalty, perhaps?' Gareth's tone was cutting.

Anger twisted her lovely face. 'Oh, what does it matter? I never meant to hurt him, but he was a fool.' She shrugged carelessly. 'Anyway, it all happened long ago. I see no point in quarrelling over it now. Let the whole business stay in the past, where it belongs.'

'I should be glad to. I'd prefer my folly dead and buried, exactly like the feelings I once cherished for you.' He looked her straight in the eye. 'I despise you, Nerys. You have the soul of a whore. Vaughn is welcome to you.'

Nerys sucked in a mouthful of air. 'You. . .you bastard!' She whirled on her heel, but at the door she paused and threw him a look of loathing. 'You'll pay for this, Gareth Rhayadar. Until now I've tried to restrain Vaughn—but no longer!'

'Just go, Nerys, and don't come back. You are no longer welcome in this house.'

The door slammed shut and Gareth took a deep breath.

It had probably been foolish to make an open enemy of her, since she had taken up with Vaughn, but by God he had no regrets. The bitterness he had carried in his heart all these years seemed to have dissolved.

He felt clean again, now that the tie which had once bound them was irrevocably cut.

Clean and ready to find Thea. He owed her an apology.

He also owed her an explanation.

As soon as their guests left tonight, he would ask his mother to release him from his promise of silence. If she protested he would point out that Nerys would almost certainly let the cat out of the bag.

It was time to face the truth.

The winding stair yawned blackly before her, and Thea hesitated. Torn between the need to follow her quarry and nervousness, she almost waited too long. When she began her descent the light given off by the bobbing candle in the distance was already fading, swallowed up by the darkness which engulfed the ancient tower.

Hurry. Hurry. Or she would lose them.

Only the faint sound of their footsteps broke the silence. Thea was wearing dainty flat-heeled satin slippers. She was sure they would not hear her, but the chill from the cold stone struck up through her thin soles like a knife.

That's why I'm shivering, she told herself, but she knew it for a lie.

She felt for the next step. The light had vanished. They must have reached the bottom. If she didn't hurry the entrance to the secret tunnel would close after them and she would never find the catch. Not without a light to guide her.

If only there had been time to snatch up a lantern, but she had acted on impulse. She hadn't expected to see Nerys when she had gone upstairs on the pretext of tidying her hair. She had needed a moment's solitude, and had hastily excused herself before the Dowager could protest.

Too surprised to call out a challenge, she had watched Nerys head for the bridge which led to the tower, and curiosity had taken a powerful hold of her senses. The older woman had not seen her.

Thea had followed. . .and had received a devastating shock.

'*Cariad*, you are early!'

Thea had come to a cautious halt, but not before she had seen Nerys cast herself into the arms of the broad-shouldered figure who stood by the stairs.

It was too dark for Thea to make out his features—she was too far away. But there was no mistaking the passionate nature of the kiss they exchanged, or the man's distinctive deep voice.

'Come, *fy llwynoges*, we had better wait a while longer. I want to be sure they are all at supper.'

Sick disgust rose in Thea's throat. John Morgan had been wrong. He had forgiven her after all.

For an instant she had been tempted to turn away, to return to her room and pack her belongings, but curiosity had been too strong. Before she left Castell Mynach forever, she wanted to confront her husband and ask him why he had lied.

Crushing the bitter hurt which had threatened to overwhelm her, she had found the courage to follow them. But now, as she reached the final turn of the stairs, her luck ran out. In the inky blackness her foot overshot the last step, and with an involuntary cry of alarm she tripped and landed on her knees.

'What was that?'

She heard Nerys call out and struggled frantically to regain her feet—but it was no use.

'*Crist*!' Hard hands hauled her upright.

'You! You have a talent for poking your nose in where it isn't wanted, my dear Lady Rhayadar.' The husky voice dripped mockery in the darkness.

Thea waited with bated breath. It was too dark to see his expression. Was he going to let his mistress insult her? Surely he cared enough to offer her a word of comfort?

His silence destroyed this last hope, and she closed her eyes to force back the tears which threatened.

Nerys became brisk. 'We'll have to take her with us. We can't risk her giving the alarm before we are ready to make our entrance.'

Still drowning in an ocean of despair, Thea kept her eyelids tightly shut and sensed rather than heard him agree. Oh, how could she have been such a fool as to believe in his sweet words even for a moment?

'I'll lead the way.' Nerys, who had set her candlestick down at a safe distance, picked it up again.

Released, Thea felt herself sway giddily. Taking a deep breath, she opened her eyes and fought off faintness.

'Move!' A rough shove propelled her towards the secret door.

A waft of cold air set the candle-flame dancing as they entered the tunnel, but it steadied once the door had swung shut, allowing Thea a glimpse of her new surroundings.

Within yards the dressed stone gave way to natural rock and the walls grew inward. Thea shivered, remembering the tons of earth pressing down above their heads, but her companions seemed oblivious. They did not seem to need the candlelight to show them where the roof dipped or the floor became uneven, but moved at a rapid pace she found hard to emulate.

Soon Thea could detect a new scent in the air—a fresher, saltier smell that warned her they must be approaching the end of the tunnel. Cati had said something about it leading into a cave above the beach. . .

They emerged into brightness, which came from several burning torches set around the rock walls. Their light revealed half a dozen or so rough-looking men standing or sitting on the sand-strewn floor.

A chorus of whistles and cat-calls greeted Thea when a final push thrust her forward. Dimly she wondered why Nerys's presence had occasioned no such reaction, but she was too busy wishing she wasn't wearing a low-cut gown to speculate.

'Quiet!' The voice behind her roared the order, and to Thea's astonishment they all fell silent.

'Well, now, and what are we to do with you, my fine lady?'

Suddenly Thea forgot her bruised knees and stubbed toes. Even the fierce ache from where she had banged her head against the roof of the tunnel ceased to exist.

His voice. Did it sound different, or was she going completely mad?

Slowly she turned round, the skin at the nape of her neck prickling with an almost superstitious dread.

The noise level in the crimson salon had risen as the level of wine in the bottles had sunk, and it was a very convivial scene which met Gareth's eye on his return. Swiftly he scanned the room, and a frown descended upon his brow.

Where the devil had Thea got to?

Spotting his sister talking to the Secombes, he sent her a discreet signal which quickly brought her to his side.

'Gareth! Mother is going frantic. She says supper will be completely——'

'Have you seen Thea?' he interrupted her ruthlessly.

Cati shook her head. 'Not since she went upstairs.'

'How long ago was that?'

'A few minutes—I'm not totally sure.' Cati's black eyebrows drew together. 'Is something wrong?'

'I hope not.' Gareth felt uneasy.

'It wouldn't be surprising if Thea is upset. You shouldn't have gone off like that with Nerys.'

Gareth curbed the blistering retort that sprang to his lips and acknowledged the remark with a curt inclination of his dark head. 'It was unavoidable.'

Cati glared at him. 'I thought you disliked her,' she accused him.

'If you must know, I detest the bloody woman,' he replied, much goaded.

'Then why—?'

'*Annwyl Crist*!' Gareth's temper snapped. 'She knows Vaughn has been blackmailing Mother.'

Cati's mouth fell open. 'Oh, I. . . I didn't know.'

This was neither the time nor the place to enlighten her. 'Don't worry, little sister. I'll deal with it.'

'I want to do something to help.'

Her anxious offer was interrupted by Howell, who came up to them to murmur discreetly that Owen wanted a word with the Viscount.

'Now?'

'He said it was very urgent, my lord.'

'I'm coming with you,' Cati declared, sensing trouble.

'No. Stay here.' Gareth could feel the knot of tension in him spiralling tighter.

'Gareth—'

'If you want to help tell Mother to order supper to be served immediately, and fob off any enquiries concerning my whereabouts.'

He strode from the room, leaving her staring after him, a rebellious expression on her narrow face.

'I see he did not tell you.'

Thea stared at him, speechless with astonishment. For an instant she wondered if she was asleep and dreaming.

He spoke again, in the voice that was almost but not quite Gareth's own, and the nightmare became real.

'Allow me to introduce myself. Vaughn Rhayadar at your service, ma'am. Otherwise known at Y Cadno.'

Thea swallowed hard to moisten her dry throat. 'You. . .you are Gareth's brother,' she croaked.

'Bravo, my lady.' He swept her a mocking bow and his men laughed.

Thea ignored them. 'It was you I saw riding to the Cwrt.'

'Aye.' He smiled, and the likeness to her husband was so strong that it made her gasp.

'And she—' Thea threw Nerys a look of dislike '—is your mistress.'

The pieces began to fall into place. It had been Vaughn she'd seen on that beach with Nerys—not her husband.

He laughed outright. 'How like a woman to think of that rather than ask how one such as myself comes to be related to the high and mighty Rhayadars.'

'I believe I can guess.' Thea had regained command of herself and she answered him with a cool disdain that set him frowning. 'You are the late Viscount's bastard.'

For an instant she thought he might strike her, but then he laughed in a harsh manner.

'What you think isn't important. I might even let you live once I have put an end to your husband and I am master of Castell Mynach.'

A cold shiver ran down Thea's spine. Now she knew who had arranged for that knife at the Druid's Circle!

'You will never succeed. Gareth will prevent it! He is worth a dozen of you!'

'Be silent!' Vaughn grabbed her roughly by the arm. 'Or I'll shut your mouth for good and all.'

'Wait, Vaughn.' Nerys broke her silence. 'She might be useful. We could use her as a hostage.'

'Good thinking, *llwynoges*.' Vaughn flung Thea away from him. 'My men can take her out to the ship while we make our announcement.'

'What are you planning?' Thea demanded, rubbing her sore arm.

'We are going to join the party.' Nerys wore a sneering smile, which deepened to wicked amusement as a pair of newcomers erupted noisily into the cave. 'Well, well. Another unexpected addition to our ranks.'

'Let go of me!' The girl was struggling and screaming. 'I hate you!'

'Cati!' Thea let out an appalled gasp.

The young man who held her sister-in-law tightly by the wrist dragged her towards Vaughn, speaking rapidly in Welsh.

Thea recognised him. It was Glyn Edwards.

'Judas!'

Her heart turned over with pity as Cati's shocked cry of revulsion filled the cavern. Vaughn's look of triumph and Cati's tearstained face provided an accurate translation of what Glyn had said.

'Tie her up and join the others. You have done well.' Vaughn handed him a rope.

Horrified, Thea watched him obey. Cati offered no resistance. She appeared half dazed, and collapsed into a sitting position against the wall when he had finished.

'Now I have two hostages!' Vaughn's tone was smug. 'What do you say now, my lady Viscountess?'

Thea wasn't listening to him. Her sharp ears had caught the sound of someone shouting.

The noise of a gun firing alerted the others.

'What the——?' Vaughn swung round with a look of surprise.

Sounds of fighting drifted up from the beach.

'I'm going to see what is going on. Take care of her, *llwynoges*.' Y Cadno flung the command at Nerys and, signalling to his men to follow him, raced for the cave's exit.

'With pleasure.' Nerys advanced on Thea.

'Stay away from me,' Thea gasped.

Nerys laughed. 'You puling little ninny! You should never have come here in the first place. You are not fit to be a viscountess.' Naked ambition flared in her face. 'I mean to have that title from you.'

Thea backed away from her. 'Even if it means taking the wrong brother?'

'Bitch!' Nerys lunged at her.

Thea swerved and ran, but found her escape hampered by the uneven floor. She didn't know the cave, and it was dark beyond the reach of the torches.

'Look out, Thea!'

Cati's warning cry came an instant too late. With a scream of triumph Nerys caught her.

The older woman was stronger and heavier, but desperation gave Thea fresh courage. With a cunning she hadn't known she possessed, she suddenly let herself go completely limp in Nerys's hold. Thrown off-balance, Nerys staggered back under her weight, easy prey to the elbow Thea drove hard into her midriff.

Choking, she doubled over, releasing her grip on Thea. Before she had time to recover Thea flung herself on her, and they both crashed to the floor, Thea uppermost.

Nerys lay still. Warily Thea sat up, expecting a trick. The redhead didn't move. For one horrified instant Thea was worried that she had broken her neck, until she saw that Nerys was still breathing and realised she had only knocked herself out.

Feeling sick, she rose shakily to her feet.

'Quickly, Thea! Untie me!' Cati's voice roused Thea.

'It won't come loose.' She worked frantically on the knot Glyn had fastened.

Cati cursed. 'Try again! Before she wakes up.'

Just when Thea was beginning to despair, the knot gave way. She leapt up. 'Come on.'

Without waiting to see if her sister-in-law followed, she ran for the mouth of the cave.

The small bay was an image from hell, lit by bright moonlight. Men were fighting everywhere, even at the edge of the water, where a longboat was drawn up on the sands. Scrambling down the path, Thea tried to make sense of the confusion. The noise was deafening. Screams in both Welsh and English echoed around the cliffs while the report of gunfire and the clash of steel made her head spin.

'Gareth!' Thea's pulse hammered as she spotted her husband. He was leading the attack!

She froze in horror as she watched him engage in a

hand-to-hand fight with a brawny smuggler. Behind him she saw Iolo, Gwen Evans's husband, tackling another of Y Cadno's band.

The smell of powder rose to her nostrils, its sharp, acrid scent penetrating her daze, and she hitched up her skirts to run to their aid.

Sanity intervened. She would be nothing but a hindrance! All she could do was edge closer and be ready to help if she could without getting in their way.

Breathless, Cati arrived at her side.

'Stay still and keep your head down!' She grabbed Cati's skirts and pulled the younger girl to her knees.

The battle raged fiercely, but, straining her eyes in the gloom, Thea realised that the numbers were almost equal. Vaughn had about eight men on the beach—most of his crew—but Gareth had rallied Owen and Dai and a couple of the inhabitants of Llanrhayadar, who had been acting as extra stable-hands for the night. Jenkins and Ifan and Tomos, the two footmen, further swelled his ranks, and they were all well armed.

What was more, he'd had the advantage of surprise on his side.

She saw the brawny smuggler fall, blood streaming down his face, and Gareth swept on. He was winning!

A few moments later and the smugglers still remaining standing threw down their arms. All except one.

'Gareth! Come and fight me, man to man!' In the sudden silence Y Cadno's cry rang out in blood-curdling challenge.

'The game is over, Vaughn.' Gareth, who had stripped off his elegant coat, wiped his shirt-sleeve across his forehead, dashing the sweat from his eyes. 'Surrender.'

'I'm not finished yet, brother. I hold your wife and sister hostage.'

From her hiding-place Thea saw how her husband stiffened.

'Don't believe him, Gareth!' she screamed, jumping

to her feet and waving her arms in the air to attract his attention. 'We are quite safe.'

A look of fury appeared on Vaughn's face, and then without any warning at all he launched himself at Gareth, who had turned to see where Thea's voice was coming from. Taken by surprise, Gareth went down under the onslaught, dropping the pistol he carried.

Thea began to run. A shriek of terror burst from her as she saw a knife appear in Vaughn's hand, moonlight glinting off its wicked blade.

Gareth managed to kick out hard, and won free when his boot landed in the older man's groin and Vaughn's hold weakened. With a snarl of rage Vaughn went after him, and both men began to roll on the sand, each seeking the advantage.

'Stop them! For God's sake, stop them!' Thea had reached Owen, and in desperation she grabbed his arm and shook it wildly.

'I can't.' His expression was anguished. 'I daren't.'

The combatants had regained their feet and were circling each other warily.

Sick with horror, Thea watched a dark stain blossom on Gareth's white sleeve.

Gareth appeared to be weakening, and Vaughn let out a howl of triumph. Once more he hurtled towards his adversary, only for the knife to be sent spinning out of his hand as Gareth feinted to the left and then followed with a blow that threw Vaughn backwards.

'Give up.' Gareth moved towards his fallen opponent, his fists upraised. 'I'll let you go free, provided you swear to leave Llanrhayadar and agree to let the other matter be settled in court.'

'All right.' Vaughn struggled to his knees, using both hands to push himself up. 'I'll do as you say.'

Suddenly his expression changed to one of unholy glee, and, realising what he had found in the sand, Thea's pent-up breath escaped with a hiss of rage.

'Farewell, *brawd*!' Vaughn raised the pistol which

Gareth had lost earlier and pointed it straight at his heart.

The shot echoed deafeningly in the silence.

A look of amazement spread across Y Cadno's face before he slumped to the ground, blood pouring from the hole in his breast.

Speechless with disbelief, Gareth turned to behold his wife standing there, a smoking pistol in her hand.

CHAPTER TWELVE

THE Viscount looked up quickly as his wife entered the room.

'How is she?'

'Sleeping. I gave her an opiate.'

Thea sighed. Glyn Edwards had been one of the few fatal casualties of the night. When his body had been found Cati had dissolved into hysterics.

'Come and sit down. You must be feeling exhausted.'

Thea denied it. A strange, nervous energy seemed to fill her, and, recognising it, Gareth did not argue. In the aftermath of battle he had seen men laugh and weep. Others became silent and withdrawn. The best thing to do would be to let Thea handle her horror in her own way.

'Will you take a glass of brandy, then?'

She nodded, grateful for the suggestion. 'But first let me look at your arm.'

'There's no need. The bleeding stopped hours ago.'

Thea glared at him. 'I think I ought to be the judge of that, sir! You get the brandy. I'll get some hot water and a bandage!'

She stomped off down to the kitchen. It was deserted. Gareth had finally sent all the servants to bed a little while ago.

Waiting for the water to heat up, Thea let her mind roam over the events of the night. She shuddered, hardly able to believe she'd had the courage to snatch Owen's pistol from him and fire it.

An image of Vaughn's sprawled body rose to torment her, but she quickly banished it.

The noise of the battle had been loud enough to reach the house. Somewhat to Thea's surprise, Angharad had coped superbly with the crisis. She had apologised and soothed, sending everyone home with such charming politeness that Thea suspected half the guests had been fooled.

Colonel Secombe knew better. In his role as magistrate he had already spoken to Thea, who had answered him as honestly as she could.

'I shall have to investigate further, my dear Lady Rhayadar, but I doubt if there will be any official repercussions,' he had told her. 'You acted to save your husband's life, after all.'

Thea had been greatly relieved. His offer to take Nerys Parry home had been even more welcome news to her ears. Thea didn't think she could have borne the prospect of spending the night under the same roof as that woman.

Nor had she been able to face sleeping in the tower until that passageway had been sealed. Her nightmares were probably going to be bad enough without the thought of someone being able to creep up those dark, winding stairs!

She had asked Blodwen to fetch a few things down to one of the guest-rooms in the most modern part of the house. It was a charming room, and Blodwen had lit the fire. By the time Thea had bathed and changed into her nightgown and wrapper it had felt warm and cosy.

Such had been Thea's state of mind that it had never once occurred to her to feel embarrassed when Gareth had eventually joined her.

He too had changed his stained clothes. Somehow he had looked younger and, in spite of everything, more relaxed than he had done for weeks.

Thea had been trying to decide if his informal attire—he wore only shirt and breeches—had anything to do with this amazing transformation, when Mrs Jones had tapped on the bedroom door and asked for her help in settling Miss Cati.

The water was hot enough now. Thea filled a basin

and, after collecting some bandages and towels, returned to her new room.

'You might as well take that shirt off. There's no sense in spoiling another one,' she said briskly, setting down her burden on the small circular satinwood table near the fire.

She busied herself moving a branch of candles to provide more light and turned back to find that Gareth had obeyed.

She swallowed hard. In the firelight his skin had a dark, satiny sheen, almost like polished oak. The flickering glow seemed to dance over his broad shoulders and chest, sculpting his superb muscles and taut, flat stomach.

'Please sit here.' She indicated a chair by the table.

'Won't you have your brandy first?'

'Why? Do you think I need it?' Thea tilted her chin at him.

Meekly Gareth shook his head, and sat down.

Thea forced herself to concentrate, and strove for detachment as she bent over him to examine his left forearm.

Down on the beach Gareth had bound the wound with his neckcloth to stop it bleeding, and when Thea carefully removed this she saw that Vaughn's knife had scored a long cut.

'Fortunately it isn't deep,' she murmured, bathing the area gently. 'But Dr Pugh should look at it.'

'It isn't hurting.'

She fixed him with a stern look. 'You must consult Pugh tomorrow.'

Gareth frowned, but finally agreed. 'I would have sent for him anyway. Cati might need his help.'

Thea paused in her task of bandaging his arm.

'She told me the whole story as I put her to bed. She overheard Owen telling you that Y Cadno's longboat had been spotted in the cove. She knew Glyn was helping in the stables so she sought him out to ask him to offer his aid. She thought you might look more kindly on him if he did, but he refused, saying that Vaughn's star was in the ascendancy. They argued and. . . Well. . .you know the rest.'

'Poor girl.' Gareth shook his dark head.

Cati had wept bitterly on Thea's shoulder.

'He only wanted me because of my rank. He thought he could use me to force money out of Gareth.' Cati had let out a wail of despair. 'Every word of love he uttered was a lie! None of it meant anything to him, Thea. Oh, I wish I were dead too!'

'She is very young. She will get over it one day.' Thea knew the words were trite, but she couldn't think of any other comfort to offer.

'I pray so,' Gareth answered solemnly.

Thea finished her task. 'I'll clear this mess up,' she murmured.

'No, leave it.' Gareth stopped her, reaching out a hand to draw her back towards him. 'I haven't thanked you yet for saving my life,' he said softly.

Thea coloured, and ducked her head in an awkward little gesture. 'I would have done the same for anyone,' she muttered.

Gareth took a deep breath. 'I don't think so.'

'I'll have that brandy now,' Thea declared, with a hint of desperation.

He was right. Love had given her the courage, but she didn't feel brave enough now to admit it.

Gareth poured two glasses from the decanter he had brought up while she had been in the kitchen. He handed one to Thea, who took a reckless swallow and almost choked.

'Thea!'

Gareth pounded her back as she coughed and spluttered, until she feebly waved for him to stop.

'I. . .I should have stuck to tea,' she gasped.

His engaging grin answered her. 'I remember. You told me once before you weren't used to spirits.'

Thea started to laugh, but then clapped a hand

across her mouth, a look of remorse spreading over her face.

'Oh, God, what am I doing? You must think me utterly callous!'

'Not in the least, *cariad*.'

Tears filled Thea's eyes, and all of a sudden she began to sob. 'I *killed* him! But I didn't mean to. I only meant to stop him.'

Swiftly Gareth enfolded her in his arms. 'You mustn't blame yourself. It was an accident.'

'No—no! It was my fault.'

Holding her tight, Gareth wished that he could convince her she was wrong. Given her lack of skill with firearms, it was a wonder she hadn't missed Vaughn completely!

'Vaughn wasn't worth your tears,' he said firmly. 'You mustn't feel guilty. He would have murdered us all without a second thought.'

Thea's sobs began to lessen.

Gareth's voice softened. 'You were so brave tonight, *cariad*. Not many women would have had such courage. I was very proud of you.'

He stroked her back in a gentle soothing rhythm, whispering encouragement and comfort until the storm had passed.

Thea fumbled for a handkerchief, and then, realising that she hadn't got one, wiped her sleeve across her face in an unconsciously childish gesture that made him smile.

'I'm sorry,' she whispered. Vaughn had been a scoundrel, but all the same, he had been Gareth's brother!

'*Duw*, you've nothing to apologise for! It is I who should say sorry, for embroiling you in such danger.' Gareth stared down into her eyes with an urgency that commanded her attention.

Her pulse began to race.

'I thought my heart would stop when he said he held

you hostage.' Gareth's voice thickened and his arms tightened around her slim waist.

They stared at one another in silence. The seconds ticked by and they both realised that he was no longer holding her to comfort her.

'Thea.' Gareth's breathing was ragged. 'Will you release me from my promise?'

'I. . .don't understand.' Gazing up into the midnight eyes burning into hers, Thea felt as if she was drowning.

'I think you do. *Wy'n dy garu di.*'

Scarcely daring to believe it, Thea said shakily, 'Does that mean what I think?'

He nodded. 'I love you, Thea. I asked you to marry me on impulse, but I was already under your spell.' A smile tugged at the corners of his well-cut mouth. 'I know I told you I was used to doing without a woman, but I hadn't reckoned on how devastating an effect you would have on me. By the time we arrived here I was going crazy with desire.'

'You hid it very well,' Thea murmured, still unable to believe her dream had come true.

'You were exactly the girl I had always hoped to find, but I was afraid to admit it even to myself.'

Gareth strove for control, but he didn't have the strength to combat his own feelings any longer. 'Oh, *lilli'r môr*, I want your answer now!' His voice shook. 'I want you now!'

Thea flung her arms around his neck. 'Oh, Gareth, there is no need to wait any longer. I love you. I want to be your real wife!'

His mouth came down on hers in swift response, in a kiss as hard and demanding as it was exciting. Helpless against the tide of desire that swept over her, Thea drew his hand to her breast.

A fierce sigh of satisfaction escaped her as he pushed aside the flimsy barrier of her wrapper and found her nipple beneath its thin covering of white lawn.

With skilful fingers he caressed her, making every nerve in her body come alive.

Thea forgot everything. The wonderful touch of his lips and hands banished all the horror and guilt, and she gave herself up to sensuous pleasure, losing herself in joyous ecstasy.

'Do you know how beautiful you are, *cariad*?' Gareth whispered hoarsely, lifting his mouth an inch away from hers.

A rosy blush coloured her cheeks. 'You make me feel beautiful.'

Gareth's conscience stirred. She looked at him so trustingly, and he still hadn't told her the full story!

'Thea, about Vaughn. I promised I would tell you——'

'Don't talk,' she begged, dizzy with longing. 'Just kiss me.'

The temptation was more than Gareth could stand. Tomorrow was time enough for talk. Tonight was for love.

Thea pressed even closer as he enthusiastically obeyed her request. With a shock of excitement she felt his virile hardness, and his arousal increased her own. Her hips writhed against his, and Gareth let out a low growl of satisfaction.

'*Lili'r môr.*' He swung her up into his arms and carried her over to the bed. He lowered her gently to the counterpane. 'Are you sure, Thea?' He whispered, settling himself next to her.

She gave him the wide, confident smile that made her dimple dance. 'I am certain, my husband.'

Gareth reached out and began to untie the bow that fastened her nightdress.

His burning gaze seemed to melt every remaining trace of her shyness. Eagerly she helped him remove it.

Gareth marvelled at the perfection of her slim figure, but Thea wouldn't let him kiss her yet.

'It's your turn,' she murmured throatily. 'I want to feel your naked skin against my own.'

It was the work of a moment for Gareth to divest himself of his garments. He shuddered from the effort of controlling his desire as she lightly ran her fingers over his chest in a hesitant exploratory fashion.

He captured her hand and lifted it to his mouth to press a kiss into her palm.

Wide-eyed, Thea watched him plant a trail of delicate butterfly kisses from her wrist to her inner elbow, before moving with leisurely enjoyment up to her shoulder.

'You have such lovely white skin,' he said softly, kissing the tender spot behind her ear.

Thea shivered with pleasure.

While he kissed her Gareth's hands moved with deft expertise. He caressed her breasts and the sweet curves of her waist and hips with a skilful attention that made Thea gasp with delight.

Her breathing quickened still further as he moved to kiss her nipples. Waves of hot, pulsating sensation rippled through her as his teeth gently tugged in turn at each tight pink crest.

'Gareth. Oh, Gareth!' Her voice sounded strange in her own ears.

A tiny chuckle of triumph escaped him, and he moved back up the bed to kiss her mouth again.

A queer ache in the pit of Thea's stomach throbbed, making her feel giddy and breathless with longing. She squeezed her eyes tight shut, scared that it might all be a dream, and clung harder to him.

Sensing that she was almost ready to receive him, Gareth let his hand drift down over the smooth plain of her stomach.

It was an incredibly arousing caress, and she sighed with sensuous delight as his fingers slipped between the cleft of her thighs and began to caress her.

Little cries of pleasure escaped her as the erotic sensations he was evoking spiralled out of control.

He moved above her, parting her thighs to admit his entry.

'Now, *cariad*, now!'

Thea's eyes flew open as he slid inside her, and she clutched at his broad shoulders in panic.

The brief flare of pain faded, and was instantly forgotten as he began to move very slowly and carefully within her.

Excitement built once more, and grew with each thrust. Heat enveloped Thea, and she could feel her heart beating fit to burst. Tiny drops of perspiration gathered at her temples, and Gareth bent to lick them away.

A new urgency began to grip Thea. Her breathing became even more ragged. Each nerve seemed to pulsate as waves of pleasure coursed through her entire body, climbing and climbing until she thought she might faint from the intensity of the sensations overwhelming her.

'Oh, Gareth!'

Delight exploded within her in a dazzling sunburst that left her dazed and incoherent with wonder.

She opened her eyes and found Gareth smiling down at her.

'Now you are mine at last,' he whispered exultantly, bending to kiss her once more.

Thea slipped quietly from the bedroom.

It was still early. Only a few of the servants were astir. For a moment Thea contemplated raiding the kitchen, but she wasn't hungry.

She would wait and breakfast later with Gareth. Happiness filled her at the thought. She was going to share the rest of her life with the man she loved!

When she had first awoken, she had watched him for a while. Sleep made him seem boyishly vulnerable, and she had experienced a fresh surge of love. In the end her need to kiss him had been irresistible, but he had stirred at her touch and, fearing to wake him, she had decided to get dressed and seek some fresh air.

It was a clear, cool morning, that promised a warm day, and Thea headed for her favourite spot in the gardens. Owen and some of the other men had removed the worst signs of the battle, but it was going to take her a while before she could brave the clifftop or the beach again.

She sat down on the wooden bench and lifted her face to the sun with a deep sigh of contentment.

'I thought I might find you here.'

Thea's eyes snapped open in disbelief.

'How did you get here?'

'I came across the sands. I hoped to catch you, but I didn't expect it to be so easy.' Nerys Parry assumed a sneering smile. 'I saw you leave the house and knew you would come here. It is your favourite retreat, is it not?'

Anger overrode Thea's curiosity. Nerys had probably overheard some servants' gossip, but it scarcely mattered how she had come by this information.

'You have the face for anything, but even you must know you are not welcome here. If you don't leave at once, I'll have you thrown out.'

'That would be foolish, my dear.' A small pistol appeared in Nerys's hand.

Thea blanched.

'Oh, don't worry. I'm not here to seek revenge. This is for my own protection.' Nerys waved the pistol gently to and fro. 'I want to put a proposition to you, and I have no wish to be humiliated by your servants.'

'Very well. Say what you have to, and then go.' Thea recovered her composure.

'May I?' Nerys replaced the pistol in the pocket of her redingote and gestured to the bench with mocking deference.

Thea nodded curtly, and Nerys sat down.

'Vaughn gave me his mother's marriage-lines for

safekeeping. Now that he is dead I regard them as my property. I am willing to sell them for the right price.'

Thea gazed at her blankly.

Nerys began to laugh. '*Duw*! You don't know what I'm talking about, do you?'

Her smooth brow creased in a calculating frown. After a moment she continued, 'I dare say Gareth didn't see any need to confide in you. It isn't as if you are his real wife after all.'

Thea felt as if a giant hand had squeezed all the air from her lungs. 'You. . .you are talking nonsense,' she gasped.

'Oh, come now. We both know yours is a marriage of convenience.' Her sneer became more pronounced. 'Frankly, I wasn't surprised when Gareth told me. You have neither the looks nor the wit to hold him. I almost died laughing when he described how you snatched at his proposal!'

'He discussed me with you?' Shock tore into Thea.

'Of course.' Nerys smoothed her skirts and smiled complacently.

'I don't believe you!'

'As you wish, my dear. But just remember this: Gareth is still in love with me, whatever he may say to the contrary.'

Thea shook her head wildly. 'Gareth loves me!'

'What gives you that idea?' Nerys viewed her with disdain. 'He doesn't even trust you sufficiently to confide in you.'

Thea winced.

Sensing she had hit a weak spot, Nerys was relentless. 'If he loved you, he would have told you that Vaughn was the real heir.'

Thea paled. 'No!'

'Oh, it's true. His father committed bigamy. Gareth is a bastard. He has no claim on Castell Mynach.' She smiled at Thea's stricken expression. 'He tells *me* everything. We are lovers.'

'You are lying. You were Vaughn's mistress.'

'Gareth only discovered that fact last night, you little simpleton.'

'You were playing them both off against each other?'

'Of course.' Nerys's hazel eyes glinted with mockery. 'I met Vaughn by chance in London. I decided to take him as my lover because he reminded me of Gareth, but when he told me the truth I realised I might achieve my ambition to succeed Angharad through him if Gareth failed me.' Her smile deepened. 'I don't intend to come out of this the loser. Thanks to those marriage-lines, I still hold the trump card.'

Thea shuddered.

'Gareth is angry with me now. It won't last, but it might be better if you put my suggestion to him. You can tell him I'm prepared to settle for a reasonable sum.' Her smile mocked. 'I'm not greedy.'

'Tell him yourself.' Thea longed to slap her. 'But I don't think he will be interested.'

Nerys's lovely face hardened. 'I know better. He wants to keep this place.'

Thea hesitated. Gareth did love Castell Mynach, but she could have sworn he would reject anything underhand.

'He will do anything to remain here. Why else do you think he planned that raid on the *Llwynoges*?'

Thea trembled. Another secret!

'He meant to kill Vaughn.' A harsh laugh escaped Lady Parry's red lips. 'You saved him the trouble. However, he knows he won't be safe until he has those marriage-lines and can destroy them.'

Thea could feel sickness rising in her throat. Perhaps she didn't know Gareth as well as she thought she did!

'Even if you are right, I want no part of it. Find yourself another messenger.' Thea got swiftly to her feet.

'Don't be so hasty, my dear. I know you hate me, but unless you do as I say I might remember I have a score to settle with you.'

Thea wished she had hit her harder!

'I can expose Gareth. Or I might decide to persuade him to seek an annulment and marry me. Either way you would lose your title, so don't annoy me.'

'Damn your blackmail!' Thea glared at her. 'I don't care if you tell the whole world.'

'You are a fool!'

'Perhaps.' She would not cry in front of this woman! 'But you are a whore. Now get out.'

Without waiting to see if Nerys obeyed, Thea turned on her heel and walked away.

A storm of emotion whirled within her. Gareth had lied to her!

Had he been lying last night?

All her instincts protested, but Thea knew that she had to face the facts. If he loved her surely he would have trusted her enough to tell her about Vaughn?

Nerys claimed that they were lovers. Whether or not it was true, Gareth had already betrayed her by exposing their private secret to Nerys's scorn.

Tears stung her eyelids. It was no use. She couldn't keep on pretending. Gareth might desire her—she didn't doubt that, in spite of Nerys's insinuations—but he didn't love her.

Once she might have told herself that desire was enough, but last night she had caught a glimpse of heaven and she couldn't bear to settle for less.

An annulment was out of the question, but there was always divorce.

Her decision made, Thea knew what she must do. If she hurried she could catch the mail-coach that left from Swansea. The landlord of the Golden Harp would look after Guinevere for her.

There was just time for her to pack a bag. The rest could be sent on later.

She would not say goodbye. Her lacerated emotions could not withstand another meeting with her husband. A brief letter would have to suffice.

Pride stiffened Thea's spine. She would not beg for

useless explanations! Gareth didn't love her. It was as simple as that!

The abbey bells were ringing out the hour of eleven when the post-chaise Thea had hired in Bristol stopped outside the house in Beaufort Square. She had also taken the precaution of hiring a temporary maid to accompany her on the last stage of her journey, to add the right note of respectability.

The ploy had worked.

In the flurry of greetings which followed, she was relieved to hear her grandmother assume that she had returned home in response to her letter.

'I thought the Viscount would accompany you,' Mrs Howard remarked, leading the way into the drawing-room. 'He does intend to follow later?'

'He is very busy,' Thea prevaricated, avoiding her gaze by shaking out the creases in her cambric skirts with more attention than the task warranted.

'You are looking well. That Welsh sea-air must agree with you—or is it marriage, eh?' Mrs Howard gave a roguish laugh. 'I'll ring for some tea and you must tell me all your news while we drink it.'

Taken aback by the effusive warmth of her greeting, Thea allowed herself to be installed in a place of honour by the fire, which was blazing forth as usual, regardless of the mild weather.

When she was seated Mrs Howard proceeded to bombard her with eager questions, and Thea gave her a carefully edited account of life at Castell Mynach. She would have to break the news that she wanted to divorce Gareth, but she couldn't face doing so just yet.

'I'm pleased to hear you have settled down.' Mrs Howard bounced her head in satisfaction, causing her many chins to jiggle. 'It's a weight off my mind to know that at least one grandchild hasn't been courting disgrace.'

Thea choked on her tea. 'What. . .what do you mean, Grandmama?' she spluttered uneasily.

A frown ploughed deep furrows into Mrs Howard's forehead. 'Your idiotic sister almost caused a scandal. If I hadn't found out in time she would have run off with a peniless rogue.' She snorted indignantly.

'An actor. She saw him on stage and fancied herself in love on the instant! Can you believe such folly, after all the warnings I've drummed into her over the years? I thought she had more sense, but as soon as this fellow started to whisper sweet words everything else went out of her head.'

Thea dropped her cup. The hot contents splattered her skirts but she didn't spare the stained cambric a glance.

'Georgy tried to elope?'

Mrs Howard handed her a large clean handkerchief. 'Attend to that stain,' she ordered.

Thea obeyed automatically. 'Is she...? I mean, did he—?'

Mrs Howard put her out of her misery. 'I caught them in time.' She snorted. 'Her virtue is safe.'

Thea couldn't think of anything comforting to say. She could see that her grandmother was really upset and her heart sank. How could she add to her disappointment by confessing the truth about her failed marriage?

'I sent him off with a flea in his ear, but nothing excuses Georgy's foolishness.' Mrs Howard shook her elaborately curled head and sighed. 'All these years I've treated her like a princess, and then she goes and lets me down.'

There was a small silence and then she coughed.

'In fact, I'm thinking that I owe you an apology, Dorothea. Anthony Harley is well enough, but he can't compare with a Viscount.'

'I'm sure he will make Georgy happy, Grandmama,' Thea said desperately, her conscience hurting.

'Aye. I suppose I should be glad Harley's so eager for the match.' A shudder shook her massive frame.

'The sooner she's safely wed the better! We can't afford any gossip.'

Thea barely stifled a groan.

Mrs Howard fixed Thea with an intent stare. 'Are you feeling well? You've turned a little pale.'

'The journey did not agree with me, Grandmama.'

'Oh, I wondered if. . . But I suppose it is a little early to hope for that.'

Guessing what she had meant, Thea hastily denied that she was with child.

'A pity, but you have plenty of time ahead of you.'

Thea winced but, wrestling with her own conscience, Mrs Howard didn't notice.

'It is you who have fulfilled my ambitions, Dorothea,' she announced solemnly. 'And I mean to show my appreciation.'

Thea waited in apprehensive silence.

'I told you once that I would leave my fortune entirely to Georgy. Well, I've changed my mind. You shall have half.'

Thea gasped. Recovering her wits, she managed a somewhat incoherent murmur of gratitude.

'No need to thank me. It is only fitting.' Mrs Howard's broad face assumed an unusually diffident expression. 'You might be Jane Ashby's daughter but you are also my grandchild—a fact I've been guilty of forgetting. You see, you are the spit of your mother. Every time I looked at you I was reminded of how much I disliked her.'

She cleared her throat. 'I was jealous of her.'

'Jealous, Grandmama?' Thea asked, her head spinning.

'Aye. Your father was mad for her. Wouldn't listen to a word I said against the match. Poor as church-mice, her branch of the Ashbys.' She sighed heavily. 'Then when she died he went to pieces. He was never the same man again. Couldn't even get over his grief for your sake.'

She met Thea's astonished grey eyes and gave a faint

smile. 'He may not have given much indication of it, but Richard loved you and Georgy. He just found it hard to show it.'

So her father had not been indifferent! Suddenly Thea's heart felt a little lighter.

'Let's not mull over the past, Grandmama,' she said slowly. 'It is over and done with.'

'Aye. We'll start afresh.' Mrs Howard laughed—a full-throated guffaw of satisfaction. 'Ring that bell and tell Dutton to bring up a bottle of the best champagne, and we'll drink to the future in style!'

Thea obeyed, concealing her trepidation behind a brittle smile.

Over the next few days Thea slipped back into the rhythm of her old life. There were changes, of course. Tut-tutting over the myserious disappearance of Thea's trunks, Mrs Howard took her shopping for new clothes. Thea tried not to feel guilty, and vowed to herself that she would repay her somehow. Her grandmother also insisted she occupy one of the big front bedrooms. It felt rather strange, but there was no denying it was far more comfortable than her old cramped quarters.

Her married status brought new freedom too. She enjoyed being able to visit her friends without the need for a chaperon, but found it increasingly difficult to fend off well-meant enquiries.

Simon Murray and his family were frequent callers, and they always asked after Gareth. She began to think that there was more gossip circulating about when Viscount Rhayadar would arrive in Bath than there were rumours claiming that Bonaparte was about to invade Russia!

One of the few persons who did not badger her was Anthony Harley. As she came to know him better Thea realised that his slightly effeminate looks concealed a sensible and determined character. He was mad for Georgy, but his obsession did not blind him to her faults. He would make an indulgent husband, but

Georgy would not be able to lead him around by the nose.

Not that Georgy seemed to have any ambition in that direction.

Like Thea herself, she had changed. Her brush with disaster had frightened her, and she knew Mrs Howard's threat to disinherit her had not been an idle one. She had abandoned her childish tantrums and become more considerate.

Thea decided that it wasn't just because Georgy was nervous of angering their grandmother. Her little sister had grown up, and become a nicer person in the process.

The rift with her family healed, Thea would have been happy if only she could have forgotten Gareth. But it was impossible! Even if she could have ignored her heartbreak, she knew a day of reckoning was inevitable.

Another week slid past, and every night she lay in bed worrying and wondering how she could explain that she had left her husband. She had tried several times and failed, but Georgy's betrothal party was only days away. Her grandmother was expecting Gareth to attend. When he did not turn up she was going to start suspecting the worst, and so was everyone else!

Sadly, this time the gossips would be right!

'You have a visitor, my lady.'

Thea, returning from paying a call on the Murrays, stared at Dutton in sudden hope.

'In the drawing-room, ma'am.'

Without stopping to remove her bonnet, Thea rushed across the hallway and flung open the door.

'Angharad!'

Her mother-in-law rose to her feet at Thea's abrupt entrance.

'I know you are angry with me, but please give me a few moments of your time.'

Reluctantly Thea sat down, trying to quell her sick disappointment.

'I came to say goodbye. I am leaving Castell Mynach.'

Thea sucked in her breath. She hadn't expected this!

'I shall stay with Cousin Mary until I can find a suitable house of my own.' Her dark eyes met Thea's with a trace of defiance. 'I have always wanted to live in London.'

'How is Cati?' Unable to frame the question she wanted to ask most, Thea asked about Gareth's sister instead. She had felt guilty about leaving her young sister-in-law; Cati would have been hurt by her defection.

'She is in low spiritis.' Angharad frowned. 'I could not believe she had been such a fool! To imagine herself in love with that boy! I asked her to come with me, thinking it might help, but she refused.'

'I wish I could have been there.' Thea had written to apologise for leaving without saying goodbye, but there had been no reply. 'I might have been able to do something.'

Angharad's usual poise seemed to desert her. 'There is something else. I want you to know that although we had been discussing what gowns everyone was going to wear, I did not realise Nerys planned to ruin your gown.'

Thea met her mother-in-law's embarrassed gaze with a faint smile. 'I guessed some time ago that she was responsible.'

Angharad shook her dark head in distaste. 'It never occurred to me that she would stoop to an affair with a smuggler.' Her dark eyes flashed. 'And so I told her!'

'You've spoken to her?'

'I wanted to give her a piece of my mind!' Angharad scowled. 'She was packing with the intention of returning to London. She had the infernal impudence to offer me a place in her carriage! As if I would accept! I am done with her false friendship!'

'Do you think she will come back?' Thea couldn't keep the anxiety from her voice.

'I doubt it. The Cwrt is to be put up for sale.'

Had Nerys given up her ambitions regarding Gareth at last? 'I'm glad to hear it,' Thea said slowly. It ought not to make any difference but it did.

Her mother-in-law smiled. 'I'm sure you are,' she replied, with her old malicious amusement. 'Just as you will be glad to see the back of me. There is room for only one mistress in any household.'

Thea did not deny it.

Angharad gazed at her intently. 'I assume you mean to return after your sister's betrothal party?'

Thea was silent.

'Why did you leave so abruptly? Were you——?'

'I don't wish to be rude, but I would rather not discuss it.'

So Gareth had not told his mother that she had asked for a divorce.

The Dowager gave a graceful inclination of her head. 'Keep your secrets, my dear. God knows, I am in no position to judge you! But I will say this: Gareth is missing you dreadfully.' She sighed. 'If it hadn't been for his wound, I think he would have come straight after you.'

'He is ill?' Thea's voice sharpened with sudden fear.

'His arm became infected the day after you left. He was very feverish for a time.'

Anguish rent Thea like a bolt of lightning. She should have been there to nurse him!

'Don't worry. He is on the mend. I waited until Dr Pugh was certain he was out of danger before I left.'

Angharad smiled faintly. 'Once, I thought Gareth had married beneath him. I was wrong. I will not ask if you and Gareth have quarrelled—that is your business. But if you have I will pray for a reconciliation.'

Thea blinked at her.

'You have been good for Gareth. What's more, I

know that you will make a worthy chatelaine for Castell Mynach.'

She rose to her feet.

'Now I must go. Give my compliments to your family, and come and see me if ever you are in London.'

With one final wave of her bejewelled hand she swept out of the room.

Thea took several deep breaths to steady her pulse.

As Angharad had rightly surmised, she had been feeling distinctly angry with her, suspecting that she had been party to Nerys's spite. She was glad to learn she had been wrong, and that Angharad didn't dislike her as much as she had thought.

But Angharad's change of heart seemed trivial compared to the fact that Gareth had been ill.

She half rose to her feet, a desperate urgency to go to his side possessing her.

Fool! Nothing has changed! she told herself. He does not love you.

Angharad's approval made no difference, and Thea knew it.

Thea surveyed her reflection in the long looking-glass. The pale greeny-blue gauze suited her, but she wished she had more colour in her cheeks.

Please God, no one would guess at her unhappiness. Only let her get through tonight, without spoiling Georgy's party, and she would find the courage to confess.

'Time's getting on, my lady.' Alice's brisk tones broke into her thoughts. She handed Thea a silver lace fan. 'Your grandmother is expecting you to join her in receiving the guests.'

'I'm ready.' Thea carefully draped her silver net scarf across her arms.

Mrs Howard, resplendent in a plumed turban and dark pewter satin, was already in position at the head of the stairs. Georgy, looking excited and prettier than ever in a dashing new gown of pink silk, stood at her side.

'No word yet from his lordship?'

'I'm afraid not, Grandmama.' Fixing a smile firmly in place, Thea joined them.

By ten o'clock both of the big drawing-rooms were full, and Thea's face was aching from constant smiling.

The steady stream of arrivals slowed to a trickle.

Anthony Harley came to claim his future bride and Mrs Howard released her.

Another half an hour went by.

Mrs Howard glanced down the empty stairs and ventured a small stretch. 'You go and join the others, Dorothea. I'll be along in a moment.'

About to obey, Thea paused at the sound of a new arrival.

A broad-shouldered man clad in dark formal evening clothes came striding purposefully up the stairs, and Thea let out a faint gasp.

Mrs Howard beamed at him. 'You are very welcome, Viscount Rhayadar!'

Gareth bowed with exquisite politeness. 'Good evening, ma'am.' He turned to Thea. 'My lady. I hope I find you well?'

Thea nodded, not trusting her voice.

Mrs Howard glanced at them shrewdly and said, 'I expect you would like a moment in private. Dorothea, take his lordship into the morning-room.' Her smile turned coy. 'But do not linger too long, or I shall send Alice to fetch you.'

Silently Thea led the way. She was very conscious of Gareth's footsteps behind her, and her pulse was beating at twice its normal rate.

The door closed behind them, and, terrified of the joy she had felt on seeing him, Thea launched straight into the attack.

'Why did you come here? I asked you not to follow me.'

'Your grandmother invited me to Georgy's party,' Gareth reminded her quietly.

'I didn't think you would remember,' she said, with a bitterness that made him wince.

'You have every right to upbraid me.' His burning gaze fixed itself upon her face and Thea's palms grew slick with nervous tension. 'I was not honest with you. I had no right to make love to you that night.'

A sickening giddiness assailed Thea and she sat down abruptly. He was going to grant her the separation she had asked for but did not want.

'*Cariad.*' Gareth made a swift move towards her and then checked himself.

Very aware of his nearness, Thea stared fixedly at her tightly clasped hands and muttered, 'I cannot live with you any longer, Gareth. We must divorce.'

'Won't you at least hear what I came to say?'

She hesitated.

'Please.' To resist the temptation to take her in his arms, Gareth thrust his hands behind his back. 'You listened to Nerys. Won't you give me a chance to tell you my side of the story?'

She nodded jerkily, her heart thumping.

'We had been married little more than a week when my mother revealed that Vaughn had been blackmailing her.'

'I guessed he had done so, and why.' Thea had worked it out during one of the long, lonely nights when she had lain sleepless.

'Until that moment I had always believed myself to be my father's heir. I realise now that I should have told you straight away, but as God is my witness, Thea, I didn't know how!' He gave a shake of his raven head. 'I was worried you might turn from me in disgust.'

'Your title has never mattered to me!' Thea said passionately. 'I would have married you if you had been a pauper. Your illegitimacy made no difference to me!'

A glimmer of hope brightened Gareth's eyes. 'Then

you believe that I didn't intentionally set out to trick you?'

'I accept that you offered to make me your viscountess in good faith, but I wish you had trusted me with the truth!'

'The shame was mine! I didn't want to lay such a heavy burden on your shoulders. I thought there would be time enough for explanations once I had dealt with Vaughn. If Nerys hadn't interfered——'

Despair welled up in Thea, and she interrupted him in a wild rush. 'How do you think I felt, learning such news from that woman? It was so humiliating, Gareth!'

'I am sorry, *cariad*.' Swiftly Gareth dropped to one knee before her, and clasped both of her hands in his.

'I would have given anything to spare you from that vixen's spite.'

Thea gazed into his eyes and, swallowing back her tears, whispered, 'She said you told her about our agreement.'

'*Annwyl Crist*!' Gareth's fingers tightened on hers. 'The cunning——' He bit back an expletive. 'I would have cut my tongue out rather than disclose any such information!'

Thea smiled tremulously. 'I should have known she was lying.'

'Nerys must have heard some servants' gossip. Jenkins and Blodwen knew we did not share a bed.'

Thea nodded. Nerys had made a lucky guess, and she had fallen straight into her trap!

Gareth moved to sit next to her on the sofa, but he kept a tight hold on her hands.

'I see now why you were so ready to believe the worst,' he said softly. 'Do I have to tell you that she was also lying when she said she was my mistress?'

Remembering how wildly she had accused him in her farewell letter, Thea coloured. 'I thought that perhaps you regretted our hasty marriage.'

'I have never regretted it for one moment. Oh, Thea,

don't you understand? I have been in hell since you left!'

She gazed at him, hardly daring to breathe.

'I wanted to make you my wife long before that final night. I hung back because I had nothing to offer you but a dishonoured name.'

'I thought you were going to confide in me the day you gave me Guinevere,' she murmured.

'I intended to, but Cati joined us and afterwards I lost my nerve. I was afraid I would lose you!' He gave a sombre smile. 'We are vulnerable when we love.'

Thea gasped, and Gareth knew that he had touched a raw nerve.

He released her and raked one hand impatiently through his hair. 'What I should have done was send you to a place of safety. I knew Vaughn was dangerous. My selfishness put you at risk!'

His mouth twisted. 'To crown my folly, I took you to bed without telling you all the facts! No wonder you ran away. I behaved without honour or sense!'

He gazed into her eyes. 'But I love you, *cariad*, and I always will.'

Thea's pulse hammered. 'How do I know you are sincere?' she demanded helplessly. 'I want to trust you, but I'm not sure if I can.'

'There is no guarantee I can give you. Either you believe me or you don't,' he replied, his deep voice vibrating with passion. 'You said you loved me. All I can do is beg you to have faith in your feelings and mine.'

She was silent for a moment. 'If I hadn't been so impatient that last night, you would have explained everything, wouldn't you?'

He nodded and she sighed.

'Then we both made mistakes. I accused you of not trusting me, but I wasn't ready to accept that your love was real. I believed Nerys because I couldn't believe you could love someone ordinary like me.'

'You are *not* ordinary!' Gareth protested. 'You are

a wonderful girl. You are pretty, intelligent and kind, and you can make me laugh!'

Thea blushed furiously.

'I won't pretend my pride wasn't hurt when you ran away,' Gareth continued. 'But if your family had encouraged you to have more confidence in yourself you would understand why I count myself very fortunate to have won your hand.'

Reading sincerity in his handsome face, Thea felt her heart lighten. 'Perhaps it isn't too late to try again,' she whispered.

Gareth's glimmer of hope grew into a brighter flame.

'You are willing to change your mind about a divorce?'

Thea managed a smile. 'I am. If you are sure you still want me?'

'How can you doubt it, *lili'r môr*?' Gareth exclaimed, drawing her into his arms.

His lips found hers in a kiss that seemed to sear her soul. A river of heat flooded through Thea's veins, melting all her remaining fears. His body was so wonderfully warm and strong. After so many cold and empty days alone she felt she had been reborn to a new life. Like a flower seeking the sun, she needed him!

'*Cariad*, I don't think I could have let you go,' he whispered, with a conviction that brought a shine of joyful tears to her eyes.

They clung to one another in a contented silence that needed no words, exchanging loving little kisses filled with tenderness until at last Gareth summoned all his resolution and gently put her from him.

'There is nothing I would rather do than make love to you,' he told her, with a gleam in his midnight eyes that made her blush. 'But first I have several things to tell you.'

'You want to rejoin the Navy!'

Puzzlement appeared on Gareth's well-cut features. 'Why should I——?' He broke off as understanding dawned on him. 'I suppose the rumour that America intends to declare war on us put that maggot into your head?'

Thea nodded, promising herself that she wouldn't try to stop him if it was what he really wanted.

'I count myself as good a patriot as the next man, but my place is with you now—not at sea.' Gareth smiled at her and her anxiety dissolved.

'I'm glad,' she said simply, leaning against his shoulder with a happy sigh.

'I was going to say that you need not worry about meeting Nerys again. She has left the Gower.'

'I know.' Thea explained about the Dowager's surprise visit. 'What of Cati?' she asked. 'Is she improved?'

'A little. I brought her here with me to Bath.'

'Where is she now?'

'At the White Hart. She wouldn't come with me tonight, but she has agreed that a change of scene would be best. The plan is for her to stay with the Murrays until it is time for her to start school.'

'Oh, Gareth, that is good news!' In that lively household, there was every chance that her young sister-in-law would start to put the past behind her. 'I shall call on her tomorrow. . .if you think she will receive me.'

He touched a gentle finger to her cheek. 'I've told her as much of the truth as she needs to know. She understands now why you left so hastily. She does not blame you for it.'

Relief washed over Thea, but it changed to apprehension as she realised that they could not close the door on the past just because Nerys had gone.

'Gareth, what are you going to do?'

He did not pretend to misunderstand her. 'I don't believe in burying my head in the sand, *cariad*. I did not buy those marriage-lines from Nerys.'

Satisfaction blazed in Thea. 'I knew you wouldn't!'

'She came to see me. Pugh had forbidden visitors, but she bluffed her way past the servants. I would have thrown her out myself if I'd had the strength, but luckily I had a better weapon to hand. The truth! She was so furious I thought she would choke!'

Thea blinked. Was she imagining that note of amusement in his voice? She turned her head so that she could see his expression more clearly.

'Vaughn was going to announce that he was the real heir that last night. He may have heard that I'd planned to drive him out of Llanrhayadar.' Gareth shrugged. 'I was determined to break his power. He hoped to ruin me first. Nerys swore she would carry out his plan if I didn't pay her what she wanted for that document.'

A sudden grin appeared on Gareth's dark features.

'I informed her it was worthless!'

'Was it a fake?'

Gareth shook his head, his smile fading. 'Soon after my mother told me about Vaughn's claim I asked my lawyers to set in motion certain enquiries. They discovered that no banns had been called before that first ceremony. Moreover, since my father was only twenty at the time, he should have had my grandfather's consent. Without it, and without proper banns, the marriage was null and void.'

'So he didn't commit bigamy!'

'And I am the real heir,' Gareth confirmed. 'What's more, knowing my father, I'm certain he was aware that the ceremony would be invalid. He probably arranged it just to keep Vaughn's mother quiet.'

Distaste mingled with Thea's relief. 'Why didn't he explain things properly to Angharad?'

'I imagine he had already grown tired of her.' Gareth shrugged awkwardly. 'He was a cruel man in many ways.'

'Please, there is no need to carry on.' Thea laid a comforting hand on his.

'Let me finish, my love, and then we need never discuss it again.' Gareth raised her hand to his lips and kissed it.

'I think it amused him to annoy her. Why else would

he have brought Vaughn to Castell Mynach, when he could easily have paid for him to be looked after in London? He wanted their estrangement. It gave him the freedom to live his life exactly as he pleased. No doubt he intended to tell her in the end, but fate had the last laugh. He had an unexpected seizure at his club and died before a doctor could be brought.'

Thea shivered. What a lot of trouble and grief could have been avoided if the late Viscount had possessed the same integrity as his son!

'Now you know the whole story,' Gareth said quietly. 'Can you forgive me for not telling you sooner?'

Remembering how impossible she had found it to explain matters to her grandmother, Thea answered him with a delicate butterfly kiss of understanding.

'Come home with me, *Lili'r môr*,' he whispered against her mouth. 'I need you by my side. I don't want anything to separate us again. Without you I'm only half-alive.'

The urgency in his deep tones sent a thrill of excitement tingling down Thea's spine. Her fingers twined themselves into the thick curls that clustered on his nape and she drew his head down to kiss him.

The loud knocking at the door finally roused them, reminding them that the rest of the world still existed beyond their enchanted haven.

'Miss Thea! Your grandmother is asking for you.'

Thea let out a groan. Her eyes flew to his dark face, only inches from her own.

'Shall I tell her to go away?' she whispered.

'What—and have your grandmother come hammering on the door in her place?' Gareth replied with wry amusement.

'It wouldn't be fair on Georgy,' Thea agreed with slow reluctance. 'Not after you failed to turn up for her first soirée!'

But she made no attempt to move out of the circle of his arms.

Gareth tilted her face up to his. 'One last kiss,' he said, and took it with a ruthless demanding passion that set Thea's nerve-endings ablaze again.

Then he stood up and held out his arm to her. 'Let's go and brave the dragons, my lady.'

Thea placed her fingers on his coat-sleeve, her eyes shining with happiness.

Her married life with Gareth was about to begin. A new life, full of laughter and joy and all the love she would ever need.

LEGACY *of* LOVE

Coming next month

THE FROZEN HEART

Laura Cassidy

Greenwich 1563/4

Anne Latimar loved her life at Maiden Court, but now her twin, George, was married, it seemed an exciting way forward to attend court as one of Elizabeth's ladies.

Never short of suitors, Anne had yet to meet the man who could match her father—and Jack Hamilton, with his brusque speech, was nothing like the Earl. Besides, Jack had buried his heart with his wife and, despite their growing rapport, Anne knew she couldn't accept second-best from the man she so belatedly realised she loved...

A COMPROMISED LADY

Francesca Shaw

Regency 1815/16

Miss Caroline Franklin had very uncomfortable memories of Brussels during the panic of Waterloo. Worse, there were moments she couldn't remember at all—how *had* she become dressed in scandalous attire with paint on her face? Thankfully, she was never likely to see again the man who had rescued her—until, back in London, her brother brought home Jervais, Lord Barnard, the one man who knew her secret.

It had felt so right to be in his arms, how *could* she now accept a proposal meant only to save her reputation...?